Silences

A Novel of the
1918 Finnish Civil War

Silences

A Novel of the
1918 Finnish Civil War

Roy Blomstrom

SHUNIAH
HOUSE
—— BOOKS ——
Shuniah House Books
www.shuniahhousebooks.com

For my parents

Mathias William Blomström
and
Agnes Hilda Maria Grönlund Blomström

CONTENTS

Part IV: WATER

PROLOGUE

The executioner always kills twice, the second time with silence.
~ Elie Wiesel

PORT ARTHUR: LABOUR DAY, 1955

THE LIGHT WIND blowing through the trees caused the body to revolve slowly at the end of the short rope. The officer examined the trees, the rope, the body. An old dynamite box that had served as a platform lay on its side a few feet away, where it had been kicked aside. The rope had been tied so as to press hard against the carotid arteries of the man's neck and cut off the flow of oxygen-rich blood to the brain without triggering the reflexive struggle against choking.

Had the hanged man so wished, he could have reached up to the branch above him and, clinging to it, swung himself to the trunk of the tree and called the whole thing off. He had not. He had been a stubborn man.

The officer could hear the nearby river. If the usual group of teenagers had been swimming at the Bend, he would have been able to hear their laughter, but it was a cool day, and they were elsewhere. He wondered how many of them knew about this place. The Finns called it "The Last Stop" and "The Hanging Tree." The police referred to it only as "the usual spot" in their reports. *Some of the kids,*

1

he decided. Some of the kids would know.

The body, having completed a quarter turn, swung slowly clockwise toward the river as if it had heard something.

Some suicides took their shoes off before they hanged themselves, concerned about making the floor of the "other place" dirty. Some did not. This one, the officer noted, had settled on a compromise. The man had a shoe on his right foot, but not on the left. Though the officer had searched the area, he had found no trace of the missing shoe.

After a few minutes he left the body still hanging from the tree and walked along the path back to the cruiser parked on Oliver Road. He called in his report and waited in the car.

PART I

EARTH

Caesar…resolved to make an example of those [the Gauls] who had risen against him. Therefore, he ordered that the warriors' hands be cut off, and he spared their lives to make more evident their punishment for rebellion.

~ Ascribed to Aulus Hirtius

1 • FINLAND, NOVEMBER 10, 1906

AS JUSSI MANTERE turned the horse-drawn cart up the long drive that led to the Solbakken house, the two ladders caught his attention, even in the dim evening light. One, which should have let a man get up on the roof, was lying on the ground in the snow. The other was where it was supposed to be—attached to the roof, right beside the chimney. Winter was the season of chimney fires in Finland, and a man might have to get up on the roof in a hurry. Jussi was sixteen, a year younger than his friend Anders Solbakken, but he knew that it was his job to tell Anders to put the fallen ladder where it would do the most good. It was something that would never occur to Berg.

Anders' father had died four years before, and Ellen Solbakken, Anders' mother, was now being courted by Harald Berg, the schoolteacher. Berg knew little about running a farm, so Mrs. Solbakken had asked Jussi to teach Anders what he needed to know.

Though it was not late, a little past six o'clock in the evening, it was already two hours past sunset, and the only light along the drive came from the waning crescent moon. A faint glow showed through the parlour window of the house—a spillover of the light from the kerosene lamps in the kitchen beyond. The house had surrendered its daytime red to the darkness; it was black with white trim now, and the road up to the house glittered a pale blue in the weak light. Yesterday's snow had melted and then refrozen to create a rutted crystal surface that refracted the moonlight, kept the warm colours for itself, and offered only cold shades in return.

Jussi clicked his tongue to encourage Viola, the chestnut Finnhorse pulling the cart, to climb the small hill up to the house, and as she toiled he drove for a short distance with his feet up high on the cart's wooden splashboard so that he could inspect his boots. *Clean, but not quite clean enough. I can wipe them off with snow before I go in,* he thought.

The two-story Solbakken house was much more substantial than

Jussi's home—a two-room cabin where Jussi slept on a cot in the kitchen and his parents shared the small bed in the only bedroom. He pulled up outside the Solbakken's small covered porch, got down from the cart, then made sure to tie Viola's reins to the hitching post. She would stay wherever he left her, tethered or not, but it was more polite to leave her secured.

At home, the neighbours could just walk into the Mantere house unannounced. To ask them to knock would have been insulting. The Solbakkens, however, were Finland-Swedes—not Finns, like Jussi's family. The Solbakkens spoke Swedish, not Finnish, and their rules were as different as their language. Privacy was highly valued, and etiquette, though no more strict than at the Mantere home, was more visible.

Jussi left Viola standing patiently in the snow and walked up the path to the porch. He bent down, picked up a handful of snow and wiped his boots clean, then opened the outer door without knocking—that much could be done within the rules. He did, however, knock on the inside door.

"Oh, thank God," he heard Mrs. Solbakken say from behind the door, but it was Anders who opened it.

"Hi, Jussi," Anders said. "Come in. Harald Berg is trying to teach us to play *Musta Maija*. Viktoria's here, too—Mamma's looking after her until her parents get back from Helsingfors. Mamma thought you were Cossacks, but I told her Cossacks never knock. Right, Mamma?" He laughed.

"I heard the *horse*," Mrs. Solbakken said seriously from behind him. Her son, good-looking, seventeen, tall and muscular, blocked her from Jussi's view. It wasn't intentional.

Jussi, though more wiry than his friend, was just as tall. He took off his gloves and put them in his coat pockets, then hung his coat and hat on a peg in the small porch. He peered around his friend as he removed his boots and placed them on the mat.

"Why Cossacks?" he asked, but Mrs. Solbakken was heading back to the kitchen already. Anders followed his mother as she led the way down the hall and past the parlour. Jussi was careful to close the inner door before starting after them.

"I told mamma it wasn't a *Cossack* horse," Anders said over his shoulder. "A Finnhorse doesn't sound *anything* like a Don."

Mrs. Solbakken stopped and turned around. "He thinks he can tell a horse by the sound of its walk."

Jussi laughed. "It might be true. He certainly knows Lovisa Finska's walk when she tippy-toes into the schoolroom." He was rewarded by a flush of red on the back of Anders' neck.

Mrs. Solbakken came to her son's rescue. "Four years ago, remember? In Helsingfors when there was that rioting, the Tsar set the Cossacks loose in the streets. I read in the newspaper about a doctor who was chased right into his house by the Cossacks, horses and all, and he had to jump out of a second-story window to get away. Almost killed himself. They were beating him with their knouts for no reason at all. And now we have all this talk of revolution again. The Tsar is going to sic the Cossacks on us, just like he always does. You just wait and see."

By her last sentence, Anders' blush had disappeared. Rescue accomplished. The three entered the kitchen.

"Herrrrr Manterrrrre," Viktoria Lassila said, rolling the *r*s in a ten-year-old's parody of Finnish speech. She was sitting at the kitchen table with Karl Solbakken. Karl was the same age as Viktoria. Ivor Solbakken, at three the baby of the family, the one everyone called "Rabbit" because of the way he liked to scoot around on the floor, was under the table examining feet. The two chairs where Anders and his mother had been sitting were empty, the cards in front of them face down.

"Viktorrrria," Jussi said and bowed his head slightly toward the ten-year-old in mock salute. *"Näytät todella kauniilta tänään."*

Viktoria smiled at him. "What does that mean?"

"I said you look very pretty today."

"Is that what he said?" she asked Anders.

"I think so. It wasn't anything bad."

"You have learned some Finnish, Anders?" Harald Berg asked.

"Just some kitchen Finnish. A few words, some simple sentences, that's all. Jussi's been teaching me."

"We should all know both languages—and fluently," Berg said in his teacher's voice. "I am ashamed to say I know almost no Finnish at all. I've picked up a few words listening to the Finnish customers at the market, but that's about it. We don't even worship together. We live here on the west coast of Finland, yet feel as if we are somehow physically attached to Sweden—even if Russia has controlled us for the last hundred years."

The company was silent for a moment, hoping that Berg would not continue.

Viktoria, bored by the conversation, now felt uneasy in the silence. "Herr Berg is teaching us to play *Musta Maija*. It's a card game that doesn't have a winner, just a loser. The winner is the game, Black Maria herself, not the people playing it. The loser goes to jail. She's like the paddywagon."

"Well, I suppose we all have to go to jail sometime," Berg said, looking at his cards and frowning. He put them face down on the table and turned to Jussi. "How's my star pupil today?"

"Fine, sir."

"Let me pour you some coffee, Jussi," Mrs. Solbakken said, effectively putting an end to what she was afraid could have triggered a litany of Berg's opinions about education in Finland.

"Thank you, but no. I just stopped by to ask Anders to do me a little favour. I'm on my way home with some supplies from Gamlaby. Can you spare him a moment?"

"Certainly," Mrs. Solbakken said. "The game can wait. But," she added, putting her hand on his arm, "so can you. We haven't seen you for a while, so sit down, just for a moment, I know you need to get back. I'll get some cookies and we can...what is it the Americans say...*sneck*."

"*Snack*, mamma," Karl said.

"*Snack*, then. What an awful-sounding word. It's like a crow's screech." She got a cup and saucer from the cupboard.

Jussi offered, "The Americans would call me 'Juicy.'"

Berg responded, "Yes, or perhaps 'Jussy.'"

Mrs. Solbakken said, "Karl, get the extra chair from the parlor." Through a small strainer held over the cup, she poured the coffee— boiled, not percolated—and set it down on its saucer at the corner of the table.

While she poured, Jussi said to Viktoria in English, "You see?" He waited. Viktoria stared at him. "It's English," he prompted. Another pause. He switched back to Swedish. "Almost. You know...for *Jussi*."

Herr Berg broke in. "But it would sound more like 'YOU see,' not 'you SEE.'"

"Yes," Jussi answered. "It is an imperfect joke."

Karl placed the extra chair at the table. Jussi sat down and reached for a sugar lump, which he placed in his mouth. He poured a little of the coffee from the cup into the saucer, set the cup on the table, and then, balancing the saucer on the tips of the fingers of his left hand, sipped the coffee through the sugar lump. To *dricka på bit och på fat*, though no longer fashionable or indicative of good manners, was permitted in the Solbakken household because, as Mrs. Solbakken's late husband used to say, it helped cool the coffee.

Mrs. Solbakken arranged gingerbread cookies on a plate and set the plate in the centre of the table. Those who had coffee took a cookie and dipped it into their cup; Karl and Viktoria used their glasses of milk.

"How was it in Gamlaby today?" Mrs. Solbakken asked Jussi. It was a signal for the children to be quiet so that their guest could speak without interruption.

"Very interesting," Jussi said. "When I was in Svensson's store, Ingvald the Communist was there telling Svensson about his time on the *John Grafton*."

"The ship that blew up at Jakobstad?" Karl asked.

"Yes. Ingvald was one of the crew members, apparently." At the Solbakken table, Jussi had learned, one speaks to children as if they are adults, and they are expected to respond appropriately.

"I didn't know that," Karl said.

"Nor I," Harald Berg added. "What did Ingvald have to say about it?"

"As I walked in, he was telling everyone about the helmsman running the boat aground last year—just before Russia lost the war with Japan."

"In the harbor of Port Arthur in Manchuria," Anders said, showing off at the cost of a reproving look from his mother.

"There's a city in Canada called Port Arthur," Viktoria whispered to Karl. "My uncle lives there."

"I know," Karl whispered back.

"Shush!" Mrs. Solbakken said. "Let Jussi talk."

Jussi continued, "Apparently when the crew was told to unload some of the weapons onto a barge, so they could be taken to Kokkola and then smuggled into Russia, they decided to do a little extra drinking and smoking before starting work, and they accidentally set the barge on fire."

Mrs. Solbakken burst into laughter.

"The cartridges got so hot that some of them started exploding, so the sailors had to dump some cargo into the sea. The next day the *John Grafton* started south again, but fifteen minutes later the helmsman ran it aground for the second time. They were close enough to Jacobstad by then that everyone in the town could see them."

"That's where the ship blew up," Karl said to Viktoria.

"I know," Viktoria said. Mrs. Solbakken shushed them again.

Jussi caught Karl's eye to quench further interruptions. "Because the boat was aground, the Customs officials in Jacobstad became suspicious, so they got in a sailboat and headed for the *Grafton*. When Captain Nylander saw them coming, he panicked. If the Customs men found the weapons, it would be game over, so he decided to blow up the ship."

"See?" Karl said to Viktoria.

"Shh," said Mrs. Solbakken.

"And when the Customs men came aboard," Jussi said, "Nylander kidnapped them."

"Kidnapped them?" Karl couldn't believe it. "He *kidnapped* them?"

"Not the smartest thing to do, but Nylander wasn't thinking clearly by this time. His men had already rigged the *Grafton* for demolition, so when the Customs men arrived, he said that he understood that they were duty-bound to report him, but he couldn't let them do that right now because he had to blow up the ship and them, too, in order to keep the weapons out of the hands of the Russians, don't you know."

"Quick thinking," Berg said, laughing.

"He made them an offer. If they promised to wait a couple of days before they reported him, he wouldn't blow them up with the ship. They agreed, of course, and then the whole bunch—Nylander and his crew and the Customs men—headed for shore. The *Grafton* exploded in a blast that could be heard for fifty kilometres, and the guns and ammunition ended up in the water. The Customs men, true to their word, gave Nylander until Sunday to get away, and he used the time to talk some of the locals into taking him and his crew by sailboats to Sweden. Ingvald stayed in Sweden for a few months, then he got homesick and came back to Finland. End of story."

"Why did the Customs men not report Nylander immediately?" Anders asked. "They were safe on shore."

"Well," Berg began, sensing an opportunity, "First of all, they had given him their word. And, second, Nylander is a popular man in Jakobstad—he's a Finland-Swede, after all. And Jakobstad is where the Customs men lived." The expected follow-up questions did not come, and Berg, disappointed, took a sip of his coffee.

"I heard the explosion," Karl whispered to Viktoria. "Did you?"

She nodded.

When the cookies had been eaten, and the coffee was all gone, Mrs. Solbakken said, "Now, Jussi, you wanted to ask Anders a favour?"

"Yes, but it's a bit personal. Do you mind if I talk to him outside?"

"Not at all."

"Is it about a girl?" Viktoria wanted to know. She knew that the time at table was over, and she could speak her mind.

"Viktoria!" Mrs. Solbakken said, nonetheless.

"Maybe," Jussi said with a smile. The blush rematerialized on Anders. "The coffee was excellent, Mrs. Solbakken, and the cookies were superb."

"Thank you, Jussi." Mrs. Solbakken sat a little straighter in her chair.

"Lovisa Finska?" Viktoria said, and Mrs. Solbakken glared icily at her.

"Maybe." Jussi gave Viktoria a smile laced with just enough smugness to drive her crazy, then the two boys left the room and went to the porch to put on their coats and boots.

Once they were outside, Anders said, "It's not about Lovisa, is it?"

"No." Jussi laughed. "It's not about her. You got a cigarette?"

Anders fumbled around in his coat pocket and came up with a small cardboard pack, beaten but still functional. From the box he retrieved two cigarettes and a match.

"Does she know you smoke?" Jussi asked.

"Lovisa?"

"Your mother."

"I only smoke when Berg is around. His clothes stink—so I use him for cover." Anders passed a cigarette to Jussi, then lit the match expertly by running his thumbnail over the match head. He lit Jussi's cigarette first, then his own. "So what's the favour?"

Jussi waited a moment before he spoke. "It's not exactly a favour. How would you like to visit Oskar Gundersson next week?"

"Gundersson? Why? What's going on?"

"I didn't tell the whole story in there."

"Oh?"

Jussi took a long drag on the cigarette. "The water's really shallow where the Grafton blew up, so the fellows in Jakobstad used the weekend to fish out as many boxes of rifles and ammunition as they could, and the Customs men turned a blind eye to it. The good citizens kept what they wanted and sent the rest out to the farmers in the countryside for safe-keeping. Berg doesn't know this, and I don't want you to tell him. He likes to show off his knowledge too much, and sometimes he's not careful about who's listening."

Anders nodded.

"Sunday afternoon the Russians showed up in Vasa with soldiers. They organized diving parties and sent them to Jakobstad to retrieve the weapons from the sea." Jussi looked at Anders expectantly and waited.

"I don't get it," Anders said at last.

"It was too late. The farmers had fished up a lot of the guns. Oskar Gundersson has about a hundred Vetterli rifles and several crates of ammunition in one of his silos, and he's giving them away to anyone who wants them, as long as he knows the person."

"For the revolution?"

Jussi laughed. "For moose hunting. Next week I'm going to town again," he said, a studied nonchalance in his voice. "Want to come along, pay Oscar a visit?"

"Sure. I haven't seen him for a while. And a Vetterli might be just the thing for bringing down a moose."

"Or a Cossack." Jussi laughed, then undid Viola's reins and climbed into the cart. The horse snorted, eager to get going once again. They had just started back down the drive when Jussi remembered the ladder. He pulled gently on the reins to stop, then turned back to Anders who was watching him leave.

"Anders," he yelled, "you need to put the fire ladder back up. It's fallen into the snow. And remember, *your* job is to clean the chimney. Berg gets dizzy." Sometimes Jussi felt more like Anders' father than his friend.

"Got it."

I hope so, Jussi thought. "Home," he said to Viola, who moved forward eagerly. She knew where she was going—home.

2 • NOVEMBER 17, 1906

"WHAT DO YOU THINK of the cart, Anders?" Jussi asked. They were well away from the Solbakken house, headed for Gamlaby on the Grötas Road. It was just past sunrise, and a light snow was falling.

"It's fine," Anders said. "Why?"

"I'll show you." Jussi had Viola move to the side of the road and stop. He got off the cart and Anders did likewise. "Notice anything?"

"No. What am I supposed to notice?"

"Look at the seat."

"It's a seat, a bench seat." Anders paused. "Oh, but you've added a box to it."

"Yes," Jussi said. He tapped the back of the seat. "I built this two days ago. The front boards are hinged, see? I can put my extra boots and gloves and scarf inside, plus food and drink. There's a latch on the bottom. Open it up."

Anders felt for the latch, found it, and swung the door upwards to see all the items Jussi had listed. "If you mean for this to be a place where we can hide the guns, I don't think it's going to work. It'll be the first place someone will look."

Jussi gave him a smile before he spoke. "Tell you what—look harder. Look closely, really closely."

Anders did. "Boots, scarf, gloves, food. So what?" He closed the door and latched it.

"You didn't notice that the box is a little smaller on the inside than it should be. There's another compartment behind the first one. You have to use a screwdriver to loosen the screws on the other side. It's just big enough for two or three guns."

Anders opened the door again. "Well. Clever. That could work."

"I don't think anyone will stop us on the way home, but it pays to be careful. When we get to Gundersson's, I'll just undo the screws and we'll put the guns inside. If we're stopped...well, we'll see."

Jussi closed the door of the box, got back on the cart, and Anders climbed up on the seat beside him. Viola started on her way again.

An hour later, they crossed the railway tracks at Gamlaby, and after a few hundred metres turned right. At the intersection of Grötas Road and the road that led to Nykarleby, they halted outside Svensson's store.

In the space normally filled in summer and fall with farmers selling produce from their wagons, a small crowd had gathered around a speaker. The man was shouting at the crowd, and they were shouting right back at him.

"It's Ingvald!" Jussi said. "Come on, you've got to see this. He puts on a goddamned good show."

They got off the cart, tied up Viola, and headed for the congregation. Because both boys were tall, they had little trouble seeing over the heads of the crowd. It helped that Ingvald was standing on a sturdy wooden box.

"All I'm saying," Ingvald shouted, "all I'm saying is that there are five kinds of people." He ticked them off on his fingers as he spoke. "People who work for others, people who own the factories that employ the workers, people who work for themselves, people who beg or steal, and people who own land and make money by charging others for its use. The owners—the ones who own the land or the factories—they control the means of production, and they get most of the money; the workers control nothing, so they get the least. And that's not fair!"

Someone near the front of the crowd shouted, "Bullshit! Communist bullshit!"

"Don't shout your ignorance at me!" Ingvald yelled back. "Just go to one of the industrial cities like Helsinki or Tampere and have a look at what goes on inside a factory and you'll see what I'm talking about. Men dying in their forties from the brutal work; men getting injured in the prime of life and having to face a future in which they can never work again. Men forced to hold two jobs, or three, just to have enough to pay the rent and put some food on the table. And the masters not lifting a goddamned finger to do anything about it because they're too busy making money and spending it on fancy houses and restaurant meals."

"This isn't Helsingfors!" the man at the front of the crowd yelled.

Ingvald realized his mistake: he had called Finland's capital

Helsinki, the Finnish name of the city. To say *Tampere* instead of *Tammerfors* was forgivable. But *Helsingfors* was Finland's capital, and in Gamlaby it was absolutely not *Helsinki*. He raised both hands in acknowledgment.

The man at the front did not accept Ingvald's "apology." Instead, he shouted, "Gamlaby doesn't have any factories, not even one! Not even a tobacco factory like in Jacobstad! Not even a tar factory!" Some people in the crowd laughed. But not all.

Jussi tapped Anders on the shoulder. "Ingvald may not be much of a sailor, but he sure knows how to make the wind blow. I'm going into Svensson's. You stay here and enjoy the show."

Anders nodded.

Viola gave a little whinny as Jussi passed her and went up the stairs. Inside, Fredric Svensson, broom in hand, stood at the front window, watching the crowd. No one else was in the store.

Jussi smiled. "Ingvald's got them all upset again, I see."

"He's been at it most of the morning."

"I was at Solbakken's place last week, and Mrs. Solbakken was worried about a revolution. Do you think that's ever going to happen?"

"Not here," Svensson said, turning away from the window. "But I've been in Helsinki." His choice of *Helsinki* was out of respect for Jussi. "The rich are a lot richer there, and the poor are a lot poorer."

He leaned his broom against a wall, then reached into a small bin and pulled out a handful of raisins and popped a few into his mouth. "And what Ingvald says about the factories is true," he said as he chewed. "Not many workers can put in thirty or forty years without being carried out damaged or dead. Up north in Kemi it's like that, too. But you know what? Those guys know what they're getting into."

Svensson glanced through the window. "Revolution? No. Not here. We don't have conscription any more. We got the new parliament this past October. No more Estates fighting each other. Women get to vote—they even get to run for office in next year's elections. Sure, the Social Democrats are becoming more powerful, but they're careful to emphasize moderation."

He put the last of the raisins into his mouth, then wiped his hands on his apron. "Ingvald is on the right track about some things, but he's completely wrong if he thinks that we're going to want more reforms badly enough to start killing each other to get them." He put on his business face. "Anything I can get you, Jussi?"

"Relax, enjoy the show. I know where everything is." Jussi set about collecting the goods he needed. Svensson went into the back room and rearranged some of the items on the shelves. Then he came back out, took up the broom once more and started sweeping the floor.

After Jussi had gathered together the supplies, he paid for them, loaded them into the cart, and went to find Anders. "Time to go," he said.

A few minutes along the road Anders commented, "Ingvald doesn't seem anything like the person you described last week. And mother thinks that he is...stupid, uneducated. But he doesn't seem that way. What's going on?"

"He's a recruiter. Did you notice that when he gives his speech, he watches his audience like a hawk? It's a speech he's given dozens of times, in dozens of places, so he knows how people usually respond to it. When it's over, he goes and talks to anyone who seems to have been really listening, and he tries to recruit him."

"For what?"

"For the communists. And he tells the Nylander story the way he does because he knows it makes the revolutionaries look less dangerous than they are—more like bumblers than fanatics. Ingvald never does anything casually."

"You think the revolutionaries are dangerous?"

"Yes. And I think Ingvald is, too."

They rode for some time without speaking.

At last, Anders asked, "Do you think Lovisa Finska likes me?"

Jussi laughed. "She likes you just fine," he said.

It was almost two o'clock when they arrived at Gundersson's farm. Gundersson came out to greet them as the cart pulled up. He was a big man with muscular arms and tree-trunk legs, a man built for throwing bales of hay. He smiled as Jussi had Viola stop in the yard.

He asked, "Jussi, Anders, what brings you here?"

"The rifles," Jussi said. "I was hoping you might have a couple for us."

Gundersson considered for a moment. "I can give one to Anders, Jussi, but you know I shouldn't give one to you."

He paused for the briefest moment.

Jussi held his breath.

Gunderson laughed. "I'm pulling your leg. You're a fine young man, Jussi, and I can't see how any harm could come from it, no matter what anyone says. They're in the silo. Come along and I'll see if I can find two good ones."

A half hour later they left, the two Vetterli rifles and several boxes of ammunition stowed safely in the cart's secret compartment.

When they got to the Solbakken farm, Anders asked, "Where do you think I should hide the rifle?"

"When are you going to use it?"

"Just when we go hunting."

"Then leave it right where it is. We'll keep both guns in the compartment. The fewer the people know about the guns, the better. And, remember, say nothing to Berg. He's a good man, but...."

"He talks a lot," Anders said. "When are we going hunting?"

"Ask your mother when she can spare you from the farm for a day. I'll be back next week, and you can let me know. Tell her that you'll be using my mother's gun."

"Your mother has a gun?"

"She hunts with my father. She's a Finn, too, remember? My family's a little different from yours."

"Not much," Anders said, "My mother is hunting Harald Berg."

Jussi laughed.

Anders didn't get out of the cart. "Jussi, why did Gundersson say he shouldn't give you one of the rifles?"

"I'm not a Finland-Swede. The rifles aren't supposed to be given to Finnish-speakers."

"That's not right. I don't understand it."

"Nor I," Jussi lied, and changed the subject. "Next week we go hunting. And remember—don't mention the guns to anyone, not even your prospective stepfather."

"Quarry," Anders said. He got down from the cart.

Jussi gave Viola's reins a flick, turned the cart around, and let her take him home.

PART II

AIR

Easy it is to descend into Hell; the gates of Death are open night and day.
But to climb back out—to follow your own trail to the upper air—
that's something else again.

~ *Dante,* The Inferno

1 • NOVEMBER 10, 1917

AS JUSSI DROVE UP THE ROAD to the Solbakken house just after sunrise he noticed that the main ladder, the one that led up to the roof, was lying on its side on the ground, outside the east wing.

Anders isn't here to remind Karl to do a walkaround once in a while, he thought. Perho, the chestnut stallion who had replaced Viola, snorted as if agreeing.

Jussi stopped the horse in front of the hitching post, then got off the cart and secured Perho. This was a horse that liked to be ridden more than it liked to pull the cart. He would not have remained there untied. Viola would have stayed put. Jussi missed her.

He replaced the ladder for Karl. Then he checked for mud on his boots, saw none, and knocked on the outer door of the porch, two short taps, a pause, and one more.

The rules were different these days. It wasn't enough just to knock.

Anders' mother opened the door after she had taken a quick look out the parlour window to see who was there.

Ellen Solbakken had begun to look old. She was not yet fifty, but farm work had stooped her shoulders, damaged her knees, and slowed her gait. Her hair was streaked with white now. Her voice, however, was still a young woman's voice, and in the rise and fall of her tones and inflections, Ellen didn't so much speak the language of the Finland-Swedes as sing it.

"Jussi," she sang out, "how good to see you! What brings you here?"

"I thought I'd stop by on the way to town and see if you'd heard anything from Anders," Jussi said. "He is still in Germany?"

He couldn't ask directly what he really wanted to know: Was Anders still alive, still unscathed?

"Yes. I got a letter from him a week ago. It was written two weeks before that. The mail is so slow now. He is well. Please, come in."

"Thank you." In the porch, Jussi removed his boots and his coat, then followed her down the hall to the kitchen.

"Coffee?" Ellen asked. "Or perhaps a little tea to warm you up?"

"Tea would be wonderful. I would enjoy that very much." *Tea would be much less expensive than coffee*, he thought—another thing they both knew, and never talked about.

Chatting as she worked, Ellen added some wood to the cook stove, fetched the kettle and filled it with water, then put it on the stove. She took two cups and saucers from the small cupboard and put them on the side table.

"I hate mornings like this. The kitchen is too bright when the sun reflects off the snow—it's too real, too bossy. It keeps insisting that the world is just as it's always been, and it makes me want to argue with it. I start to wonder what Anders is doing, how the fighting is going at the Eastern Front, and when I'm going to see him again."

Jussi understood. Anders was with the 27th Jäger Battalion. The Germans were training him to fight the Russians, preparing for the time when Russia's soldiers and Cossack battalions would sweep into Finland. Anders and the Jägers would shore up the country's western and southern coasts. That was the scenario, the plan. Everyone knew it; few talked about it.

"I blame those damned Boy Scouts, you know," Ellen said as she sat down. "Harald got all carried away by Baden-Powell and that stupid Boy Scout Movement. When he heard about it, there was nothing for it but to form a troop and make himself its Scoutmaster—and this was *after* the government had made it illegal to be a member of a quasi...what is it called?"

"Quasi-military organization," Jussi filled in for her.

"Yes. And that place, what was it called, Maffy something—that African place?"

"Mafeking."

"That's the one. Harald was so...*enthralled,* I suppose, by the story that Baden-Powell had trained boys to carry messages in that war, and he wanted his own students to learn how to be military scouts, too. Imagine! Young boys."

Jussi nodded. "Like those in the siege of Mafeking."

Ellen couldn't stop. "Harald read about it the year after, and next thing you know, he's talked Anders, who was twenty-three but still knew almost nothing—he's talked him into being his Assistant Scoutmaster. And two years ago when the Germans said they would train some of the young men of Finland—the Scouts, they meant—to be soldiers, Anders and a couple of the older boys packed their bags and off they went. *Dammit!*"

Ellen inhaled and then managed a shrug, a mother's resignation. "Sorry for babbling. It makes me angry."

"You say you got a letter from Anders?" Jussi didn't want a long and uneasy silence. "What is he up to?"

"They've pulled the boys back from the front again," Ellen said, her voice becoming a monotone. "Now they're teaching them all about artillery. Anders doesn't tell me much about it—not even where he is. They read his letters."

"He's probably very busy," Jussi said. Sometimes he couldn't believe he'd ever been worried about Anders keeping a Grafton gun. It seemed that Anders had taken to the military. He'd become a soldier. "What about Karl and Rabbit? I see Karl at Svensson's, but I never seem to catch Rabbit."

Ellen laughed. "Nobody catches Rabbit. He's fourteen—fifteen in a few weeks—and still into everything."

"He's a smart boy."

"He is. But he's much too trusting, and far too kind. He's always trying to help people. Harald has him tutoring some of the slower ones at school, and Rabbit just loves it. He'll make a good teacher someday."

The rising whistle of the kettle sent her to the stove. She filled the teapot with water and then added the loose tea to it.

"My mother used to tell me that one must never scald the leaves by pouring hot water on them," she said. "The leaves must learn to swim."

She sat down at the table once again. "Fredric Svensson has Karl doing the ordering, now. Rabbit went into town with him. You know, I think Svensson would like it if Karl took over the store sometime. Fredric doesn't have any children to leave it to, and his wife has no interest in running it."

"I hope it works out that way," Jussi said.

"So does Viktoria." Ellen laughed, shaking off her melancholy. "Karl's proposed to her. Did you know that?"

"No, but that's good news. What's the date?"

"They haven't set one. The Lassilas are in Helsingfors again, and I don't think Victoria has talked to them about it yet."

Ellen got up and peeked into the teapot. Pronouncing it ready, she poured some of it through the strainer into Jussi's cup. "Sugar?"

"Thank you, no. This is fine." As Jussi raised his cup, he heard thudding horse hooves, and a moment later a loud, unpatterned knocking at the door.

Ellen hurried into the parlour and looked out the window. "It's Inga Svensson. She's come on horseback. She hates to ride. Something must be wrong."

She went to the door, with Jussi right behind her. As soon as the door was opened, Inga Svensson rushed in and immediately shut it behind her.

Her eyes were red. "Fredric is dead, Ellen, and Karl is hurt, but not badly. They wore red kerchiefs over their faces. Jussi, you have to go to the store and help!" The words rushed out of her, tumbling over each other, gaining momentum as if they were boulders pushed off the top of a steep hill.

"Karl is hurt?" Ellen asked. "How?"

"Robbers, bandits. Jussi, you have to go right now. Right now!"

"Go," Ellen said to Jussi. "Do what you can to help."

"You'll take care of Inga?"

"Yes, yes." She turned to Inga. "Jussi will go to the store, and you will stay here tonight."

Outside, Jussi released Perho and got into the cart. An hour later, he was at Svensson's store.

A small group of men stood around Karl, who sat in a chair. He looked as if he had taken a beating but would be none the worse for it in a few days.

Jussi said, "Are you okay?"

Karl nodded. "They killed Fredric. I tried to stop them, but there were at least four of them. They got him with their knives. One of them hit me with something and knocked me out. I don't know why they didn't kill me, too. When I came to, they were still here, taking things, and I started yelling, and they ran. That got the attention of the men. Herr Berg was first. He's in the storeroom with the body."

"Where's Rabbit?"

"He went over to Lassila's as soon as he and I got here. Viktoria was going to lend him some of her books. He's probably still there. I kept anyone from getting him until we knew what's what."

"Good," Jussi said. "Did you recognize anyone?"

"No, but I got a shoe. I grabbed someone's leg as he ran out." Karl used a handkerchief to wipe away some blood that still oozed slightly from a cut above his left eye. "A trophy." He pointed to the shoe sitting on the counter. It was a right shoe, well worn. "Is Inga all right?"

"She's at your place. Your mother is taking care of her. Has anyone gone to Jacobstad to report this?"

"Johannes. He telegraphed first, though."

"Good. Let me see Fredric."

"We'll leave you to look after things," one of the men in the store said. Jussi, they felt, would know what to do.

"Thank you." Jussi followed Karl into the storeroom.

Harald Berg was looking at the shelving but turned as they came in. His left eye was blackened, his left cheek bruised.

"Jussi, they killed him. Four men. Reds, I think. Karl's got a shoe one of them was wearing."

"You're hurt."

"Not much. I was coming into the store and one of them gave me a couple of good ones before he took off. Here." He passed a piece of paper to Jussi. "This was stuffed in the front pocket of Fredric's apron. I can't read it. It's in Finnish. What does it say?"

Jussi looked at the writing. "Reds."

Karl asked, "But what does it say?"

"It's some of Ingvald's poison," Jussi said. "It's Marx. 'From each according to his means.'" He looked around the storeroom. Very little was left on the shelves—mostly non-food items.

Harald noticed Jussi looking. "They couldn't take much. There wasn't much left to steal."

Jussi nodded.

"Now what?" Harald wanted to know.

"They didn't write the message here," Jussi said. "The paper is folded. They came here with it in someone's pocket. They meant to kill Svensson, I think, not just steal food. The message is bullshit. It's meant to throw us off the scent."

He turned to Karl. "Baking powder, yeast, cheese. What else is missing?"

Karl examined the shelves. "Salt, crackers, flour—the last we'll be getting for a while, I'm afraid—tobacco, and tobacco paper. Those things for sure. We haven't been able to get any coffee from the suppliers for half a year now."

"Still, mostly food. Did any of them look familiar?"

"No. They weren't from around here. Their clothes and boots hadn't been bought here. We don't carry what they were wearing."

Jussi glanced out the window. "They'd probably scouted the village—maybe a few days ago."

He turned back to Karl. "One of them—a lookout, perhaps—might have been quite young."

"What makes you think that?"

"There are candies on the floor by the counter out there. The young one likely helped himself to a handful from the candy jar. He might have been their spy. Do you remember anyone watching the store in the last few days, maybe from across the street? A youngster?"

"No. And the ones in the store were older. None of them was younger than me."

Jussi looked at Harald. "You must call a meeting, Herr Berg. This...." He shook his head. "It's time to form a White Guard unit. Whoever did this will try something like it again if we don't. Are you willing to take charge?"

Harald looked down at Svensson's body. "Yes. Go back to the house and tell Ellen and Inga that I'm going to stay with the body until the authorities arrive from Jacobstad. Take Karl with you so that his mother can see that he hasn't been hurt too badly."

"Yes, sir. I'll take Rabbit as well. Karl, go find your brother, then come straight back here."

Karl nodded and left. Harald and Jussi stood in the doorway between the storeroom and the main part of the store. From there they could keep track of both rooms.

Once he was certain they were alone, Harald asked, "Who do you think did this?"

"The note is meant to tell us it was the Red Guard, but I don't think we should take it at face value. It could just as easily be anyone. If Fredric had any enemies—" He let the statement hang. "There's no real law enforcement any more, no visible government. People take advantage—"

Then he had a sudden thought. "Excuse me a moment." He walked to the store's main display window and looked across the street, careful to stay out of the direct sunlight.

"Harald," he said, keeping his voice low, "there is a young boy, eleven or twelve years old, maybe—he could be older—standing beside the blacksmith's shop, looking this way. Move slowly and don't let the sun give you away, but come over here so you can see him."

Berg stood behind Jussi.

Jussi asked, "Do you see him?"

"Yes. He's not from here. I've never taught him, at any rate."

Jussi backed away from the window. "Harald, take the broom and start to sweep the store. When you get to the doorway, start to sweep the steps outside so you catch his attention. I'm going out the back to see if I can grab that kid."

Berg took the broom and began sweeping.

Jussi went into the storeroom and out the back door. *God, give me speed*, he thought. When he judged that Harald Berg had started on the front steps, he exploded from around the side of the building and ran at the young boy. But the child was just as quick and ran behind the blacksmith's shop before Jussi had time to cross the street. Jussi came around the corner of the smithy a little too late. The boy had a horse, a Don, a Cossack horse. He was out of sight in less than a minute.

"Dammit!" Jussi said. He went back to the store.

"Well?" Harald asked.

"The boy is a horse thief, and a damn good one. He rode off on a Don. I don't think he'll be back."

"So, now what?" They went back into the store. Jussi picked up the shoe.

"This. We'll start with the shoe. Tomorrow I'll go to Nykarleby to see if any of the cobblers recognize it as their work. But right now, Herr Berg, stay at the store with the body until the sheriff gets here from Jacobstad. If it's taking too long, send someone to get him."

Through the store window, Jussi saw Karl and Rabbit across the street, coming at a run. He went outside to intercept them.

"Rabbit," Jussi said. "You stay right here on the street. Don't go into the store. Karl, give your key to Herr Berg so that he can lock up the store when he leaves. Then we'll all go to your home so your mother can see that you are okay. Did you tell Viktoria?"

Karl nodded.

"Good," Jussi said.

2 • DECEMBER 6, 1917

JUST AFTER NINE O'CLOCK that evening, five men had arrived at the Solbakken house. They were now seated around the kitchen table. Ellen came down the stairs from the smaller of the two upstairs bedrooms.

"Is she asleep?" Harald asked. He poured himself a little tea, then carefully put the teapot back on a warm part of the cookstove.

"I think so," Ellen said. "Almost a month later, yet she still doesn't really believe Fredric is dead. I'll check on her in a few minutes. I don't want to disturb you, so I'll leave you men here to your business and work a bit in the sewing room."

"Thank you, Ellen." Harald waited to give her time to leave the room and joined the others at the table: Jussi, Karl, Oskar Gundersson, Emil Almquist from Jacobstad, and Johannes Norlund who had come by train from Vasa. Karl, at twenty-one, was the youngest and had no idea why Jussi had asked Harald to put him on the committee.

Harald introduced himself, then each person in turn. Almquist, a writer for the *Jacobstads Tidning*, the weekly newspaper, knew the ins and outs of Finnish politics. Johannes Norlund had connections to the White Guards and to the politicos in Helsingfors.

Almquist had a thick set of notes on the table before him. He glanced at them, then put them aside.

"This has been a very...disconcerting year. In February, there was the army revolt in Russia, and here the Reds started their attacks on their employers, their neighbours. Anyone they didn't like, anyone they thought was anti-revolutionary. Even the teachers of their children." He looked across the table at Harald Berg.

"In mid-March," Almquist continued, "Tsar Nicholas was removed and, for a while, the more conservative elements in Russia were able to control the Duma and the Provisional Government. That was good for us, but everything else kept breaking down,

28

especially the economy. Russia stopped buying things from us, and our government was a mess."

Karl found himself listening to his mother's sewing machine. He tried to concentrate.

"And so when the Social Democrats got into power," Almquist was saying, "they tried to be fair to everyone by balancing the new Senate—six socialists on one side, six non-socialists on the other. Result? No way to compromise, no way to solve problems. We got street councils and employer organizations and strikes and mass meetings, everybody trying to run the government except the government. Grain imports from Russia stopped. Up went inflation, down went production. In came price-fixing, the black market, and demonstrations in the streets."

And Ingvald on his soap box, Karl thought, *and Svensson losing money all the time and dying in the storeroom.*

"Excuse me, Emil," Johannes Norlund said. "There is something I'd like to point out here."

Almquist hoped Norlund would keep his comments short. Norlund, like an academic in a lecture hall, sat with his hands folded neatly on the table.

"Our problems aren't just political. Consider. In theory, if you have a farm, you can grow your own food and sell what remains to city-dwellers. If they have no money to pay for it, however, you either have to give it away and risk losing your farm, or you have to sell your produce for less than it costs you to grow it, and hope the banker isn't going to notice. Either way, the tension builds between you and the townsman. The Red raids and attacks on the farms exploit and magnify this tension."

"Quite right." Almquist said quickly. "And remember, in March we first heard that Russian soldiers had murdered a number of their officers. The chaos isn't restricted to the civilian population. Then in April, Germany thought it could bring about a revolution in Russia if it gave Lenin safe conduct to travel to Petrograd. Lenin, Germany believed, would convince the Russians to sue for peace. But Lenin's take on it was a little different."

All but Karl laughed. *You must pay attention to everything*, Berg had once told him, *so that you acquire common knowledge. It is what makes us a people.* He wished he had followed this advice more closely.

"In May, the Reds in Finland thought a copy-cat revolution might work, so they divided their Workers' Guards into two parts, the Security Guards and the Red Guards. The Red Guards organized secretly in the more industrialized villages and towns—Helsingfors, Tammerfors, Åbo, Viborg, and others. We should have countered with White Guards, but we didn't."

"Because?" Karl asked.

"Because we didn't believe it would get really serious. But it did. This past month almost thirty people were killed by the Reds, and maybe two hundred more had their homes and farms burned. And, contrary to what most people think, there was no direction from the Red leaders for the gangs to start getting their hands bloody. Nobody of any rank ordered them to do this. The workers, the peasant farmers, the dispossessed, they did it on their own.

"Then, in July, the Social Democrats came to their senses, and they introduced the Power Act which finally gave enough power to our Parliament to govern effectively. But the act was never ratified by Russia. Instead, the Russians sent more troops to Finland. And Lenin, who had been agitating in Finland for revolution, just ran away."

There was light laughter around the table. This time, it was Jussi who remained solemn.

"By autumn," Almquist said, "we had organized close to a hundred and fifty Civil Guards, what we call White Guards now."

Harald Berg stifled a yawn and sneaked a peek at his pocket watch.

Almquist continued, "We had enough White Guards to keep the peace for a while. But in October and November, the workers' revolution in Russia put the Bolsheviks in a position to seize power. All of a sudden the Reds in Finland wanted to remain part of Russia. We on the White side wanted sovereignty instead—control of our destiny—but not independence because, after all, Russia was, and remains, the main market for Finnish goods. Real independence would have brought economic disaster.

"And then, at the end of October, some of the Finnish Jägers arrived from Germany."

"What?" Harald said. "The Jägers have returned?"

Ellen emerged from the sewing room. "Is Anders back?"

"*Some* of the Jägers have returned," Almquist said. "A very few. I am sorry, but it is unlikely your son will be among them. They were on the *Equity* when the ship brought a cargo of German weapons to Finland. I don't know why this particular group has returned. It may have something to do with the Cavalry School, or with the distribution of the weapons, I don't know. I will make inquiries, however."

"Thank you," Ellen said. "I—I'm sorry for disturbing you. I'll get back to my sewing. Thank you." She retreated to the sewing room, but her hands were trembling with such force that needlework was beyond her.

"I, too, am sorry," Harald said quietly when Ellen had gone. "It did not occur to me that she would be listening."

"Quite all right," Almquist said.

In the sewing room Ellen cried quietly.

"There is more I want to tell you," Almquist said, "but I would prefer if Herr Norlund gives you the latest."

"Oh, for God's sake!" Harald Berg burst out. "This isn't the Finland I grew up in! What the hell is going on? This happens, and that happens, and then something else happens, and it's all supposed to make sense? Are the circus clowns in charge? It doesn't matter *why*. All that matters is what is happening *now*, and what we're going to do about it."

Jussi put his hand on Harald's arm. "Good point. But let us allow Herr Norlund to speak."

Norlund showed no sign of being upset by Harald's interruption. "On the seventeenth of November, Lenin and the Bolsheviks revolted, which means that we can expect no moderation of Russia's...fervour."

Unexpectedly, Norlund smiled. "The good news, for us at least, is that on the seventeenth as well, the German submarine UC-27 brought home a few Jägers and an agreement that will see the White Guard receive seventy thousand rifles in the near future and the return of the Jäger battalion to Finland."

He had hardly finished his sentence before Ellen reappeared in the kitchen. "The Jägers are coming back?" she said excitedly. "The rest—they're coming back?"

"Yes," Norlund said, "and your son should be among them, though I don't know exactly when they will arrive. But from what I hear, the Finnish-speaking lads who have been training with them will not be returning at the present time. There is some fear that there may be...compromised individuals among them. Red sympathizers."

Jussi said nothing.

"But Anders will be back?" Ellen asked.

"Yes."

"Thank God," she said quietly. "I'm going to check on Inga." She went upstairs to the little bedroom.

"Let me get to the point, as the English say," Norlund said. Karl wondered if he could. "On the twenty-seventh this past month, the Social Democrats met and voted to stick with the idea of a socialist revolution in Finland. The Labour movement asked for its own military force, but I don't know what happened to the request.

"And...." Norlund thumbed through his notes. "Stalin, Joseph Stalin was at the meeting, but he couldn't get them worked up enough to start the revolution then and there. Oh, and Stalin promised that Finland would be granted independence."

"Not likely," Harald said.

Norland smiled. He put away his notes. "More likely than you think," he said. "The Conservatives under Svinhufvud hold power now, and they have decided both to separate from Russia and to strengthen the White Guards."

"Well," Harald said. "I certainly had not expected that. But—"

"And today is December sixth," Norlund said nonchalantly. "And in case you haven't heard, there is now an armistice between Germany and the Bolsheviks."

He waited for the words to take effect, but his audience sat waiting for an explanation. After a moment, he added, "Right now, perhaps even as we sit here, Finland is declaring itself an independent state."

For a moment, no one spoke, then they turned as one toward Emil Almquist for confirmation.

"It will be in tomorrow's *Tidning*," Almquist said. "We are no longer a Russian Duchy. We have our country back." He rose to his feet. "Long live Finland!"

The men at the table immediately stood. "Long live Finland!" they shouted in response—all but Jussi, who stood with them but could not speak. His mind was full of thoughts of war. The Reds would think that the country had been given to *them*; the Whites would think it was *theirs*.

Harald Berg slapped his hand down on the table. "This is

wonderful!" he said.

"What about Russia?" Karl asked, as they sat down again. "Will they let us stay independent?"

Almquist answered, "Lenin will support independence, I think. In his April Theses he argued for the self-determination of all nations. If he doesn't weaken, Finland will no longer be part of Russia."

"Long live Finland!" Harald Berg shouted, and the men at the table rose once more and repeated the words in loud chorus.

Ellen came down the stairs, anger in her voice. "What is going on? You'll wake Inga if you keep that up."

"Finland is independent," Harald said quietly. "Herr Norlund just told us. I'll talk to you about it later. It's wonderful news. But now, Herr Norlund is going to tell us how to form a White Guard unit." It was a signal for Ellen to leave the room, but she remained where she was.

A civil war is coming, Jussi thought.

Inga Svensson appeared on the stairs behind Ellen. Ellen turned. "Inga, you need to be in bed."

"I heard the noise," Inga said. "I—I was dreaming and I thought Fredric was....He's still dead, isn't he?"

Ellen nodded. "Go back to bed. I will be there in a moment."

Inga slowly but obediently climbed the stairs. The men went back to talking.

3 • JANUARY 23, 1918

IN THE STORE, THE SHELVES were nearly empty. Karl finished sweeping the floor in the storeroom, put the broom away, then went into the sales area to check on Inga Swensson. She stood behind the counter, going through the week's receipts, tallying the figures.

"How is it going?" Karl asked.

"It's hard to learn, but I think I'm getting it. I used to watch Fredric doing this, but I never thought to help him. It wasn't something I wanted to learn. Now I have to."

"I talked to Jussi yesterday," Karl said. "He said Mannerheim has been made Supreme Commander of the White Guards."

"He was a general, once, wasn't he? In the Russian army?"

"That's him."

"I never paid much attention to politics. I thought it had nothing to do with me."

Karl pretended to be occupied by his sweeping. He waited a minute before speaking. "Mannerheim's trying to disarm the Russian garrisons. He needs their weapons. Quite a few of the Russian officers are helping him."

"Why?"

"I don't know. They trust him, I guess. Jussi thinks there's going to be a war—a real one. Already the skirmishes around Viborg have turned into pitched battles. Ali Aaltonen and Lenin have apparently decided to ship weapons from Petrograd to Viborg, and that means having to first take control of the railroad between the two cities."

"Aaltonen is the drunk, isn't he? The one who wrote articles as Ali Baba?"

"That's him. Jussi says he's a hell of a general, though."

"Jussi knows a lot, doesn't he?"

"He's the smartest person I know. Even smarter than Anders."

Inga smiled. "That's high praise. I know how you feel about your brother. But do you think Jussi's right about the war?"

"Yes." Karl was silent for a moment.

Inga Svensson went back to examining the receipts.

"Mrs. Svensson," Karl said. It was time to broach the subject. She looked up. "Jussi thinks that when the war comes, there will be conscription again."

Inga was puzzled. "And?"

"If there is conscription, I will have to join the White Guards. I won't be able to take care of the store for you."

"I see," Inga said.

"Jussi thinks Aaltonen can muster a hundred and fifty thousand men. At most, we can manage seventy thousand, and that's only with conscription."

Inga looked around the store. "Well, it's not like we have much to sell."

"I'll stay on as long as I can."

"I know you will. You're a good man. Your mother, you know, is a saint—I can't believe she let me stay with her for a month. You take after her. Have you told Viktoria?"

"About conscription? No."

"You need to tell her. Soon."

#

When the five horsemen, each with a red armband on his right arm, arrived, there were no tracks in the snow on the road to the small farm. They had expected to see cart tracks.

"He might not be there," one of the men said to their leader in Finnish.

"If he's not there, we'll wait," the leader replied.

"He'll see our tracks," the youngest said.

"He'll still come. And you're not coming. I don't want you involved in this. Go back to Gamlaby, but stay out of sight."

"Why can't I?"

"Enough! Do as I say. And if someone does see you, don't let him catch you."

The youngest turned his horse around and headed for the village. The others approached the house. They stopped just out of earshot and dismounted.

"Shouldn't we put the bandanas on? She'll see our faces," the tallest said.

"It doesn't matter if she does, you stupid shit."

The leader took his rifle from its sheath, and the others did likewise. He walked toward the house, the others following, their weapons ready. The door was unlocked, but he kicked it in anyway, and entered.

The first shot caught him in the forehead before he spotted the woman sitting under the kitchen table. The man immediately behind him was so startled that he dropped to the floor behind the body of the leader, and the woman's second shot got the third man instead. The last to come in shot her in the chest. She lay wounded in the kitchen, the rifle at her side.

The man who had been the second to enter scrambled across the floor toward the woman, flung the table against the kitchen wall, and picked up her rifle. He passed it to his companion, then knelt on the floor beside her.

"Your son?" he asked. The woman shrugged and gave him a defiant and ironic smile. "Your husband," he said, "where is he?"

"Tar," she said, and a bubble of air and blood came from her mouth.

"What did she say?" the shooter asked.

His partner looked up from the woman. "*Tar.* I think she means that her husband's gone north to work a tar pit. Am I right?" he asked, turning back to the woman.

She answered by slashing at him with a kitchen knife she had hidden behind her. The blade caught him across the nose and cheek and tore flesh from bone.

"Bastard!" the woman yelled. She spit blood at him. The knife fell from her hand.

"Bitch!" the man shouted. He grabbed the knife on the floor and then violently stabbed her several times in the chest.

"I didn't see her get the knife," the shooter said calmly from behind him. It was neither apology nor concern, merely an observation.

"She had it ready."

"She got you good. I'm going to have to sew those cuts. Wait here and watch the door. I'll see if I can find needle and thread." He headed into the small bedroom. In a minute or two he was back with needle, thread, and scissors.

"Alcohol," the slashed man said. "Look for alcohol. You need to disinfect the wounds."

The shooter started to search. Neither in the kitchen nor the bedroom did he find any alcohol. "Nothing." He shrugged.

"What's wrong with these people? Go look outside in the horse's shed. Get horse liniment if you have to. Anything!"

The shooter left the house. As the door slammed shut, the slashed man heard a shot. "Marku, are you all right?"

No answer. He got up, wiped some of the blood from his face, and then pulled the woman's corpse out from under the table and propped it up as a shield in front of him. He crouched low behind her and trained his gun on the door.

He was certain that it was Jussi Mantere who'd fired the shot. Now Jussi would kick in the door, but he'd still be little a sun-blind from the snow outside. That would make Jussi an easy target for someone low to the floor and behind the body of a woman. He waited, ready.

The shot that killed him came from behind, through the small kitchen window.

Jussi entered the kitchen a moment later, holding the old Vetterli. His mother was dead. He felt distant, emotionless, his ears still ringing from the noise of his gun. *There will be time for grieving later.* His mind worked mechanically. He stepped over the body of the man his mother had slashed, and as he did so, he noticed the man's new shoes. He rolled the body over onto its back, put the front of the Vetterli's barrel on the man's groin, and pulled the trigger.

#

Just before five o'clock, Karl saw the cart pulling up in front of the store. Jussi did not immediately get off.

Karl turned to Inga, who was in the middle of restocking some of the shelves. "Jussi's here, but something's wrong. I'll be right back."

Inga stopped working and went to the window.

As he came down the front steps of the store, Karl saw the bodies in the cart.

"They killed my mother," Jussi said. Though his face was streaked with tears, his voice held no emotion. He got down from the cart and began to pull one of the bodies out. He yanked on it until the body

37

slid off the cart and onto the street.

Karl put his hand on Jussi's shoulder.

"No!" Jussi shouted. "They killed my mother. They belong in the dirt." Another body landed on the ground.

"Then I'll help," Karl said. He pulled the third corpse off the cart. If this was what Jussi wanted, then Karl would help.

Two men came running across the street from the telegraph office. Another emerged from the smithy.

Jussi pulled the last body out of the cart. The face had blown apart where the bullet had exited, and Karl noticed the groin.

As the body hit the ground Jussi said, "There was another—the boy, I think, on a Don. He got by me. Cowardly bastard!"

The man who had come from the blacksmith's shed said, "I know this one." He pointed at the man Jussi had first dragged out of the cart. "Seppo...something. He has an older brother, in Helsingfors, I think. They are not from here. This one has been staying with his uncle on a farm, near Esse maybe. I'm not sure."

Karl turned to the man. "Find Herr Berg," he said. "He will still be at the school. Tell him what's happened and ask him to go home to my mother immediately. She's there alone. There may be other raiders around." To the pair who had been in the telegraph office, he added, "You two take care of this—" He pointed at the bodies. "This garbage. Get others to help."

He put his hand once more on Jussi's shoulder. This time, Jussi did not shake it off. "You'll stay at our place tonight, Jussi."

"My mother," Jussi said. "She's still on the kitchen floor. I could not—it is *her* kitchen. I have to—"

"*We* have to," Karl said. "But first we'll go to my place to pick up what we'll need. Then we'll all go to your home. We need to telegraph your father, too. All of us will help. Okay?"

"Okay," Jussi said. And he allowed himself to weep.

4 • FEBRUARY 2, 1918

THE SMALL FINNISH CHURCH overflowed with mourners. They sat in the pews, stood along the walls, crowded the doorways. Those who had arrived late or who, by choice, had given up their seats to people who needed them more, stood outside as close to the open main door as they could get.

All of Gamlaby seemed to have come to this place that most of them had never seen—this Finnish church at the intersection of two farm roads only twenty kilometres from the village. The Finnish farmers, tenant farmers, tradespeople, and peasants looked uncomfortably at the strangers in their midst, and those among them who could speak a little Swedish wondered if it would seem too forward to approach these *ruotsalaisia*, these "Swedes" who were their neighbours, whom they did not really know.

Inside the church and outside its walls as well, islands of Finnish-speakers and islands of Finland-Swedes had formed. Here and there a man who knew both languages tried to mingle, usually unsuccessfully, with people he did not know but with whom he could speak. The women, less likely to have a second language, kept to their own groups. All wore black.

Jussi and his father, dressed in suits borrowed from Svensson's store, sat in the front row with Jussi's uncle and three older women whom Karl, sitting in the row behind him, did not recognize.

Pastor Niemi entered through a side door off the altar and climbed three steps to stand in the pulpit. The abrupt silence of the congregation poured out of the main door and flowed over the people standing outside.

"*Isän ja Pojan Ja Pyhän Hengen nimeen.*" In the name of the Father, and of the Son, and of the Holy Ghost.

"Amen," the Finland-Swedes said in unison with the Finns. Everyone recognized that these were the familiar opening words of the funeral service, but only the response would sound the same in

39

both languages. *Amen.* So be it.

Jussi did not want to picture his mother lying bloodied on the kitchen floor, but it was all he could think about. Karl and Inga had gone with Jussi to pick up Ellen, and the four of them had gone to Jussi's home. They had gone to his home where his mother.... Jussi forced himself to disengage. He concentrated, instead, on counting the posts supporting the communion rail. There were twelve. *Was that deliberate?* he wondered. Twelve apostles—with Judas hiding among them?

Pastor Niemi had reached the part of the service where he and the congregation recited the psalm—he said a line in Finnish, and the members of the congregation responded in Finnish or Swedish; this, too, was a part of the funeral service everyone expected and understood.

Jussi began to listen now in both languages, concentrating first on the Swedish and then on the Finnish. *Be elsewhere,* he thought. *Go elsewhere.*

"The Lord is my Shepherd."

"*Ei minulta mitään puutu.*" I shall not want.

"He maketh me to lie down in green pastures."

"*Ja vie minua virvoittavan veden tykö.*" He leadeth me beside the still waters.

"He restoreth my soul."

The languages did not blend easily. Their rhythms were dissimilar, the sounds dissonant as if one language were made of waves cresting, the surf rushing toward a beach, and the other were built of rocks on the shore being shifted and rearranged by the power of the waves.

"*Ja vaikka minä vaeltaisin pimiässä laaksossa,*" Yea, though I walk through the valley of the shadow of death...

"I will fear no evil."

"*Ettäs olet kanssani;*" for Thou art with me.

"Thy rod and Thy staff..."

"*Sinun vitsas ja sauvas minun tukevat.*" Shall comfort me.

Jussi's father reached up and put his hand on Jussi's shoulder. He gripped it hard as if trying to pull strength for himself from its muscles and tendons. Jussi stopped listening to the psalm and let his eyes find comfort in the whitewashed vertical boards behind the communion rail. He sat, motionless, for a long time, then came to himself once more when Pastor Niemi was reading the gospel.

"Through the tender mercy of our God; whereby the dayspring from on high has visited us, to give light to them that sit in darkness and in the shadow of death, to guide our feet into the way of peace."

Luke, Jussi thought, and he went back to looking at the wall.

Just before the homily, Jussi's father took his hand from Jussi's shoulder. *We are much alike*, Jussi thought, and he began to listen to the service. Time slowed, folded itself over onto itself, and they were outside the church in the small parish cemetery, ringed by mourners. Though it was not bitterly cold, Jussi shivered as he stood beside the coffin his father had made and Inga and Ellen had lined with the comforter from the bed. The wood still smelled of fresh stain and varnish.

Pastor Niemi had found a man who could translate his words into Swedish at the committal.

"*Maasta sinä olet tullut*," pastor said. "*Maaksi sinun pitää jälleen tulla. Jeesus Kristus, Vapahtajamme, herättää sinut viimeisenä päivänä.*"

The translator said, "From the earth you came, and to the earth you must return once more. Our Saviour, Jesus Christ, will wake you on the last day."

The men handling the ropes guided the coffin into the ground, then Jussi and the others who were part of the family stepped back. The mourners filed past the open grave, tossing in flowers. Jussi made himself think about the digging of the grave, he and his father beginning the work by shoveling the ground free of snow, then using the pick to break up the frozen soil. A thin layer of blossoms formed on the lid of the coffin.

After the committal service, the mourners went down into the basement of the church to get coffee and sandwiches and to give their condolences to Jussi, his father, his uncle, and the aunts. Coats were piled on chairs set against the walls; the conversation was now less somber. Each family offered Jussi a card containing hand-written words of remembrance—a story, a reflection on the character of Jussi's mother, an anecdote about a lesson learned, or a few well-chosen words about what Jussi's mother's life had meant to them. Jussi promised that the card would be read when there was time and, yes, he would explain to his father what the Swedish ones said.

#

Long after most of the mourners had left for home, a group of men lingered in the church basement. Jussi was not among them. Pastor Niemi, with the help of his translator, had organized the meeting. He had been careful in his selection of the people he felt could safely be invited.

"What news?" Pastor Niemi wanted to know.

At first, no one spoke. Harald Berg, conscious of the awkward silence, stepped in. "You've heard that Mannerheim disarmed the Russian garrisons last month?" The translator immediately went to work. "On the twenty-fifth we found out that the Helsinki Red Guard had been activated."

Others joined in. Despite the need for translation, after a while the conversation felt seamless.

Karl Solbakken, invited because the store was a clearinghouse for news and gossip, added, "And we know that a Russian train with a large number of weapons set out from Petrograd to Viborg." He shook his head slightly. "Sorry, Viipuri. The train had a couple of hundred Red Guards as an escort."

"How many weapons?" Pastor Niemi asked.

Karl began to tick off the list on his fingers. "Fifteen thousand rifles, thirty machine guns, two million rounds of ammunition, ten field guns, six boxcars full of artillery ammunition, and two armoured cars."

"Merciful God!" Pastor Niemi exclaimed. "Did it get through?"

"The White Guards attacked it and forced a delay, but in the end the train got through. The Reds have the weapons."

"That's why the Red Guards decided to take control of Helsingfors on the twenty-eighth," Harald Berg added. The translator substituted *Helsinki* for *Helsingfors*.

"Wait, please," Pastor Niemi said. "Helsinki has fallen to the Reds?"

"Yes," Harald said. "It's the capital of Red Finland now."

"But we've disarmed the Russians in Ostrobothnia," Karl put in.

"What...what is *our* capital?" Pastor Niemi asked.

"The Senate has been moved to Vasa, so I guess it's Vasa," Karl said.

For the first time Emil Almquist, the editor, spoke. "Yes, and General Mannerheim has made Vasa his headquarters as well. At least for the time being."

Like a schoolboy in a roomful of teachers, one of the Finnish-speakers raised a hand. "Matti," said Pastor Niemi, and the translator took over.

"In the north, in Kemi, the workers are all going over to the Reds," Matti said. "I am wondering how many of us will be White and how many Red when each side is full."

"I may be able to answer that," Almquist said. "At most, the Red side will be able to arm a quarter of a million against us. That includes women and children. Some of them, we know, will fight alongside their men. At best, we can manage seventy thousand. Realistically, they'll put a hundred and fifty thousand in the field. And Mannerheim will force conscription. It's the only way he can raise the numbers he needs."

"He can conscript as much as he wants," Matti said, "but my neighbours will vanish into the bush when Mannerheim's men come knocking on the door. They won't follow him. Not many, but a few, will join the Reds. In the south it will be very different. Almost all the Finns, the Finnish-speakers, will fight for the Reds. I am sure of it."

"What about Sweden?" Karl asked. "Can we get weapons from there?"

Almquist answered. "It does not look good. The easiest way for them to send us arms would be by rail through Haparanda and Tornio in the north, but the railway gauge is different in both countries, as you know, so the weapons would have to be unloaded from a Swedish train onto a Finnish one, and the workers who would do that are mostly Red. The Swedes are trying to help, but not much is getting through."

Karl broke the silence that followed. "Where is Jussi?"

The translator addressed Pastor Niemi, who said a few words in Finnish. Matti nodded his head.

"Jussi is with his father," the translator said. "They have gone for a walk. This is a bad day for us, but it is much worse for them, and Pastor says it is time for us to go home and leave them to their grief."

5 • FEBRUARY 8 AND 9, 1918

"NOW, WHAT IS IT you want to tell me?" Ellen Solbakken poured herself a cup of coffee and then came to sit at the kitchen table with Rabbit. "Something about Karl?"

Rabbit folded his hands on the table. He tried to sound casual so that his mother wouldn't be alarmed. "Karl says that Mannerheim is going to announce that Finland is going back to conscription—the 1878 conscription act. Any day now."

"Oh?" Ellen forced herself to be calm. "And how does Karl know this?"

Rabbit shrugged. "That committee he joined. He says every able-bodied man is to be conscripted."

"Lucky for you, you're only fifteen," Ellen said, but she didn't believe in the weight of her words. Boys lied to get in, died to get out.

"Karl says it's not going to matter much how old you are. Anyone who is able-bodied will be conscripted."

"I'm sure that's not going to happen," Ellen said. "It would leave the countryside with just women, old men, and children. The farms would fail, the raiders would return." She tried to put her coffee cup down gently so that Rabbit would not notice her shaking hand, but the cup clattered on the saucer as it settled.

"There's a man coming to the store tomorrow. He's signing up volunteers for the White Guard, for the army. If you are conscripted into the army you don't get a choice of what you want to be. If you volunteer, they give you some choices."

"Darling Rabbit, you're fifteen," she said again. "You won't be conscripted. They can't make you fight." She wanted to believe it.

"I don't want to fight. I don't want to kill. That's something I could never do. But I want to help. I want to be a cook. I'll be far away from the fighting and I'll be doing something I like to do. I'm not a soldier—I know that. But I have friends who are already eighteen, and they'll be conscripted. And they'll have less chance of dying if there's someone like me who cooks for them. If I do the cooking, the soldier whose place I take gets to fight, and he'll do that much better than I. Karl says...he says an army fights on its stomach."

"*Marches* on its stomach," Ellen said. "Napoleon said it first." She wiped her hands on her apron to give herself time to think. "Ivor," she said after a moment, "Karl is your brother, and he knows many things, but this is something he does not know much about. War is...it's not fair, Ivor. There are no rules. And people lie. They tell you anything just so you will do what they want, what they need you to do."

She had not meant to say the last sentence. She had wanted to say something else, but whatever it was had gone from her before she could put it in words. It had been something about conscription and that it was morally wrong in a war like this one, but she couldn't think why.

"Karl says that the conscription man is one of the Jägers. He came on the submarine. Do you think he knows Anders?"

Ellen reached for the coffee cup and willed her hand to behave. She took a sip and then put the cup back down gently, quietly in the saucer.

"He may," she said, "but there are a lot of young Finnish Jägers in Germany." She was silent for a moment. "I guess it wouldn't hurt to ask."

"I will find out," Rabbit said.

Dear God, what have I done? Ellen thought. *Have I lost him? Just like that?* She wanted to pull him close to her, have him sit on her lap so that she could explain that he must not go to war, but he was...he was...he was *Rabbit*—under the table, untying people's shoelaces. In his world, no one would ever kick him.

Rabbit went back into the parlour to read. Ellen went outside to weep.

#

Just inside the front door of Svensson's store early the next morning, Karl helped Warrant Officer Nils Lundmann set up a small table and two chairs. It was still dark outside. On the table Lundmann placed an ink bottle, pens, blotting paper, and the two reams of documents he had brought with him, then the two men sat down at the table. The first of the volunteers showed up almost immediately.

By three in the afternoon, the sun was dropping in the sky, turning orange, readying itself for sunset. Earlier, there had often been a lineup of men outside the store. Now five or six minutes could pass between the departure of one recruit and the arrival of the next.

"I've heard that some of the trainers can be pretty tough on the new guys," Karl said. "Is that true?"

Lundmann considered. At length he said, "Well, there are two main types: there's the fellow who yells at the troops and tells them they're stupid, and there's the one that explains things to the troops and encourages them. And there's nobody in between."

"Which one is better?"

"I don't think there's much difference. Half the recruits are like mules who need to be hit over the head to make them pay attention, and the others are eager little puppies all set to learn. It's too bad that we can't sort them beforehand and give them to the appropriate trainer."

Karl laughed. "My stepfather is a teacher. You and he would get along very well." He paused for a moment. "So, what sort of trainer are you—a head basher or a puppy petter?"

Warrant Officer Lundmann smiled, but instead of answering the question he said, "I don't suppose you have any coffee?"

"I could look in Inga's kitchen, I suppose. The store hasn't been able to find a supplier for a year, but she probably has a bit of her household stock left. I'll look."

"No, no. That is much too much trouble. Tea?"

"That we have." Karl got up from his chair and went behind the store's counter. "You're not one of those people who insist that the water be heated in a samovar, are you?"

"We're independent, now. Haven't you heard? No more fancy silver samovars and Russian affectations."

"No more flour, either," Karl added. "Though it's not bad here. I've heard that in Helsingfors they've started to add potato flour to the bread."

"Times are tough. One good piece of news, though—there's going to be an artillery school in Jacobstad, and that's only a few kilometres from here."

"I've heard the rumours."

"The rumours are true. There's a fellow from the Swedish Brigade—the volunteers from Sweden—by the name of Adolf Hamilton who'll be in charge." Lundmann smiled. "His wife is the Countess Ebba Maria Augusta Mörlander, and his father, I think, is a professor of some kind. Hamilton's a career officer."

Karl kept his face blank, to give no indication of what he thought of an aristocrat in general or this man in particular. "When will the school start?"

"A couple of days. Hamilton is supposed to arrive on the tenth. I don't think they'll have all the cannons by then, but he could certainly start with the theoretical stuff as soon as he's at the school."

"Most of the students will be from Jacobstad?"

"The first batch. After that I don't know. It sounds, though, as if the plan is to turn loose the first graduates in the space of a week and send them off to the front—wherever that is. They're needed right now, fully trained or not."

The door opened and Rabbit walked in. "I've come to volunteer," he said immediately to Lundmann.

"Oh no you haven't." Karl came from behind the counter. "Even I haven't volunteered, and you're a kid. This isn't something you should get involved in. Does Mother know?"

"I talked to her about it."

"I didn't ask you if you'd talked to her. Does she know that you've decided to volunteer? Does she know that?"

"Not exactly." Rabbit stood completely still. "I told her that I was thinking about volunteering to be a cook for the Guard, for the army, and that I would try to find out when Anders might be returning."

"While cooking, I suppose," Karl said. "God in Heaven, Rabbit."

"Rabbit?" This from Lundmann. "He's pretty tall for a rabbit."

"Sir," Rabbit said, "I have heard that volunteers will have some say in what kinds of jobs they will be given in the army. Is this true?"

"They will have some say, but the final decision will always be in the hands of the senior officers."

"Wait a minute," Karl said. He had forgotten about the tea and now the kettle on the potbellied stove had begun to whistle. "Wait." He took the kettle off the stove and placed it on a trivet on the counter. The whistling quickly died away.

He looked at Rabbit. "You're fifteen. You need to be at least eighteen to be conscripted. Isn't that right?" He looked to Lundmann for confirmation.

The warrant officer shrugged. "Mannerheim needs seventy, eighty thousand men. He won't be picky about age. He's looking for the able-bodied. There will be a lot of men who are just boys. Fifteen's pretty young, though. If Mannerheim does what he's been talking about, conscription will theoretically involve just those who are between twenty-one and forty. At least to start. After that...." He shrugged.

It was not the support Karl had expected.

"Sir, I wish to volunteer," Rabbit said. "To be a cook."

Lundmann pushed a sheet of paper at him and indicated the pen. "For now," he said, "we just need your name, where you live, the date, and your signature."

"I can be a cook?"

"It's likely that you'll be in my unit. I'll see what I can do."

"Goddammit!" Karl suddenly yelled, coming to the table. He put both hands on it and leaned forward. "Get your own goddamned tea!"

Lundmann stayed seated.

"Goddammit," Karl said once more. There was a moment of strained silence. "Give me the paper. Rabbit's not even a man yet. He's going to need someone to look after him. His mother—" Karl wrote rapidly. When he finished he said, "His mother needs to know that I'll be with him." He looked at Rabbit, who found he could not meet Karl's gaze.

"Sir," Rabbit said, looking steadily at Lundmann instead, "do you know when the Jägers are returning? I promised I would ask."

"The twenty-fifth, soldier," Lundmann said. "Perhaps you'll see—Anders, was it?—then, or a few days later. The Jägers will likely be given leave to visit their families before being assigned other tasks."

He turned to Karl. "The *tea*, if you don't mind, *soldier*, then you and your brother can go home. You've got some explaining to do to your mother. I'll finish up here. I'm sure Mrs. Svensson will be here soon. You'll be notified about when and where you have to report."

Karl went back to the counter, poured the tea into its small cup, set the cup on a saucer and carried it back to the table. Some of the tea splashed into the saucer as he set it down in front of Lundmann, who pretended not to notice.

Karl took his coat from the clothes rack beside the door, put it on, and went outside with Rabbit. They stood on the deck that ran along the front of the store. Karl leaned against the railing. Rabbit waited for him to say something.

Finally, Karl said, "I'd better go see Viktoria first. My wife is going to kill me. Then we talk to Mother." They went down the three steps to the street. "And Mother is going to kill the both of us, you know."

"I don't think you have to worry about the second murder," Rabbit said. "You won't feel it once Viktoria's finished with you." He put his arm around Karl's shoulder. "Thank you, brother," he said.

6 • FEBRUARY 11, 1918

JUSSI AND HIS FATHER stood in the darkness at the west side of the long shed that served as the artillery school. Both were smoking, trying to keep warm, waiting for the first class to begin. The others, some boisterous, some subdued, all nervous, were mostly Swedish-speaking.

"You heard about Suinula?" Jussi asked.

His father nodded, pinched off the end of his cigarette and put it in his pocket. He indicated one of the groups of men with a nod of his head. "They're teaching me some Swedish. I know the word *butcher* now."

Jussi had been told the story on the day of his mother's funeral. It was the wrong time, the wrong place, the wrong story, but Jussi listened politely to the man who told it to him, then thanked him.

The man's version of the story—there were many—was that early in January, a troop of the White Guard had escaped from Tammerfors—the place the Finns called Tampere, an industrial city a hundred and seventy kilometres north of Helsinki—and had made it to Suinula, twenty kilometres east. Their plan was to head north into the safety of White territory beyond the Red lines, but the troop ran into trouble. In Suinula they stopped and occupied the Aitolahti People's Hall and stayed too long. Three hundred Red Guard riflemen led by Valdemar Sammalisto were sent from Tampere to Suinula. Sammalisto promised that if the Whites surrendered they would not be harmed, so they surrendered.

A couple of weeks later, a Red reinforcement of two hundred riflemen led by Tuomas Hyrskymurto was sent from Tampere to support Sammalisto's troops. They arrived on January thirty-first. When one of prisoners spoke out of turn, a Russian officer slashed him with his sword, and in the tumult that followed, and despite Sammalisto's objections, Hyrskymurto gave the order to kill all the captives. Seventeen of them died, twenty-six were wounded, only fifteen escaped. Of those, only five made it to the White front line. And Hyrskymurto became the "Butcher of Suinula."

"And now it begins," Jussi's father said. He turned to look at the others milling about in the yard, nodded in their direction but kept his voice soft. "They burn with rage."

Jussi threw the butt of his cigarette into the snow. He pointed at the large cannons standing between them and the wall of the shed. "Where did these come from?"

"Nykarleby, I think. Seventy-six millimetre, looks like, and the breech blocks are missing."

"Breech blocks?"

"See the hole at the rear end of the barrel? That's where the cartridge goes. The breech block locks it in. When the Russians were disarmed in Nykarleby, they hid the breech blocks. By the time our boys realized something was missing, it was too late."

"So the guns won't work?"

"They'll work once the breech blocks are replaced. A good machinist can make the parts."

In the southeast the sun was still below the horizon, but the sky was becoming lighter.

"Jussi!" The voice belonged to a man who had just come around the end of the shed. He hurried toward them, then touched his hat and addressed Jussi's father first.

"Herr Mantere, my sympathy to you on the death of your wife. She was a wonderful woman. And to you, Jussi. There was no one better than your mother." His accent was Swedish, but he spoke Finnish fluently.

"Father," Jussi said, "this is Arvid Grönhagen from Nykarleby. He is—"

"A machinist," Jussi's father finished. "You were at the funeral. People say you do good work. You are here to fix the guns?"

"Yes, sir. I've come to make breech impressions and to verify the bore and model of each gun. I've been told that I can borrow parts from some working guns, but there is no guarantee that the others are identical to these." He pointed to the guns just now becoming visible in the dawn against the background of the shed.

"How long will the work take?" Jussi asked.

"Two days, maybe three. I told your commander that I can have them firing by Thursday at the latest—sooner if the Nykarleby White

Guard can find where the Russians hid the breech blocks."

"Not likely," Jussi said. "Those guys can't find their pants in the morning."

Grönhagen began to laugh, but stopped when Adolph Hamilton, the man in charge of the school, appeared in full dress uniform.

"Men," Hamilton said, "the school bell has rung. Let us go inside where it's warm."

Jussi raised his hand to get Hamilton's attention. "Sir, some here understand no Swedish. May I translate?"

"Yes," Hamilton said. "By all means. How many Finnish-speakers are there?"

Jussi asked, and three men—his father included—raised their hands. Jussi explained to them what was going on, then they entered the school. Later in the day they learned to march, more or less.

#

"Well," Rabbit said to Karl as the train out of Gamlaby began to pick up speed, "that didn't go as smoothly as I would have liked."

"Mother was upset," Karl said.

"Mother was doing her best to hide it. Now, Viktoria...."

"Viktoria will have calmed down by the time we get to Vasa."

"Four hours? I think she'll need more time than that. The wedding may have been last month, but the honeymoon is now officially over, dear brother."

Rabbit turned around in his seat to address another passenger. "I'm Ivor Solbakken, and this charming fellow is my recently-married brother, Karl."

"Erik Andersson," said the man sitting by the window. He reached over the seat to shake hands with Rabbit and Karl.

"Antti Myllysilta," said the young man beside him, and shook hands as well. "Sorry, I poor on Swedish. But understand."

"Milly...sorry, I did not understand it all." Rabbit said.

"Silta. Myllysilta."

"Thank you. Myllysilta. I know we go to Vasa first, but then where?"

Antti shook his head. "First, Seinäjoka, then Vasa. Spend Vasa training couple days then Vilppula maybe, maybe Rouvesi."

Rabbit turned to Karl for help. "Where? I don't—"

"Vilppula and Rouvesi are by the big lakes, south and east of here, in the middle of the lake country. Lundmann, the recruiter, told me that the front line runs through there now, and what Mannerheim probably wants to do is firm up the front line and then push south from there to get down to Tammerfors. Tampere," Karl said so as not to offend.

"I think that's right," Erik said from the seat behind. "And the Russians want to make us go the other way." He laughed.

"You have gun, Ivor?" Antti asked.

"No," Rabbit said. "I'm going to be a cook. But my brother does. He's got our older brother's Grafton gun. It still shoots."

"I have no gun," Antti said. "I hope get one of Vasa."

"Me, too," Erik said. "I'm not much good at throwing stones."

"Throw at armoured trains, I think," Antti said. "Tough nuts to crack."

Rabbit looked at Karl for explanation. Karl gave him a warning look. "The...Russians are using armoured trains at Vilppula. They have cannon."

"Oh," Rabbit said. He found it impossible to picture a battle with a train. It was, he considered, better to remain silent than to demonstrate how little he knew. If opposing trains were both heavily armoured, what would they do? Try to bump each other off the tracks?

After a few more minutes of small talk with Antti and Erik, Rabbit turned around and sat looking out the window for a while.

At last, he nudged Karl and whispered. "Erik said we're fighting the Russians. You did, too."

"It's what he's been told." Karl kept his voice low. "It's better that way."

The train clattered through the swampy Finnish countryside, a land of small lakes, bogs and spruce. Once in a while they passed a hardscrabble farm or crossed a road—often more a raised path than a route for a carriage—and then the train dove into the forest once more.

Swaying with the rhythm of the train, Rabbit fell asleep and woke just before Vasa. It had begun to snow.

#

Viktoria crossed the street and climbed the three steps to enter Svensson's store. Her mother-in-law, Ellen Solbakken, was there with Inga Svensson.

Inga came from around the counter and hugged her as a mother would hug her own child. Ellen, who had been making tea, put down the kettle and came over.

"You said goodbye to Karl?" Ellen asked.

Viktoria gently broke off the hug. "Earlier," she said. She left unsaid the fact that she had not been able to make herself watch Karl get on the train. Ellen, she knew, understood. She did not know if Inga would.

"It will be all right," Ellen said. "Don't worry. He'll come back."

Viktoria nodded—a nod of politeness, if not belief—and turned to Inga. "I want to help," she said. "May I help you with the store? I—"

She didn't know how to say that she wanted to be someplace that made her feel as if Karl was close by. Or that, if he died, perhaps his ghost would come to the store sometime, looking for her. She knew that the idea was crazy, but there was comfort in the touch of madness.

"Of course," Inga said. "Take off your coat."

"I brought my shoes," Viktoria said.

"Good. So coat off, shoes on, and we'll start cleaning up the storeroom."

7 • FEBRUARY 13, 1918

ALMOST AS SOON as the train stopped, the door of the boxcar was opened from the outside. It took a moment for Karl's eyes to adjust to the bright light.

The man who had opened the door yelled, "Everyone out!" He was dressed in the winter clothes of a working man, but wore a white armband on his right arm. "Form up in front of the car in two lines facing me." He indicated where they were to stand.

Karl was the second man out, Rabbit the third. They had not seen Erik or Antti since boarding the train in Vasa. Karl had tried and failed to spot them as the men lined up to get into the boxcars. They did not appear to be in this lineup, either.

"Squad, attention!" The men, a little slow to react, came to attention.

The man wearing the white armband shook his head. "You'll have to do better than that, boys. At ease!"

Those who had rifles rested the butts on the ground. Those without pretended.

"Squad, attention!" The men came to attention promptly this time. "The lieutenant will speak to you shortly. Look smart. Now follow me. And at least try to march. Left, right, left, right. Don't keep looking at the ground. You're not on the farm."

They followed him as he strode ahead, leading them past the station to an open space beside it, where their leader ordered them to halt beside an open wooden crate. Those without weapons picked up a rifle from the crate and got back in line. In a few minutes two hundred men stood, more or less at attention, in front of the railway station.

Two men, one a Jäger officer, dressed in grey melton winter uniform, white fur hat, and calf-high lined leather boots, armed with sword and pistol, came out of the railway station. The other man, dressed in common winter clothing except for the white armband, walked a little behind the Jäger. The two stood in front of the assembled crowd. Karl thought about risking a look for Erik and Antti, but the squad leader caught his eye, and Karl looked straight ahead.

"Eyes front!" the Jäger officer yelled at someone else.

"Sir?" It was Rabbit. He had put up his hand as if still in Harald Berg's class. "I am a cook, sir. I have a note from Warrant Officer Lundmann in my pocket. Where should I go?" Some of the men laughed.

The Jäger officer approached. "Soldier, this isn't school." He dropped his voice. "How old are you?"

"Eighteen, sir."

"Not likely." The officer paused. "How old are you really?" His voice was kindly.

"Fifteen, sir. But I was told I could be a cook."

"Let me see the document."

Rabbit took it out of his pocket, and the officer examined it.

"We have a cook, a few cooks actually." He looked steadily at Rabbit, who kept his eyes front. "I don't think you're a cook, not yet, but you might make a good cook's helper. Will that do?"

"Yes, sir! Yes, sir! I will do my best, sir."

"Go into the station, ask for Ruupeni—he's our chef." The officer laughed. "And give me back your rifle. It's not much good for stirring, and we can use it."

"Yes, sir. Thank you, sir." Rabbit handed over his rifle and hurried into the station.

"Thank you, sir," Karl said to the Jäger.

"He is young," the officer replied. "I will try to have him assigned to food preparation, but I cannot promise you anything. War breaks all promises."

"I understand, sir," Karl said.

The Jäger raised his voice to address all the men. "At ease!" The men relaxed slightly. "I trust there will be no more cooks requesting employment."

Some light but nervous laughter came from the assembly.

The officer let it die down before he spoke. "Before I begin, I want to introduce my translator, Seppo Koskinen." Koskinen inclined his head but remained silent. "I am Lieutenant Nils Munson and in charge of this station."

He waited for Koskinen to translate, then continued, pausing between sentences so that Koskinen could translate into Finnish. "Tomorrow you will face the enemy for the first time in combat." He gave time for the words to sink in.

"So far there have been three serious attempts to take Vilppula. Each has been repulsed."

A few of the men cheered.

The officer waited for quiet. "In the last attack on our position—just south of the village—the revolutionaries were backed by a Russian-crewed armoured train, Russian field artillery, and over twelve hundred men. Had the train made it this far, we would have been overrun, the northern front line would have vanished, your wives and your children would have been killed, your farms and your homes burned. When the attack began, we could muster only three hundred able-bodied men at the front—not nearly enough to stop the Red advance.

"There is a dam near here, fortunately, and as a last resort we opened the gates to flood the land to the south, slow the Red advance, and make it impossible for the armoured train to get near enough to use its cannons. This was not, I will tell you, part of some master plan we keep in a closet for emergencies. We were desperate, and it was all we could think of to do at the time. Fortunately, it worked, but the revolutionaries remain just ten kilometres south of here at Lyly railway station, and the land is drying out. We won't be able to flood it again anytime soon, and we still don't have enough men.

"God sends us just one miracle a month, so now it's up to you to hold the line. We can't let them break through. If they get past us, Vasa will be overrun, and the war will be over.

"Three days ago one of our patrols tried to blow up the Siitama railway bridge. They were not successful, though they did some damage. That is how it is here. We can damage, but we can't yet destroy. We know another attack is coming, but we don't know when or where. The Russians may attack here, or they may already be on the march to Ruovesi, which is only thirty kilometres east of here, but devilishly hard for us to reach. Some of the men who trained with you, however, are on their way there from Haapamäki. We hope they will arrive in time to be useful."

Erik and Antti, Karl thought. *Tomorrow they could be dead*. He tried to push them from memory. *Worry about Rabbit, instead,* he told himself.

Munson continued, "Tomorrow you go to the front. It will be a difficult, if not long, march. Tonight some of you will be berthed in the railway station here, and others in homes in Vilppula and some of the nearby villages and farms. There is food and drink for you in the railway station. Once you have eaten, your squad leaders will call the roll and take you to your quarters. Do not expect to sleep in a bed or a bunk tonight. In war any dry floor is a luxury.

"Dismissed." Munson turned from the men and strode into the railway station. In time, under the direction of their squad leaders, the recruits followed.

Karl looked for Rabbit in the station, but he was nowhere to be seen. Ruupeni had, Karl heard, sent him by sledge with another helper to scrounge supplies from a nearby farm.

#

Jussi was uneasy. Adolf Hamilton had ordered the men to return to their classroom at the end of the day. Chairs were set out in front of a makeshift blackboard on which Hamilton had sketched a map of the Vilppula/Ruovesi area. The Finnish-speakers made sure to sit near Jussi so that he could translate without disturbing the whole class.

"As you have heard," Hamilton said, "the enemy is trying very hard to continue the Red push north along the railway from Tammerfors to Vilppula. So far it has not been successful, but we do not have enough men and weapons in the area to hold it for long unless we can reinforce the positions. Thus far, the Reds have been repulsed, but we have received word of a formidable battle being fought west of Vilppula at Ruovesi. My understanding is that the Black Guard is involved."

The Swedish-speaking students reacted first. There were whispered questions and answers. Hamilton waited for Jussi to translate and explain the situation to the Finnish-speakers.

"The Black Guard is made up of Russian sailors—anarchists, mean as hell, almost uncontrollable," Jussi whispered. "Suicidal. They fight at Ruovesi."

Hamilton continued, "In the next few weeks, the war will be won or lost. Right now the enemy has superior firepower, far more men, and better access to supplies. It also has at least two, possibly three armoured trains—that means artillery, machine guns, and rapid attacks along the railway, deep into our lines.

"We are scrambling to assemble what artillery we can, and put it on flatcars so that early next week we can send you boys into the thick of things. If Ruovesi holds, if the men there can buy us the time we need, there is a chance we can start to push back.

"Tomorrow, we are going to form four-man teams and work on the responsibilities of each man in the team. You won't just be learning your own job; you will be learning everyone's job. I don't think I need to tell you why. You are dismissed for the day."

#

Karl and his squad leader, Olavi Karppinen, were sent to a small house at the edge of Vilppula. The owner and his wife were in the tiny bedroom; Karl and Olavi shared the kitchen floor. It was warm enough, if hard. They spoke as equals.

"Olavi," Karl said as they lay in the dark, "you are Finnish, but you speak Swedish, too, with a southern accent. Where did you learn?"

"My mother," Olavi said. "She was Swedish from Helsinki—sorry, Helsingfors—and my father was a Finn from Tampere. I speak a little Russian, too—enough to get by."

"Russian?"

"I volunteered to serve in the Russian army when the big war broke out four years ago."

"Ah," Karl said. He left the direction of the conversation in Olavi's hands.

Olavi explained that when the war had started, some of the Finns had supported Russia, since Finland was then still part of Russia. But other Finns had supported Germany in the hopes that if Germany won, Finland could become independent.

"I put in some time on the eastern front, got a little wounded," Olavi said, "got discharged back to Finland. And when the revolutionaries took the cities in the south at the end of January I had to head north."

"You fought for Russia, but now you fight against them?"

"My father is—was—the owner of a small textile plant. The Red

Guards said he was a capitalist and a member of the bourgeoisie, so they killed him and they killed my mother as well. I found the bodies the day after."

There was a long pause.

Olavi added, "I was neither Red nor White then, but I can tell you I'm White now. A lot of the men that are White officers now were volunteers in the Russian army."

"It's a good thing," Karl said. "Most of us don't have any idea what we're doing, and you can show us what we need to know. You have experience."

"Yes. And I can tell you from experience that you need to sleep now. You need to learn to sleep whenever and wherever you can."

But Karl had another question. "The Red Guard and the Russians, the ones that are south of us. Where do they sleep? In the open? There aren't many towns or even farms south of here, as far as I know."

"Boxcars. At Lyly there's a siding. The Reds sleep in the boxcars; the lucky ones get the passenger carriages. That's why even though they push hard during the day, they retreat before nightfall. They want to get back to the cars. If they tried to sleep outdoors, winter would kill them in their sleep."

8 • FEBRUARY 22, 1918

FOR KARL, THE MATH OF HUNGER WAS EASY. Twenty-five hectares equals three or four cows and their calves, two horses, a couple of pigs, two or three hundred chickens, a potato field that can produce half a tonne of potatoes, and a vegetable garden that will provide enough vegetables to last a small family through the winter, as long as there isn't a major crop failure and the animals stay healthy and don't run out of feed. It is not enough to feed an army—or even a small part of one—for one day.

Because grain no longer flowed from Russia, there was little if any bread. Jars of preserves—blueberries, strawberries, and lingonberries—could add a little sweetness and colour to the diet, but they couldn't vanquish a soldier's hunger for bread, never mind protein.

The math of death was more complex. The Reds were advancing north, a few kilometres here and a few more there. The previous week, Längelmäki, south and east of Vilppula, had fallen as the Reds outflanked the Whites. In Tampere, the Reds were bringing in more armoured trains from the Fredriksberg factory in Helsinki, and constructing improvised armoured trains of their own, the sides protected with sandbags and bales of paper—a trick they'd learned from Latvian volunteers who supported the Reds.

Each day brought a new story, real or invented, of some atrocity. It arrived in the wind and seeded itself in the men of the White front. In X, the Reds had stolen everything a farmer owned, then burned his house and barn before killing him. In Y, a teacher had been hanged. In Pori, eleven prisoners had been shot in a schoolyard. In Varkaus, hostages had been taken by the Reds and shot when the Whites attacked.

All good news arrived contaminated with bad. When Varkaus had fallen to the Whites, fifteen hundred Reds had surrendered without incident, but one group of Reds who had been occupying a factory building raised a white flag, then came out of the building—"surrendering" under the protection of the flag—and then opened fire. Fifty or sixty Whites had been killed.

Now, because a white flag meant nothing, Red prisoners were being summarily executed. "We shoot the Reds because we have no choice," the men said. "We don't have prisons to put them in, guards to guard them, or food to feed them. And, besides, that's what they'd do to us. That's what they did in Suinula; that's what they did in Varkaus. Sure, their commanders tell them that they must not execute prisoners, but they do it anyway. And if they don't need to obey their commanders, we don't, either. And you know what else? If I'm in a fight and I get surrounded, I'm not going to surrender, because there's no difference anymore between surrendering and being killed."

Karl and Olavi now shared the kitchen floor at night with four others—reinforcements from Vasa. Though more reinforcements kept arriving, there were never enough of them. The Reds from their enclaves in the south could always send double the number of men that the Whites could muster.

Karl was awake. As usual, his stomach did not want him to sleep. Someone was snoring, too. What was his name? Ensio? Yes, from Kaskö on the sea. He snored too much at night and laughed too much when he was awake.

Karl didn't try to remember his surname. Already too many people, whose names he had learned, had died. They came to him unbidden in his sleep, and sometimes made him recite their names. And always they asked for bread.

Sometimes Jussi's mother came, too, and stood beside them and said, "I can make blood pancakes if you kill the pig. Four decilitres each of blood and milk and barley flour, one egg and something sweet, a big pinch of salt, some pepper if you have it, and butter. They must be fried in butter."

Jesus, Karl thought, and he got up as silently as he could and went to get a drink of water from the pail on the kitchen table. Jussi's mother had actually made him blood pancakes once. She believed that anything that could be eaten must not be wasted, including the pig's blood. He had tasted them—it would have been an insult to refuse—and then he had asked for more. Even in his nightmare they had still sounded good.

He was just about to drink when the farmhouse door flew open, and cold air poured in. The men were already awake when the messenger yelled, "Everyone up, rifles ready, and outside in five minutes. The word is that the Reds are going to attack with a train." The messenger disappeared into the darkness.

"Up, boys!" Olavi shouted. Ten minutes later the men stood in formation outside the railway station. Half an hour after that they were in position along the tracks.

#

Jussi and his father had arrived at Vilppula the previous day and set up the big guns on a hill a little more than six kilometres south of the town. Ahead of them lay a straight section of track. To the right, the tracks curved around the hill.

Tired from piling sandbags to build revetments and protect their positions, they waited for the sun to rise. They had been up since six o'clock and it was now a quarter after seven and already the sky was quite light. Half an hour to go.

Some distance ahead of the artillery, the men whose job it was to tear up the tracks were still at work. Behind Jussi and his father, out of sight, the horses that had hauled the old 87-mm guns into position stood hobbled and waiting.

"This train," Jussi's father said, "what do you know about it?"

"Not much. We know that the Reds are using a transport train to get their troops up here, and it's likely in Lyly now. They might be thinking to outflank us, but I don't think the main force is here yet. The armoured train, though, is coming to test our defenses before there's any kind of major offensive."

Jussi's father laughed. "You talk like a general." He pointed to the wooden crates stacked nearby. "Did you count the shells?"

"We don't have many. We'll have to stretch out the ones we have."

"Hey, I forgot to tell you. That younger brother of your friend—I think he's in that group ahead."

"Karl?"

"Yes. Looked like him. He was carrying a shovel and a pry bar—rifle, too. I didn't see the kid, though."

"Well, if Karl's here, Rabbit will be somewhere close by."

"He's the one who wanted to be a cook?"

"He did." Jussi was quiet for a moment. "This is no place for a kid."

"This is no place for anyone." Before Jussi's father could say more, they heard the clatter of machine guns.

"The train's coming," Jussi said. "It's strafing the trees in case we have riflemen lying in ambush."

"Do we?"

"I don't know."

"How far away is it?"

"Position!" the lieutenant in charge of the battery yelled. "Elias, what do you see?"

From high in one of the trees came the spotter's reply. "It's just coming into view at the bend." He prayed that no snipers had been sent in advance of the train. Spotters seldom lasted long.

The lieutenant checked a map. "Number one, distance twenty-three hundred metres. Four degrees left. Fire when ready."

The gun crew loaded the shell, then positioned the gun. There was a tremendous roar. The crew immediately set about reloading.

"Elias!"

"Three hundred metres short, a hundred wide and right. I think there are some soldiers on the right hand side of the train, using it for cover. And our guys are on the way back. Most of them are keeping to the edge of the tree line, but there's a small group just walking along on the ties."

"Jesus Christ!" the lieutenant swore. "Number two, twenty-six hundred metres. Three degrees left. Fire when ready."

The battle had begun.

#

An hour before sunset, the armoured train withdrew. On the hill, the last shell of forty had been fired. Three members of the battery had been wounded, one killed, no guns lost. All of the wounded could be patched up.

Jussi's ears rang in the aftermath of the thunder of artillery fire. Perhaps, he hoped, the sound wouldn't be there in the morning. His father was all right, there had been no serious attack by Red troops, and Karl and the other men who had torn up the tracks seemed to have escaped unscathed. Some White guards, positioned to defend against an assault, had been killed under shelling, but "casualties were light," as some official report would no doubt say.

"How many shells did they fire at us?" Jussi's father asked.

"Maybe a hundred, maybe more. They're not serious yet about picking a fight. But next week, or the week after...."

Both he and his father knew what he was unwilling to say.

Vilppula was, to the Reds, a minor roadblock. The real attack would be on the village of Haapamäki, a crossroads. There, the railway that ran east to west and formed the southern limit of the White front line met the railway that ran south to Tampere.

The Reds couldn't advance north if Haapamäki was in White hands, and they couldn't get enough weapons and men to the railway station there except through Vilppula. Rouvesi was a secondary target—no railroad ran through it—and roads, especially in winter, did not lend themselves to the quick transport of large guns by teams of reluctant and exhausted horses.

#

When Karl got back to the small house, he found that four more men would share the kitchen floor. That night he dreamed again of the blood pancakes.

PART III

FIRE

It is our duty still to endeavor to avoid war;
but if it shall actually take place,
no matter by whom brought on,
we must defend ourselves. If our house be
on fire, without inquiring
whether it was fired from within
or without, we must try to extinguish it.

~ *Thomas Jefferson*

1 • MARCH 15, 1918

THE REAL WAR, the war of tens of thousands of men on opposite sides, began with a shared dream—a massive frontal assault that would send the enemy fleeing.

The Reds, with better arms and more troops, would attack the heart of the White front line with armoured trains, then mount a flanking attack on Vilppula. This strategy would draw the Whites away from Haapamäki, and the Reds could capture the railway junction and sweep north.

The Whites believed that with better-trained troops and with Mannerheim in charge, they would be able to repel any attack and inflict huge losses on the Reds. They focused on holding the line. If they held the line, the Reds would give up; the war would be over.

Mannerheim—the man, not the idol—was neither a romantic nor a dreamer. He was a strategist. The Reds, he knew, would not give up just because it was a reasonable thing to do. They would have to be killed by the thousands, run down and trampled, and shot when they surrendered.

On the first of March, the Reds had begun to move men and trains north. On March 10th, with fifteen thousand men committed to the northern advance and the capture of Haapamäki, they had attacked the village of Vaskivesi, west of Vilppula, but as the Reds entered the village from the south, the Whites entered it from the north and drove them back. On the 11th, some seven hundred students of the Vöyri training school joined the Whites at Vaskivesi and ensured that any counterattack by the Reds would fail.

On March 12th, Mannerheim had decided that it was time to stop holding the line. It was time to move south from Vilppula and mount the main attack on Tampere, seventy-five kilometres away. Tampere would become Tammerfors once more.

On the same day, a rumour had swept through the Red lines. At Vilppula station, the story went, the Whites had a train loaded with explosives and ammunition. And since the tracks were again sound between Lyly and Vilppula, the Reds decided to send a locomotive and three flatcars on an unmanned run into the village. The flatcars would be loaded with pyroksite explosive and boulders. The little train, its safety valves closed, its throttle set to top speed, would crash into the Whites' ammunition train, blow up, send boulder shrapnel flying everywhere, and destroy the Whites' explosives and ammunition and the railway station itself.

But the rumour was false—there was no ammunition train at Vilppula. The next day, when the Reds' bomb train arrived in Vilppula, it smashed into the buffer stop and came to a sudden halt, but its pyroksite did not explode and neither did the locomotive's steam engine, though its safety valves had been closed. Two railroad employees ran out of the station, opened the safety valves, and shut down the angry train.

When the amazement and the amusement had subsided, the Whites realized that the failed attack was likely the prelude to the arrival of another armoured train and a large force of Red soldiers. They were right, and when the train arrived, it was met with artillery fire, machine guns, and rifles. After Jussi's battery hit the locomotive, the train's crew backed the crippled train to safety behind the Red lines.

On the same day, Mannerheim gave his troops their marching orders. It was time. On multiple fronts, twelve thousand men prepared to head south.

#

Karl was the first of the dozen men in the house to come awake. He got up as quietly as he could and went outside to the outhouse. As he was returning to the house, he saw the messenger, a boy of about Rabbit's age.

"Sir, you and the men in the house are to report to the railway station immediately. Mannerheim has given the order."

Karl knew what he meant. "I'll tell them."

"Thank you, sir." The messenger then headed for his next stop along the road.

Karl hurried back to the house. "Everybody up!" he said as he opened the door. "We're moving today."

Olavi groaned. "Who the hell gave you *my* job?" He got slowly up from the floor. "And where the hell is that woman I was dreaming about?"

The others began to get up as well, jockeying for room to put on their boots and outer garments. When one man opened the door to go to the outhouse, another yelled, "Can't you wait until we're at least half dressed? You're letting the cold in!" He promptly shut the door and waited anxiously while the men slowly dressed.

"Is the village being attacked?" Olavi asked Karl.

"No," Karl said, "I think we're the ones that will be doing the attacking today. The kid said it's an order from Mannerheim himself."

"Gather all your belongings, men," Olavi said. "You might not be coming back."

Just then the woman of the house came out of the bedroom. "You're leaving," she said. "But you're not leaving without some coffee."

"Coffee?" Karl said. "You don't have any coffee."

"Today, I do." She went back into the bedroom and came out with a jar of green coffee beans, then got out a frying pan to roast them. "What I don't have is enough cups. You'll have to share." She pointed at the door. "You all have business to do out there, I'm sure. There'll be time for a cup."

Her husband appeared in the doorway of the bedroom. "And one for me," he said.

His wife set about frying the coffee beans. Part way through she said, "Karl, take over here for a minute. I almost forgot. I have a present for you."

Karl took the frying pan and stirred the beans as they began to brown.

In a minute the woman was back from the bedroom. She carried a pair of woolen socks. "For you. Wear these over your old ones—the ones with the holes. We are not out of winter yet." Karl traded her the frying pan for the socks. "Stay alive and try to keep your boots dry."

"You sound like my wife," Karl said. He would have liked to say more, to thank her for her hospitality, for letting him remember such things as families and homes existed. But he did not.

"Good. Now get out of here."

#

For Jussi and his father, the morning began with the arrival of an artillery battery of two howitzers, plus the eighty men and fifty horses that were needed to transport, defend, and fire them.

"*Haupitsi!*" Jussi's father said when he saw the howitzers.

The Jäger in command of the howitzer battery heard him. "I am Second Lieutenant Lars Larsson," the Jäger said in Swedish.

"Jussi Mantere," Jussi said, "and my father, Raimo Mantere. We are gunners, sir."

"Both Swedish-speaking?"

"Only I, sir. But I am happy to translate."

"*Kiitos*," Larsson said. "*Puhun suomea huonosti.*"

"Not at all, sir. You speak very well."

"Thank you," Larsson said. "But I am afraid that I have used up half of what I know."

"Sir, you are one of the Jägers who returned last month?"

"Yes, on the twenty-fifth."

"Do you know Anders Solbakken?"

"Very well. He is a First Lieutenant in charge of a rifle company. I believe his company is still in Haapamäki, guarding the railway station."

"Will there be trouble there?"

"Perhaps. First, however, the Reds have to capture Ruovesi. Mannerheim is sending almost all available men from Haapamäki to Ruovesi. He's holding back very few. It's over forty kilometres to Ruovesi from there, and there aren't many villages along the way. If those fellows can't find somewhere to sleep, they'll have to march all night. Mannerheim wants a thousand men in Rouvesi by tomorrow. The Reds, he thinks, are going to attack with three or four thousand. Do you have a cigarette?"

"What? Sorry...yes." Jussi reached into his coat pocket and shook a cigarette out of a beaten pack, then he found his match box. "Can we stop them?"

Larsson lit the cigarette and drew deeply on it before answering. "Yes," he said slowly. "But stopping them isn't enough. We have to go after them. We have to make them believe that we have far more men than we do and more weapons. We have to make them think we've come to set the house on fire. We have to make them start running."

"I don't think—" Jussi began.

Larsson cut him off. "Don't think. It will get in the way of the killing." He pinched off the end of the cigarette. "Thank you for this," he said, putting the butt in his pocket. "May I also have a match for the next time I light it?"

"Of course." Jussi opened the match box and gave him three matches. Then he shook another cigarette from the pack, and passed it over as well. There were two left.

#

Near the railway station, as Olavi was marching at the head of his men, Karl caught sight of Rabbit running toward them.

"Karl!" Rabbit yelled and swung about to march with them.

"Squad, halt!" Olavi commanded.

"Thank you, sir," Karl said.

"I'm to go to Ruovesi," Rabbit blurted. "They need a cook, Karl, a real one. And I get to go. I've written mother to tell her. I told her you were well. I—oh hell, I have to go. Good-bye, brother. Take care of yourself, and don't worry about me."

Then he was gone, back the way he had come.

"Squad, forward march," Olavi said, and the men moved on.

#

Mid-March...winter's back is broken, Pastor Niemi thought. *The snow has begun to melt.* He sat in his kitchen looking out the window. There was still enough snow for the horse-drawn sleighs to be used, but by the end of the month people would have put away the sleds and roads would be full of wheeled carts and carriages.

He turned away from the window and went back to looking over Sunday's sermon. The church, he knew, would be half-full at best—women, children, old men. Already, only a couple of months into the rebellion, his congregation had at least five young widows—five who knew their husbands had been killed, and probably five more who didn't.

The door opened. His wife came in carrying kindling and logs for the woodbox. She opened the lid of the woodbox with one hand and expertly dropped the load in, logs on the left, kindling on the right. She closed the lid and said, "Paavo Pajari is coming up the road. What do you think he wants?"

Her husband put down his pen. "I don't know. Viivi, is Lyddia up?"

"Yes." Something in her husband's voice made Viivi Niemi anxious.

"Tell her to come down. Make sure she's dressed."

Viivi Niemi hurried up the stairs to their daughter's bedroom.

Downstairs, Pastor Niemi heard Paavo bring his horse and sledge to a halt. In a moment he knocked on the door. Niemi opened it immediately.

"You must leave." Paavo said. He made no move to enter the house.

"Raiders?" Niemi asked.

"Yes. *Lentävä osasto.* They're coming to burn down the church, and worse. You, your wife and daughter will be safe at our place. But you have to hurry. They're almost here. I have blankets in the sledge."

"But why? How do you know—?"

"It's random. They're thugs. I'm a Red. I hear things. But I can think for myself. You're a good man, Niemi—even if you are a supporter of the Church—and what the raiders do is wrong. It's wrong on both sides of this damned revolution."

In just a few minutes, the full Niemi family—Pastor, Viivi, and daughter Lyddia—was seated on the rough plank floor of the sledge and had started down the road. Half an hour later, from the Pajari farm, they saw the smoke rising from the direction they had come.

"You can rebuild the manse and the church," Paavo said quietly. "The graveyard will not burn."

#

On both sides, the war stalled.

Mannerheim ordered Lieutenant-Colonel Appelgren to advance south, but the advance was stopped by the Reds moving north up both sides of Lake Kyrösjärvi, northwest of Tampere.

The Reds made no progress at Ruovesi at the north end of Lake Näsijärvi, but almost got through at Väärinmaja on the east side of the lake.

Colonel Wetzer, though under orders from Mannerheim to start an offensive, needed reinforcements. He waited for them to arrive.

In Jämsä, east of Väärinmaja, the Whites were unable to attack, and the Reds were unable to move. The Whites, however, saw an opening for their men to move south to Orivesi.

A tipping point had been reached.

It was the Ides of March.

2 • MARCH 17, 1918

THREE LAKES—Lake Kyrösjärvi, Lake Näsijärvi, and the complex of lakes that becomes Lake Päijänne—all run more or less north-south in south-central Finland. From far above, they look like scratches made by the palsied hand of a sculptor working with rock and forest, scratches that reveal stretches of surface water as the ice melts. Their edges are rough and uncertain, their shorelines formidable barriers to rail and road.

At the south end of Lake Näsijärvi lies Tampere, the large industrial city that has become the target of the Whites, the haven of the Reds. It is no longer Tammerfors. Swedish is absent from its streets.

Two armies march along and between the three lakes—the Whites moving south, the Reds heading north, both sides attacking, both sides unaware that the tide of war has turned.

Mannerhiem, unlike Caesar, has survived the Ides of March.

The Reds, unwilling to be ruled by any one man, march into battle under the direction of men who were elected to be generals—men with so little military training that they don't understand the need to keep troops in reserve. Hugo Salmela, the most competent of their leaders, was a sawmill worker and sometime actor. His friend, Gustav Salminen, was a painter. In less than two weeks, Salminen—perhaps deliberately, perhaps not—will throw a live grenade into a box of grenades in the headquarters of the Reds in Tampere. Salmela will be killed; Gustav Salminen will lose his legs.

The Red leadership has divided the Tampere area into three defensive zones, but the zones are under the command of two machinists, Aatto Koivonen and August Dufva, and a railroad worker, Jukka Merlö.

Four days from now, champion wrestler Mikko Kokko, another emergency commander picked by the Reds, will send an improvised armoured train north to Suinula. Kokko's troops will capture the railway station, then charge farther north, straight into the main force of the White army. The Reds will be routed and will flee south to the apparent safety of Tampere—and so will all the Reds between them and the city.

As Tampere falls, Anders Hilden, a labourer from Helsinki, will be put in charge of the defense of the Messukylä Ridge, a little southeast of the city. His forces will be overrun, and he will be executed by the Whites. Robert Oksa, a wrestler and future Olympic coach, fights for the Reds, and after the war he will become the model for Waino Aaltonen's sculpture of The Hero, a celebration of the White "liberation" of Tampere. But The Hero will not have Oksa's Red face; Aaltonen will replace it with that of his own White brother-in-law.

That morning, however, none of these events can be foreseen. At ground level the war seems routine, mundane. Tomorrow, everyone believes, will be much like today.

But today, the War of Independence, the War of Freedom, the War of Liberty, the War of Brothers, the Class War, the Red Rebellion, the Finnish Revolution, the Finnish Civil War, has become for the Reds the Amateurs' War, and it will soon be clear to them that they will lose.

#

The road to Ruovesi had been cleared of danger. Ski patrols skirting the forest on both sides of the road had determined that no Reds lay in ambush.

Still, Rabbit worried. Who knew for sure?

In Ruovesi, well after dark, the sledges were unloaded by half a dozen men. Partway through the unloading, another man joined the group and approached Rabbit.

"Ivor!" he said. "Is you?"

Rabbit recognized the broken Swedish before he recognized the man from the train. "Antti! Antii Myllysilta!"

"Yes! You remember! I hear someone comes from Vilppula so I want to hear news. I never think he will be you."

"Erik," Rabbit said. "Is Erik here, too?"

Antti hesitated for a fraction of a second. "He is dead. Almost a week ago. There has been much fighting."

"I'm so sorry."

"He was friend. And brave man."

Both stood awkwardly for a minute as behind them the unloading continued.

"You are delivery boy now," Antti said finally. "Groceries." He allowed himself a little laugh. "I am put in Ylihärmä Company. Everyone is speaking Finnish language. No Swedish."

Rabbit was quiet for a moment. "How did Erik die?" he asked at last.

Antti considered his answer carefully before he spoke. "He stop shooting." He looked down at the ground as if seeing the memory in the snow. "We are being attacked. Reds are coming at us and yelling. And Erik, he just stop pulling trigger. I don't know why. He just watch the Reds coming, and he is killed."

It was Rabbit's turn to be silent.

"And yesterday, when Reds come again, we lose battle and have to retreat. But when we are fighting I see how thin, how skinny, Reds are. And that they are farmers like us. Jäger who leads us, he tell us all the time that we are fighting Russians from Tampere, from barracks there, but he is lying. We are killing only Finns. Everybody sees this. Now all of Ylihärmä Company want to go home. This is not what they sign paper for."

"Will they try to do that?"

"Maybe, but I think we won't be let home. Jäger puts machine guns behind us. We do like Erik and die, or we shoot to stay alive."

Antti took off one of his mitts and fumbled in his coat pocket.

"*Saatana,*" he said. "No cigarette." Then, to Rabbit, "Be careful of this Jäger. I point him out to you tomorrow. He is not good man. He is liar. Reds have lots of liars, too, but this one is our liar and all liars are dangerous."

#

Early that morning, Paavo Pajari wakened Pastor Niemi, Vivvi, and their daughter, Lyddia. It had become dangerous for the Niemi family to stay with the Pajaris any longer. Before the sun rose, they left Paavo's home for Gamlaby. Paavo stopped half a kilometre from the town and asked the Niemis to walk the rest of the way.

After leaving them, he did not go back home, however. Instead, he waited an hour and resumed the journey to Gamlaby. The town was not free of Reds. Had he been seen bringing the family into the town, his own home would have been burned. The empty sledge, he reasoned, was "proof" that he had not aided the Niemis.

Inga Svensson took in the Niemis, and they spent the day at the store.

At eight o'clock in the evening, darkness had gathered. The sun had slipped below the horizon more than an hour earlier. Inga and Viktoria brought chairs from the upstairs family quarters and set them in a rough circle in the storeroom around the small wooden table normally used when stocking the shelves. The Niemis gathered there.

Ellen Solbakken positioned herself close to the storeroom door. Beside her, against the wall that separated the customer area from the storage room, she had propped Fredric Svensson's loaded shotgun. She sat listening for sounds outside the store where the streets were dark and, she hoped, empty.

"I have an uncle in Jacobstad," Viktoria said to the Niemis. "Tomorrow he is coming to take you there. He has a big house and there is a lot of room. You will stay with him until this war is over."

"We can't—" Pastor Niemi began.

Viktoria cut him short. "Yes, you can. He will be honoured."

"Thank you," Vivvi Niemi said on her husband's behalf. "Jacob, you remember what you always say?"

"Grace before honour."

"Yes."

"How long will the war last?" Lyddia wanted to know.

"It's over when it ends," her mother said.

"Not this one," said Pastor Niemi. "I am afraid this one will fester. It will end in sores that do not heal." He turned to Viktoria. "You also have an uncle in Canada?" he asked.

"In Port Arthur. It is a city on Lake Superior. There is another city, the same size, to the south. They lie rump to rump, my uncle says."

Niemi laughed. "Two cities? How did that happen, I wonder."

"He says they are growing together. Now only a few streets touch, but sooner or later they will be one city—like Siamese twins joined at the rump." Viktoria smiled. "Mind you, my uncle thinks there will be some 'festering' there, too, before that happens."

"There are Finns there?"

"Lots. Both kinds, Finnish and Swedish-speaking."

"And they get along?"

"That," Viktoria said, "I don't know."

#

All day the rumours have grown in the Red camps. *The Whites are coming down from the north and will overrun every place between the old front line and Tampere. White troops are approaching from the east and west as well, and will cut us off unless we abandon our positions immediately and withdraw to Tampere. If we allow ourselves to be cut off and surrounded, the Whites will torture and kill us, will take no prisoners, will....*

On the White side, Colonel Hjalmarson, having taken the village of Kuru without much opposition, believes the Reds will be ferocious opponents and gives his troops two days' rest before battle. Colonel Wilkman's forces move south, but stop just short of taking over the railway station at Orivesi. Colonel Wetzer feels that his own men are worn out and refuses to press south until he hears what Colonel Hjalmarson is doing.

None of the colonels realize that the Reds are on the run. The White advance fizzles out.

Commander-in-Chief Mannerheim spends much of his free time yelling at his aide-de-camp. His subordinates are using every excuse they can think of to delay the advance. *It is time, it is time, dammit, to attack! What the hell is wrong with them?*

The Red commander, Salmela, spends all his time trying to keep his troops from fleeing. At Vilppula they are pulling back. In Orivesi they are holding protest meetings. They don't want to be killed; they want to run away.

Every Red has heard the stories. *They are being pursued by the "butchers." No prisoners are ever left alive by the Whites. And it is not safe to eat anything because the Whites have secretly poisoned Red food rations. Red Guard units are selling out, giving up, joining the enemy. Their commanders have betrayed them. And the proof? None needed. Along the roads and rail lines that lead south to Tampere, one need only to look around. The Red troops from the north, the ones who have been at the front lines, the ones who know, are streaming past.* So they join in, and the retreat becomes a river of soldiers flowing south, in darkness, to the "safety" of a city that is doomed to fall.

3 • MARCH 28, 1918
BLOODY MAUNDY THURSDAY

ON THE ISTHMUS separating two frozen lakes—Näsijärvi to the north and Pyhäjärvi to the south—Tampere woke to the start of the third day of fighting.

On the first day of the fight, Commander-in-Chief Mannerheim had come with his staff to watch the battle from the hill at Leinola on the eastern flank of the city. He expected the city to fall without much opposition. But at the end of the second day it was obvious that the Reds, with substantial artillery support and protected positions, would not give up the city without a real fight. There would be no more running.

Mannerheim had realized he needed fresh troops, and unless he used the men he counted on to win the war in Karelia—the new conscripts, the Swedish brigade, the 2nd Jäger Regiment—he might lose the city, and to lose it would be to lose the war. The momentum would shift to the Reds. They would chase the Whites north on the very roads and rail lines that the Reds had used to flee south.

So Mannerheim had canceled his plan to keep the Jägers and the Swedes in reserve for Karelia; Tampere was more immediately important. Karelia, the buffer between Finland proper and Russia, would have to wait its turn. Nothing much was happening there anyway. The two armies were nose to nose, dug in, shooting but not moving.

Now, on the third day, Mannerheim stood once more on the hill and waited for the sun to rise.

The plan he had formed was for Wilkman to attack the Red southern front while Wetzer pushed east. The Jägers, the five hundred men of the Swedish brigade, and the conscripts, of course, would go in on Wetzer's left wing. Their battlefield would include the

Russian barracks and the Kalevankangas cemetery in eastern Tampere beside Lake Lidesjärvi.

#

"The sun is coming up," Jussi said. His father merely nodded.

"Ready!" Corporal Hedmann, the artillery officer, yelled. "Thirty minutes of fire, remember, then no more. We don't have enough ammunition to shell the hell out of them and, besides, we don't want to shoot our own men when the attack begins. Fire on my signal."

They waited to start.

"It's Maundy Thursday," Jussi said.

"If you were the Pope," his father said, "you could be getting ready to wash men's feet."

"It would be better than this. My ears never stop ringing. My head is full of bees and church bells. I think I would rather be in Rome than here. You think the Pope would wash my feet since I'm not Catholic?"

"Number one, fire!" came the command, and immediately the gun to the right of them roared. Jussi waited a moment and then fired. Down the line, each gun crew followed suit in turn. When the last finished, the first was ready again.

Thirty minutes later, the guns went silent. There had been no return fire.

"That's that," Jussi's father said.

"We didn't do much damage, I think. Half an hour is not much time to make a mess of things."

"Where do you think the shells fell?"

"Not the Russian barracks," Jussi said. "We were pointed just a bit left of them. If the angle of the guns was just a little higher we'd have been shooting at the cemetery. I'm guessing it was the ground—the hill—just short of the cemetery itself."

"No sense killing the dead, I suppose," his father commented. "Think there are still Russians in the barracks?"

"Nope. All gone home except for a few hundred crazy volunteers. Do you think the city will fall today?"

"Not today. All those Reds we chased south are in Tampere, and they're scared silly. They're going to fight like hell. Mannerheim's come to watch, again—bad luck for us."

"He's had to throw in the Jägers and the Swedes. You remember my friend, Anders Solbakken? He's one of the Jäger officers, now. At least that's what Hedmann says."

"What about that other one—Karl?"

"I haven't heard what's happened to him," Jussi said. "Not since Vilppula."

"And the young one?"

"Rabbit. The last I heard he had become a cook for the guys at Ruovesi."

Jussi looked for Hedmann, the artillery officer. When he spotted him he said, "Sir? Do you want us to start loading the guns for transport?"

"No, not yet. Take it easy for a while. I've sent a courier to see what's going to be needed of us. It will take some time before he gets back."

#

It took Karl a second or two to realize that the cannon fire had ended. "That was short," he said softly, almost to himself.

"Too short," the man beside him said. He didn't look at Karl but stared straight ahead.

The seconds dragged on. A minute or two after the firing ceased, the infantry charged—the Second Jäger Regiment in front, regular infantry and conscripts following.

The Reds opened up on them almost immediately with rifles and machine guns, and the Jägers began to fall. The Swedish Brigade, too, was suffering heavy casualties as, on the right, it charged uphill across open fields and without cover toward the cemetery.

Each side, Karl knew, could hear the screams of the other as men fell, ripped apart in the fusillade.

By noon, exhausted from the uphill battle, the infantry had reached the eastern outskirts of Kalevankangas Cemetery. The Reds, behind the formidable red wall of the cemetery, fired down on them.

The Jägers, just ahead of the regular infantry, had the job of scaling the wall at its lowest point. Many of them did not make it over. But there was no point in seeking an easier place to get over the wall—there was none. Ahead of them on the left, the ground dropped away precipitously. A retaining wall, perhaps ten metres high, rose above the path and was topped by the red brick of the wall proper. It would have been impossible to climb.

Behind Karl, some of the conscripts began to flee. Their officers, revolvers in hand, drove them back into formation, pushing and kicking the men ahead of them, firing into the air, striking them with their revolvers. The officers herded the conscripts like sheep toward the cemetery to keep the attack going.

"Fight or die!" one of the officers yelled, "Or don't fight and still die, you cowardly sons of bitches! If you stand still, I'll kill you where you stand! If you try to run away, I'll kill you on the run!" At the end of each sentence he fired his revolver in the air.

A short distance away, the little river that paralleled the cemetery had begun to collect the dead. Bodies littered its banks or floated downstream; blood stained the snow and turned the river's water red.

At last, the Jägers managed to gain access to the cemetery and push the Reds back a bit.

Karl followed the leading edge of the infantry over the wall. Once in the cemetery he began to run through the trees and, when he came out of the forest, continued to run, using the gravestones for cover as the Reds fell back.

There was no letup in the hail of bullets. Shards of granite exploded off monuments, the trees behind him suddenly lost some bark, bits of spruce branches fell to the ground. His body felt as if it could no longer move.

He dropped behind one of the gravestones to steal a moment's rest, and sat with his back to the stone, to let his heart slow its pounding, to allow his legs to get back some strength, to see if under all the fear he could still find some courage.

On his left, a few steps back, a statue on one of the monuments had taken a number of hits. What had once been an angel in black granite had become a ghoulish thing without face or hands, one wing gone.

Musta Maija, he thought, and smiled grimly, remembering the card game from long ago. That night, his brother Anders and Jussi had been cooking up some plan about guns—the Grafton guns. Meanwhile, he'd been focused on Viktoria.

All he'd ever wanted was to protect the life that seemed possible then—a life with Viktoria in Gamlaby, where he worked for Fredric and Inga Svensson in the general store and perhaps bought them out one day. A life in which Anders took over their family farm and got bossed around by some worthy woman when their mother became too old to do it. A life in which Ivor, the Rabbit, could grow up all the way into manhood without having to fight in a war.

A life in a country that knew how to make room—both for his Finland-Swede family and for Finns like Jussi Mantere and his parents, and the rest. A Finland that used to be and could still exist. In essence, a Finland where he and Viktoria could have children and raise their family in peace.

Karl shook his head. The men behind him were emerging from the trees. They must not see him just sitting here, hiding. They would think him a coward, or worse yet, they would think that if *he* could hide....

He rolled out from behind the gravestone, flattening his body on the wet ground as much as possible, getting into firing position, seeking a target. Suddenly, the world turned white. The noise of battle was silenced.

#

The courier, later than expected, had returned. He spoke at length to Hedmann, the artillery officer, and then Hedmann signalled for the gunners to gather so that he could address them.

"I know some of you have been speculating about the target of this morning's action. It was a Red position just north of Lake Lidesjärvi."

"Not the Russian barracks, then," Jussi whispered to his father.

"Though the barrage hit its mark, we now know that the action was not long enough to do much damage." He paused for a moment. "Frankly, the attack by the Second Jäger Regiment and the Swedish Brigade, supported by volunteer and conscripted infantry, went quite badly. We believe that something close to one thousand of our troops were killed and, perhaps, another thousand or more wounded. The commander of the Swedish Brigade is among the dead.

"In just one battalion, the Jägers lost over twenty of its thirty-two NCOs and nine of eleven officers. In some of the Jäger companies, the death toll was over fifty percent. I can tell you, however, that we now have control of the Kalevankangas cemetery as well as the Russian barracks to its north. The front line is now on the far side of the cemetery at the south-east corner of the city. Questions?"

"Has the city fallen?" Jussi asked.

"Not today."

"And tomorrow?"

"We bury our dead. Mannerheim has said, apparently, that before we next attack, our artillery will flatten the city."

"How can we help in the meantime?" Jussi asked.

"This battle's over," Hedmann said. "There's a shipment of German ammunition coming by rail. You can go pick it up."

"We have horses, wagons—we can help collect and identify the dead," Jussi persisted.

"They can wait. Their comrades can take care of that."

"What did he have to say?" Jussi's father asked when Hedmann finished speaking. Jussi told him.

When he finished, his father nodded. "So be it," he said, and then, "Do you know what they will do with any prisoners?"

Jussi shook his head. "I don't know," he said. "But I am guessing that they will shoot many of them—put them on trial first, maybe, find them guilty and then shoot them."

"Mannerheim doesn't want that, does he?"

"Mannerheim is a general. He doesn't have much say in what the soldiers actually do. If the war goes well for us, there will be a lot of prisoners—tens of thousands of them—and no place to keep them, and no food. They will be defenseless and surrounded by angry men who will make each other more angry each day."

The men in the artillery battery were following Hedmann down the road to the area where the horses and wagons waited.

"We should go," Jussi said, and he and his father followed the rest.

#

It was Olavi who found Karl's body. It was lying flat on the ground, the hands still holding the rifle. Part of the skull had been blown away.

"*Perkele*," Olavi said. "*Perkele*." He noticed that one of Karl's boots was missing. *What the hell?* He looked around to see if it was nearby. It was not.

Olavi knelt down and looked more closely at the corpse. He saw two holes close together in the back of the greatcoat but only a little blood. Someone, Olavi realized, had shot Karl's body in the back—after he was dead.

Olavi stood up. He had asked Karl to let his family know if he died, and Karl had agreed and asked the same in return.

There were two brothers, Olavi remembered—Anders, the Jäger; and Ivor, the boy who wanted to be a cook. And a friend, Jussi Mantere, who was in the artillery. He decided to formally identify the body to his superior officer and then try to find Jussi when there was time.

As an afterthought, he removed Karl's remaining boot. He would give it to Jussi if he could find him. A man should not look undignified in death. What kind of asshole would steal just one boot?

4 • MARCH 31, 1918
EASTER SUNDAY

IT WAS THE SECOND DAY of the bombardment of Tampere. The city had begun to burn the previous evening, the red glow in the sky growing ever more pronounced as house ignited house. Now, louder than any churchbells would have dared ring, the cannons boomed and the shells fell again on the neighbourhoods of Tammela and Kyttälä in the heart of the city.

The artillery battery had been moved into a more advantageous position, but still Jussi had no direct view of the damage it was doing. He and his father loaded and fired, loaded and fired, and watched as the smoke rose above the city. Overhead, from time to time, a small plane flew, dropping leaflets. *Surrender!* the leaflets demanded, and almost as an afterthought promised, *We do not kill our prisoners as the Reds do.*

Jussi had seen one of the leaflets. *We kill them differently*, he had thought, holding it in his hand.

The prisoners, those who were not being immediately executed, were being held under guard in the Russian barracks. Built for a thousand men—all of whom, except for a few volunteers, had left for Russia, for home, in the middle of March—the barracks were now being prepared to house ten thousand.

Despite his best efforts, the Red commander, Rahja, who had managed to raise a force of thirty-seven hundred men to provide relief to the Red troops in the city, had been unable to break through the White encirclement.

Tampere would fall in a few days—it was now inevitable.

#

At the Easter service in Gamlaby, Pastor Niemi and Pastor Carlson shared the duty. Pastor Niemi had come from the safety of Jacobstad especially for the service. Though the congregation was composed mainly of Finland-Swedes, a few Finnish people had also come to worship.

Pastor Niemi told himself that more of his former congregation would have attended, but Gamlaby was some distance from the church that had been burned, and only half of the service, after all, would be understandable to the largely unilingual Finnish-speakers. He tried hard to suppress the thought that many of his flock would have felt as if they were entering into a den of wolves. The thought, unvoiced, peeked from around a corner of his mind, however, and his eyes anxiously watched the faces of the people he recognized.

News of the battle in Kalevankangas Cemetery had come to Gamlaby by telegraph the previous day. Everyone knew that the casualties on both sides had been large. Few knew if their sons or cousins or neighbours had fought, but all knew that the battle had occurred on Bloody Maundy Thursday.

As the congregation entered the church, the Swedish-speakers went to their familiar pews; the Finnish-speakers sought out places where other Finnish-speakers had gone to sit, and where they formed little islands of Finns in a lake of Swedes.

Both groups hoped that the service this Easter morning would be short. Just after noon, they knew, someone from the telegraph office would post the lists of dead and wounded on the outside wall of Svensson's store.

Ellen Solbakken and Harald Berg, Inga Svensson, and Viktoria Solbakken all sat together in a pew on the right-hand side of the church. Harald looked about from time to time, noting that even in these surroundings, many of the Finns had chosen the left side.

Viktoria wished that her parents were with her, and prayed that they were still safe in Helsingfors, where the start of the war had trapped them. She did not dare let herself wish for Karl's safe return. *Sometimes God punishes us for taking up too much of His time*, she thought.

Ellen thought of Anders and Karl and Rabbit, and told herself to trust in God to keep them out of harm's way.

#

On the hill overlooking Tampere, Jussi was praying that all the civilians had left. He did not want to be shelling people in their homes and in their churches; he wanted them to have run away to safety. But he knew that many civilians would have stayed behind in the belief that the Red fighters would run away, would give up in the face of superior force, and that it would not be necessary for their White soldiers to use cannon fire to drive the fighters out of the streets and redoubts and basements.

But it was necessary, and shell after shell left the mouths of the cannons to land on the houses and businesses of Tampere, and Jussi and his father, caught up in the maelstrom of war, helped send them on their way.

#

After the service, the congregation did not linger. It streamed from the church, split into multiple groups and made its way by this route and that to Svensson's store.

The list had already been posted. It took forever for Ellen and Harald to get close enough to read it. They found Karl's name among the dead. Inga took Viktoria by the hand, Harald put his arm around Ellen, and they went inside the store where their grief would not be public.

Once inside the store, Ellen broke down. "Is this all?" she cried. "His name on the list? Is this all we are going to know?"

"For now," Harald said. "Just for now. We will hear more when more is known." He tried to comfort Ellen, tried to be strong, but tears ran down his cheeks.

Viktoria sobbed while Inga held her. Her husband, her childhood friend, the man she had loved from the earliest day she could remember, was lost to her, lost to everyone. Unbidden, the thought came: *Who will look after Rabbit now?*

Outside the store, someone began to weep. A short time later someone else cried out.

5 • APRIL 3, 4, AND 5, 1918

"NEXT THING YOU KNOW," Jussi's father said, "they're going to wake us up before we go to sleep."

It was just after midnight, and for the third night in a row, the men of the artillery battery were moving into position. Mannerheim, who had once more come to watch the fall of the city, was on a hill in the Vehmainen district on the east side of Tampere. He had given orders to start the bombardment of the city at two-thirty a.m. The infantry would attack half an hour later.

The isthmus on which Tampere lay was split north to south by rapids. Significant portions of the city lay both to the east and to the west of this dividing line.

Mannerheim's plan was to attack the eastern part of the city from three directions—east, north, and south. The spine of the eastern part of Tampere was the railway line that ran north and south. To the east of it lay the Tammela section of the city; to the west was Kyttälä. The troops would pierce the enemy lines north and south, then follow the railway line to penetrate the city and place themselves behind the enemy lines. From the railway they would then spread east into Tammela, west into Kyttälä. The Red forces trying to defend the city would be divided in two and trapped.

The bridges across the rapids posed a significant problem. To facilitate an attack on the western half of Tampere, the bridges needed to be intact, and the Reds had surely mined them. Mannerheim needed to capture the bridges. He also needed to catch the Reds sleeping, hence the early morning bombardment and almost immediate attack.

"Mannerheim's back up on the hill," Jussi said.

"He brings bad luck," his father commented. "I think the Reds fight harder when they know he's watching."

"Maybe so. But we've left them little to fight for."

"It's going to be street to street, today."

"Mannerheim's going to be disappointed," Jussi said.

\#

By late afternoon it was evident that not all had gone according to plan. The bridges had not been captured. Nor had the Reds blown them up. The troops assaulting from the south had sustained heavy casualties and had bogged down in the street fighting, but the attack from the north had gone well, and block after block of the northern parts of both Tammela and Kyttälä had been cleared of the enemy.

At nightfall, news arrived of a "successful" and "heroic" action. Under Captain G. Melin, a company of Jägers from the 6th Jäger Battalion had managed to cross the rapids on a dam and had dashed into the centre of the city, then headed straight north and onto the ice of Lake Näsijärvi. From there they had gone northeast to Näsilinna and seized the museum building.

For the whole day, they held off the enemy and cut off access to a railway bridge. A Red armoured train, consequently, could not be used to support the Red defence of Tampere. At night, having fought all day without food and water, they abandoned the museum and fought their way back across the ice to the main force. The price—half a hundred wounded and almost three dozen dead.

At the end of the day it felt as if the city were a jungle, and every tree, every thing that moved, a threat.

What the Whites did not know was that the Red central command structure had collapsed. The will of the Reds to fight was breaking; formerly brave and idealistic men had taken to hiding in cellars. The Red women, those in the women's units of the Red Guard and those who were the wives or girlfriends of the men in the basements, had to drag them out of their hiding places and shame them into continuing to fight. The Red artillery, as well, was running out of ammunition; the big guns were falling silent.

\#

The next day, April 4th, it was obvious that Tampere, though not felled, was certainly falling. White troops reoccupied Näsilinna after their cannon fire had blown holes in the south wall of the museum, and when a Red armoured train showed up, it was forced to retire to the western part of the city where White artillery put it out of commission. Refugees and deserters began to flee the eastern parts of Tampere to seek food and safety.

Overhead, an aircraft, a Red one, dropped leaflets. *"Try to hold on a little longer,"* they said. *"Help is near."* Almost everyone who read the message looked up, but by then the sky was empty.

A more useful and truthful message would have been *The Germans have landed at Hanko* for, indeed, they had. The first of what would become fifteen thousand German troops had arrived at the invitation of the Vasa senate, the White government in exile from Helsinki.

At night a column of Reds, their families with them, tried to break out through the White lines south of the city. Though the advance guard managed to escape, the rest—men, women, and children— were targeted by machine-guns, and the survivors were forced to flee back into the city.

#

The following day, by noon, only the Town Hall remained untaken. There, a unit of Red Guard women and some Russian volunteers managed to hold out until late in the afternoon. At eight-thirty that evening they asked for terms of surrender.

In violation of Mannerheim's order that prisoners "not be shot out of hand," Ausfeld, the White commander of the troops that had taken the Town Hall, ordered that after the Reds surrendered, all Russians, commanders, and "agitators" would be executed. The rest would be tried by the courts.

Not surprisingly, Ali Aaltonen, the Red commander, tried to escape with a few hundred followers at night on the ice of Lake Näsijärvi. Surprisingly, he succeeded, taking Aatto Koivunen, the Red Guard leader, and Verner Lehtimäki, the other Red commander, with him.

6 • APRIL 6 AND 7, 1918

AT NINE O'CLOCK A.M. on April 6, 1918, the Reds in Tampere formally surrendered. By the time the surrender took place, the Whites had already begun to deal with the huge number of prisoners.

Initially, they had brought the captured to the warehouses by the railway station and held them there. But soon there simply wasn't room enough in the warehouses, and so they began to execute them.

Spectators gathered on the overpass above the tracks to better see the executions taking place. They leaned against the railing in the bright sunshine, watching as the prisoners were lined up and shot against the brick wall of the office area. As promised, all the Russians were killed as soon as they could be identified, as were the Red commanders and anyone who could have been an agitator.

Those lucky enough to escape being shot were marched to the city square. It took almost the whole day to round up the eleven thousand prisoners from multiple locations in the city, line them up in rows, five men wide and filling the entire square, and then count them.

Men, a few women, and children—mostly boys—showed up to watch. The children were fascinated by the machine guns placed at the front of the lines, manned by White soldiers to help keep things orderly and block possible escape routes. Many of the prisoners stood in the sun and melting snow of the square all day with no food or water before they were marched to the Russian barracks north of Kalevankangas cemetery.

The following day, Sunday, work started on collecting the dead and transporting the bodies to the cemetery. Fifty Red bodies made a pile; one pile equalled a mass grave, and twenty-four graves were needed to swallow twelve hundred men. The math was simple. The prisoners dug the graves; the executions continued.

#

Early Sunday morning, Olavi Karppinen found the artillery battery. He carried a large paper bag with something inside it.

Olavi approached the first man he met and said, *"Etsin Jussi Manteretta."* The blank look told him he needed to switch to Swedish, but then the man, suddenly understanding, pointed to a young man sitting with an older one beside a field gun. Like schoolboys, the two were sharing a cigarette.

"You are Jussi?" Olavi asked, walking toward them.

"Kyllä, olen Jussi Mantere. Ja kukas sina olet?" Jussi said, smiling and getting up. He knew from the man's accent that he was a native Finnish-speaker.

Olavi immediately extended his hand. "I am Olavi Karppinen, and I am very pleased to meet you," he said in Finnish.

"Father," Jussi said, and his father got up, pinched off the end of his cigarette and pocketed the butt. Jussi introduced the two formally, let them shake hands, and waited for Olavi to speak.

"I am afraid I bring bad news," Olavi said. "Your friend, Karl Solbakken, died in the attack on Kalevankangas."

The war, so distant at times to the men in the artillery battery, was suddenly too real and too near.

"I was his squad leader." Olavi swallowed. "We were billeted together as well, so we talked often."

Jussi heard the soldier's words and reacted appropriately to them, but he felt as if something in the nature of time had changed. He made himself concentrate, made himself think of the man's full name so that he would remember details.

One day, he knew, he would talk to the Solbakkens, and he would need to be able to repeat the story to them, word for word. Everything that was happening now, everything that Olavi Karppinen was saying, must not be forgotten.

But all he could think to ask was, "How did he die?"

"It was near noon," Olavi said. "We were just inside the walls of the cemetery. I was ahead of Karl, moving from gravestone to gravestone for cover, so until the battle was over I could not check to see who had fallen among our boys. I found his body."

"If I want to find the place he was killed, how will I find it? His family—they—" Jussi broke off.

Olavi understood. He thought for a moment. "It is at the crest of the hill, just out from among the trees on the east side. There is a statue on a gravestone—an angel in black granite. He was between it and a gravestone just south of it."

"How did he die?"

"A bullet in the head."

"It was quick, then."

"Yes." Olavi searched for his next words. "There is more," he said after a pause. "Someone...after Karl was dead, someone put two bullets in his back."

"He was shot in the back after he was dead?" Jussi could not think of anything else to say.

"Yes."

"By the Reds? A counterattack?"

"There was no counterattack. I think...I think he was shot by one of us."

"But—"

"And someone had taken one of his boots. I looked all over for it. I even went back to the place where we had climbed over the wall, but I couldn't find it."

"Had taken *one* boot? Nobody takes just one."

"I looked everywhere. I thought that perhaps the thief had thrown the boot away in anger. It wasn't anywhere within a hundred metres of where your friend died."

"A trophy, then?"

"Perhaps."

"There are such men," Jussi's father said. "They fight on our side, even kill their own if they have to—spies, assassins...evil, evil men. Killing is a pleasure to them." He shook his head.

"Karl told me about the murder of his boss, the shopkeeper, in the store," Olavi said to Jussi. The statement hung in the air for a moment. "The shoe he managed to grab."

"Ahh," Jussi's father said. "Someone who knew the story of the shoe, then."

"I have the boot—the one that was left behind." Olavi gave the paper bag to Jussi. "Perhaps you should keep it. You are the only one I have told of this."

"Yes." Jussi took the boot out, turned it over, put it back in the bag. "Karl carved his initials into the leather sole," he said. He was silent for a moment. "I will keep this. And you," he said to Olavi, "Keep your ears open."

Olavi nodded. "I have to get back," he said.

The three men shook hands once again, then Olavi turned around and started down the path. He turned around after a few steps.

"His brother...Rabbit? He has disappeared. Karl was trying to find out where he was, but no one seems to know. If you see him...."

"I will tell him," Jussi said.

#

In the afternoon, Jussi and his father got permission to visit Kalevankangas cemetery. Already, a double line of bodies stacked three deep ran from one cemetery wall almost half way to the next, and Red prisoners had started the work of digging the trenches in which the corpses would be laid.

Some of the bodies were without any clothing; many of the rest had lost only their warm outer garments or boots to the scavengers. There were, after all, no white armbands on any of the corpses, and that had made the bodies fair game to anyone who didn't mind stealing from the dead.

Along the line of bodies a few people from the town walked slowly, alone or with a companion, looking for a son, a father, a friend amidst the fallen. The townsfolk had dressed in their best clothes—the clothes they always wore when visiting a cemetery. Those who had come by horse and carriage had left the animals tied outside the cemetery gates.

Here, though, despite their best efforts, there was no dignity for the deceased. Nothing that friends and relatives could do, nothing they could say, would help. White soldiers, standing around in groups of three or four, watched idly, gave orders, told jokes, smoked their cigarettes, and yelled obscenities at the visitors.

Jussi turned away and decided to try to find the place that Karl had died.

A few minutes later, he stood beside the black angel. All around it the grave markers were scarred and chipped by bullets. Karl's body had been removed.

It was only a week, a little longer, since the battle had taken place, and yet it seemed as if this part of the cemetery must always have looked as it now did, must always have been scarred.

Time is different here, Jussi thought, *among the dead*. He stood for a long while in silence, then said, "Good-bye." He did not want to pray here, did not want to say Karl's name in this unspeakable place.

He touched his father's arm, and the two made their way quickly back to the main entrance.

Across the road, groups of soldiers were transforming the Russian barracks into a prison camp. They had begun to dig post holes for fences, and to bring in barbed wire.

As Jussi watched, three wagons arrived with some barrels of water. *But no food yet,* Jussi thought.

Jussi's father pointed at the work going on at the barracks. "This is not good," he said.

An hour later, Jussi and his father were somewhere on Hämeenkatu, one of the main streets of Tampere. They stood on the street corner, staring at the devastated buildings, the carnage.

Jussi's father asked, "Did you know your mother and I came here once?"

Jussi shook his head.

"It was not long after we had married—a year, maybe two, before you were born. Your mother thought that maybe if I saw the city I would want to live here, be a tradesman, a clockmaker, perhaps, something more than just a poor farmer." He was quiet for a while. "I know we walked on this street," he said at last, "but I don't know where we are. We are on the street corner but...there is nothing that looks the same; it's all destroyed."

In the road a horse lay dead on its side. It still wore its leather collar but was no longer attached to the wagon it had been pulling. The wagon was farther down the street, under the rubble of a house roof. The wheels on one side of the wagon had remained intact; those on the other had collapsed when the roof had fallen into the street. The horse, Jussi decided, must have been wounded in the explosion that brought down the roof. It had broken loose from the wagon, run a hundred metres or so, then fallen down and died of its wounds.

Two bodies—two people—lay in the street between the horse and the wagon. They had, Jussi could tell, been killed by artillery fire, just like the horse.

All along this part of the street, there had once been elegant houses and businesses. Now, almost nothing of the buildings remained except for their chimneys, ten-metre stacks of block and brick standing in the rubble, giant tombstones erected to mark the death of the city.

On the opposite side of the street, three soldiers posed for a photographer. Men and women had come to look for their dead among the bodies that had not yet been loaded into wagons and removed from the streets. Some stopped to stare at the photographer and his equipment before continuing their search.

"We did this," Jussi said. He felt ashamed. He shivered, and his hand went of its own accord into his coat pocket in search of a cigarette.

"Yes," his father said. "We did."

When Jussi lit the cigarette, his hands shook.

An hour later they were standing on the steps of the Church of Russia, the Orthodox church. It had been heavily damaged on the outside.

"This wasn't here when your mother and I first saw Tampere," Jussi's father said. "I think they finished building it in '99. You were, what...nine, ten?"

"Nine," Jussi said.

"That big brick building on the left, down a few blocks...that was here back then. It was a factory—broadcloth, I think. But not the theatre." Jussi's father pointed at the only other recognizable building some distance away. "They didn't start on that until—"

"1904," Jussi said. "Harald Berg was all excited about it because it was going to be a *real* theatre." But the memory of Berg's enthusiasm could not overlay the present reality of the damaged building—he felt suddenly guilty again. The grey buildings and the cracked cobblestones of the road drove the cold deep inside him.

Between the steps of the church and the only two recognizable buildings, the chimneys stood at attention like soldiers of the dead, and he thought of Karl and the dark and damaged statue of the angel. *Black Maria*, a part of his mind whispered.

"The theatre is not far from here," Jussi's father said. "It's next to the market square. Shall we go look? From here it doesn't seem to have taken much damage."

"Yes," Jussi said. The thought of Harald Berg pushed aside the image of the black angel and made him curious to see the theatre.

When the war was over, when they were home once more, Berg would ask him about it. If they went to see it, he would have something to tell him. And yet.... Jussi imagined the scene in the Solbakken home. If he told the story of this walk with his father through the streets of Tampere, he knew he would have to add lies to it to fill in those parts of the story that needed to be buried.

"First," he said, "let's see what the church looks like inside."

They entered the narthex.

"What the hell?" Jussi's father said.

They were in a fairly large room with chairs set against the walls. Two large ornate stands, each meant for holding a dozen candles, lay on the floor. The candles, some of them broken, were scattered everywhere. An elaborately decorated lectern had been pushed over.

"The candle stands are called *manoualia*," Jussi said.

"They look like upside-down chandeliers. And why is there a lectern here?"

"It's called an icon stand," Jussi told him.

"For what?"

"Icons."

"Which are...?"

"Special religious things—statues, relics. This one probably held a book of some kind." Jussi looked around the narthex. "But someone seems to have walked off with it."

"Looters," his father said. "They may still be here."

The doors ahead of them were closed. "These are the Royal Doors," Jussi said. "On the other side is the nave."

"How do you know that?"

"Berg," Jussi said. "'A church is basically a theatre,' he'd say to drag us back to what he really wanted to talk about. He was keen on teaching us to try to see *through* things—not just look *at* things."

"Berg?" Jussi's father shook his head. "I think it was the *talking* that he was really interested in."

Jussi opened one of the doors and they walked into the nave.

"Oh, my God!" his father said as he entered behind his son. He had lowered his voice almost to a whisper.

The nave was at least three stories tall. Above them hung an enormous golden chandelier. Toward the front, huge columns anchored magnificent arches that supported the ceiling. On the far side of the arches, the ceiling opened up to reveal windows placed high in the east wall. A set of steps ran between the columns and a gilded partition wall in which were set three doors. The centre double door was flanked by two life-sized icons—the Virgin Mary on the left and Christ on the right. The other two doors were to the left and right of the iconic figures.

"The sanctuary is on the other side of the wall," Jussi said. "The middle doors are called the Beautiful Gates. The other two are the Angels' or Deacon's Doors."

"I've never seen a place so beautiful," Jussi's father said. He glanced around, trying to take everything in. "Where are the pews?" he asked at last. "There's those wooden chairs around the walls, but no pews."

"The congregation doesn't sit down. The seats are just for the old or the infirm. Most people stand."

"For how long?"

"If they're lucky, an hour and a half. If not, several hours. Sometimes they have to prostrate themselves, too. They kneel on the floor like the Muslims and touch their foreheads to the ground."

The floor was covered in plaster and bits of wood that had fallen from the ceiling. Jussi's father looked at the debris. "I don't think I'd want to do that just now. Did you notice the onion-shaped cupolas on the roof outside? Somebody's been using those things for target practice."

"Artillery," Jussi said. "Not the fellows we're with, but you know we're not the only Whites with artillery in the city."

Jussi's father did not comment. He stood looking at the structure of the building as he might when deciding if a tree should fall this way or that way when he cut it down.

After a moment he said, "After the war...you know what I think? I think they'll rebuild the church. The foundation is still good. The walls are in bad shape, but that's mostly cosmetic. And roofs and cupolas can be fixed if everything else is okay."

"You think they'll repair it?"

"Churches are symbols. We'll rebuild our churches—the ones that the Reds burned—and the Reds will do the same."

From the back of the church they heard the sound of men. Five White soldiers and the photographer that they'd seen taking pictures on Hämeenkatu came through the Royal Doors and began walking toward the sanctuary entrance. They were speaking Finnish.

"Picture time," one of the Whites said, and he pointed to the photographer who followed with his camera and gear.

"This is a mess," Jussi said to the speaker off-handedly.

"Too bad," the soldier replied. "But it's a God-damned Russian church, and the Reds hid in it."

"Pretty, though," one of his companions offered.

Jussi held his right hand up to stop them. "Don't take anything," he said. "And don't do any more damage."

"We'll do what we want," the leader said. He took a step toward Jussi.

For a moment, Jussi didn't move. He could feel the blood rushing to his face. He clenched his fists but didn't raise them.

"Fight him if you must, Jussi," Jussi's father said, "but don't kill him." He pointed at the photographer. "This one can take his picture when you're done."

Jussi turned his head slightly but kept his eyes on the leader. He addressed the man's companions. "Are you in or out?" he asked.

"Out," one of them said. "Fair fight. It's his quarrel—not ours."

"And you?" Jussi asked the leader. "How badly do you want your picture taken?"

"This is bullshit!" the leader said as he brushed past Jussi and headed for the exit, his friends and the photographer in tow.

Jussi put his arm out and stopped the photographer. "Leave the dead their dignity," he said, then let the man pass.

His father waited a minute or two, then steered his son to the door. When they were outside he looked around to make sure the gang had gone then said, "That was foolish. Their leader...."

Jussi nodded ruefully. "Sorry. You're right. I shouldn't have...."

They stood near the entrance to the church for a minute.

Finally, Jussi said, "It's not far to the theatre. Can you stand some culture?"

#

The theatre was just off the market square where the Red prisoners had been assembled the day before. From the outside it did not look damaged, but inside it was very dark, too dark to see clearly. The city was without electricity, and the auditorium, Jussi knew, would be windowless. He opened one of the doors off the lobby and they walked into the auditorium. After their eyes became accustomed to the darkness they could make out the two balconies behind them, and the stage with its orchestra pit, but not much else.

"Did you know," Jussi's father said, "that they had a celebration of Finland's independence here in the middle of January? Representatives came from lots of different countries."

"And two weeks later, we started killing each other." Jussi stood for a moment. "Let's go. There's nothing to see here."

As they were leaving, his father stopped for a moment to stare down some steps that led into the basement. "The Reds were hiding in here, too," he said.

Two unclaimed bodies lay at the foot of the stairs.

"This is a hell of a day," Jussi said.

He and his father made their way back to camp in silence, not even sharing a cigarette.

7 • APRIL 14, 1918

RABBIT WAS LOST, running for his life in the darkness. From time to time the waxing crescent moon shone through the trees, but the night was still too dark for him to keep from stumbling and falling. What little snow remained on the ground had lost its crust in the growing warmth of the last few days, and it was hard for him to run now—his legs felt like leaden weights, and his feet were wet inside his boots.

If the Jäger-devil had sent a squad along the road to find him, they might notice the spot where he had cut into the woods. He had to run until he could run no more. If they caught him, they would kill him, and he didn't want to be killed. Not now.

What had happened had happened, and when it was over he had wanted to die. It could not be erased; it could not be forgotten; and it could not be told. But it also could not be allowed to end his life. He was the Rabbit—he could outrun it.

At last, long past the point where he should have fallen for the final time, he dropped into the snow and could not get up. His body begged for sleep, but Rabbit knew that if he allowed himself even a moment of unconsciousness, he would never wake again. And if he let his feet freeze in his boots, he would not be able to run. He needed to risk a fire.

For a few minutes he lay on his back and stared up through the trees at the night sky. Here and there clouds obscured the stars, but sometimes he could make out the figure of the constellation, Karlavagnen, whose last two stars point to the North Star.

Otava, he thought, framing the word in Finnish, the frying pan, or was it salmon net? He shook his head. He was falling asleep. He made himself roll over to see if he could spot a birch tree. He had a knife—he could strip off some bark, find a fallen spruce, cut some dry branches, build the fire where the ground was bare.

Half an hour later, he had a fire going. And half an hour after that, he had built himself a nest of boughs to keep his body off the cold ground. He had taken his boots off to let them dry beside the fire.

If I have to die, he thought, *I will die tomorrow, not tonight.* The fire sat atop a small pile of thicker branches and broken dry spruce. The base would catch fire sometime in the night, and would keep him warm until morning. He let himself fall asleep.

He woke shivering before sunrise and put on his boots. They were not warm, but they were dry. The sky, he saw, had grown light enough for him to be able to pick an easy route through the woods. But to where? He had no idea in which direction—if any—safety lay.

He got up, then stood quietly listening. The woods were quiet. If he went south, his pursuers—again, if any—would be reluctant to follow. Best for them to stay out of Red country until the White army had conquered it. He allowed himself a smile, then tore the white armband from his sleeve and headed south. The sky gave him directions.

#

It was Hedmann, the artillery officer, who broke the news. "It's going to get busy again," he said, addressing the gun crew. "Tomorrow we're moving out. I can't tell you where."

"Karelia," Jussi's father whispered. He gave his son a light jab with his elbow.

"Ahvola, then," Jussi whispered back. "That's where they need the artillery right now."

When Hedmann had finished his speech and given them their orders of the day, Jussi and his father set to work. In the evening, in their lodgings near the railway station, they had time to talk. Everyone knew that during the day Helsinki had finally fallen to the Whites and, of course, to the six thousand German soldiers who had done most of the fighting.

"How do you know it's going to be Karelia?" Jussi asked. He was sitting on the floor of their lodgings next to his father, their backs against the wall.

"That's the talk," his father said. "The Germans have driven the Reds out of Helsinki, so Karelia's got to be next. It's funny. If you ask one person what he guesses, you get an answer that's wrong most of the time. But if you listen to everyone...after a while, you know."

His father took a long pull on his cigarette, silent for a moment. "It's always been Mannerheim's plan to secure Karelia and make it tough for the Russians to take back Finland."

He pinched off the end of the cigarette and put the butt in his pocket. "This is my last one," he said. "How about you?"

"Yesterday," Jussi said. "I smoked it."

"What about *snus*? Got any?"

"No."

"Damn war better end soon. You think we're going to Ahvola?"

"I know it," Jussi said.

His father raised a quizzical eyebrow.

"Okay, I'm guessing," he admitted. "But I'll tell you something interesting—not about Ahvola, though. You know that fellow, Borg, the one with the girlfriend in Helsinki?"

"The new guy."

Jussi nodded. "His girlfriend's a telephone switchboard operator in Helsinki."

"So?"

"So here's what he says. Almost all the switchboard operators in Helsinki are Finland-Swedes. They're White."

"Ah." His father knew what was coming.

"They've been listening in on the conversations of the Reds and passing the information up the line to Mannerheim."

His father laughed. "I should have known it was something like that. Mannerheim's no genius, you know. He doesn't build his battle plans out of thin air." He thought for a moment. "What about the telegraph operators?"

"Same, *and....*" Jussi drew out the word like the Master of Ceremonies at a music hall. "Guess where the ministers, Talas and Louhivuori, were hiding."

"I thought they were either dead or captured."

"No, they were disguised as patients in Mehiläinen hospital in Helsinki, along with Ståhlberg, the politician."

"Because most doctors and nurses are White."

"*And*...here's a funny one. There were Red guards in the hospital, of course, and when they got bored they looked out the hospital windows at a house across the street. There was a Red checkpoint close by, and day after day students carrying violin cases would go through the checkpoint and into the house for their violin lessons."

"So?"

"The guards never checked the violin cases. If they did, they would have found that the cases were oddly heavy. The violins they used for their lessons were stored in the house along with...."

Jussi's father grinned. "Guns?"

"Yes. The ones they carried in the cases. And ammunition. Borg figures that when the Germans got into Helsinki they had the support of two full battalions of a White resistance army with a couple of thousand rifles plus some machine guns and a quarter of a million cartridges."

"And lots of extra violins, but no artillery."

"That would have been asking too much. Of course, the case for a bass fiddle is pretty big. It would have been possible, I suppose. Ten men carrying one bass on their shoulders like a coffin...."

For a while neither of them spoke. At last, Jussi said, "I hate it when war makes me laugh. I wish it would just end."

"War never ends," his father said. "Just ask the Irish."

#

Night was closing in. Rabbit's travels had brought him to a road that ran east-west. He was, he thought, somewhere between Hämeenlinna and Lahti. Tampere had to be at least fifty or sixty kilometres north and west of where he was now.

He had been on the run for, what, five days? Six? He wasn't sure. He hadn't eaten for almost three days and didn't completely trust his sense of time and distance. He was south of the big lakes—that much was clear—and there were more farms, and he hadn't crossed any railway tracks since he had got off the rail bed a little east of Tampere.

But he was still lost, and from his hiding place on the north side of the road he watched an endless caravan pass by—people on foot or in carts or on wagons piled high with household goods, farmers herding or leading animals, women with young children walking beside them, men carrying the tools of their trade—and all of them heading east.

He'd been watching for at least an hour as the river of the defeated flowed past, its flotsam and jetsam eerily silent. When anyone spoke it was in Finnish, in a voice low and tired. No one laughed, no one shouted greetings or told a joke. If Rabbit wanted to stay alive—and he did—he would have to join the eastward march with this caravan. Perhaps someone would have food to share.

When he saw a small break in the line he got up and made his way almost to the edge of the forest, then turned around so that his back was to the road. He undid his fly and urinated against a tree, then buttoned it up and walked slowly to the road and inserted himself into the midst of a farm family, the husband walking behind the wagon, his wife controlling the reins, two children—a young boy and a girl a little older than Rabbit—keeping watch to make sure that nothing fell off their ark.

The husband said something in Finnish to Rabbit, and Rabbit pretended not to hear it. When the farmer touched his arm, Rabbit feigned fear, then pointed to his ears using both hands, and shook his head. For the rest of this part of the journey, he would be deaf.

He pantomimed eating and gave the farmer a pleading look. The farmer shouted something to his wife, who said something to the girl, who reached into a burlap sack and found some bread and cheese, and passed the food to Rabbit.

Kiitos meant *thank you*, Rabbit knew, but how might a deaf person try to say it? His mother sometimes put her hand over her heart to show gratitude. He did the same. The farmer nodded and smiled.

Rabbit considered his situation. He couldn't play deaf forever, and he couldn't reveal himself to the Finns as a Finland-Swede. He was alone, and while he was young, he was not as young as some of the Red Guards—they would think him a spy. He needed to find someone who spoke Swedish, someone he'd be able to understand and who could tell him where he was and where everyone was going.

He began to walk more slowly, letting people get ahead of him. He listened for Swedish. It took an hour before he found a family who used it. They were not rich, that was for certain. There was no wagon, no animals, just a man, a woman, and a boy a bit younger than Rabbit. Both the woman and the boy were carrying battered leather suitcases. The man had a canvas pack on his back and a rifle in his right hand. There was a red armband on his sleeve. Rabbit hoped the man would not notice the stitch marks that his own white armband had made on his left sleeve.

"You speak Swedish," Rabbit said as casually as he could. "I thought I was the only one."

"There aren't many of us," the man said. "I'm Anders Marklund." He pointed to his wife and son. "My wife, Lisa-Maija, and my son, Markus." Each gave Rabbit a slight nod of the head.

"I am Gustav Rudeberg," Rabbit said, extending his hand. He had become used to lying proficiently. "I have a brother named Anders." And he knew that a little truth always helped the lie along.

"Pleased to meet you." Marklund transferred his rifle to his left hand so that they could shake hands. "What do you know of the war?" he asked.

Rabbit had been ready for the question. "I know that Tampere has fallen," he said quietly.

"Yes," Anders said. "That is what I believe, too, but it is not something you should say too loudly. We have been told otherwise, officially."

"Oh?"

"Our leaders have promised us land in Olonetz. We are to evacuate the west and central areas of Finland and start colonies in Russia."

"In Olonetz? In Russia? How are you supposed to get to Russia?"

"Walk." Marklund was quiet for a moment. "Now, I have a question for you," he said finally. "How is it that you have not heard of this?"

"I thought we were just running from the butchers," Rabbit answered quickly. "When was this order given?"

"A few days ago. We are from Riihimäki. It's south and west from here, and there's a train station there. The day before yesterday a train from the west arrived, and it was full of refugees—lots of civilians, even though it was supposed to be only for fighting men, no families allowed. I told my wife it was time to go."

"Do you think there will be safety in Olonetz?"

"It doesn't matter what I think. The butchers are behind us, and they will kill anyone they catch. I think we're close to the front of the line, but I don't know. Maybe there are as many ahead of us as behind. There was a man on horseback that came past us this morning. He said that at Hämeenlinna people keep arriving from the west, and there's no place for them to sleep, so they sleep on the streets. Thousands are on the move. And nobody seems to have any food."

"I was in Tampere a week ago," Rabbit said. That much, at least, was the truth. "The Whites have taken the city and they're moving south." It wasn't exactly the truth, but it would do. "I tried to stay ahead of them."

"We've heard there are Germans...." Marklund probed.

"They landed a week ago at Hanko. That's all I know."

"Helsinki is lost, then," Marklund said. He walked mechanically along the road.

"What road is this?" Rabbit asked after a few minutes. "Where does it go?"

When Marklund didn't immediately reply, his wife spoke up. "Originally we walked along the tracks from Riihimäki, but as soon as we could we went north, then east. This road leads to Lahti. If Lahti hasn't fallen by the time we get there, the route to Karelia and to Russia should still be open."

Rabbit merely nodded, and they walked slowly on.

#

In Gamlaby, Harald Berg was with Ellen, Viktoria, and Inga in Svensson's store.

"First Karl, and now Ivor," Ellen said.

"Perhaps it is a mistake," Harald offered. "Such things happen. He—he was behind the front lines. He was—he *is* a cook."

"He is dead," Ellen said. "His name is on the list."

8 • APRIL 20, 1918

HAD IT NOT BEEN for the insolence of the White's Major Kalm, Rabbit would likely have died a Red.

Kalm, a hot-headed and impetuous major, commanded a battalion of White Guards at Padasjoki, a small town fifty kilometres north of the factory city of Lahti. He was given orders after Tampere fell to head for the town of Mäntyharju, east of Padasjoki and on the other side of Lake Päijänne, a trip of close to a hundred and fifty kilometres. Furthermore, he was told he would have to serve under Toll Löfström, a commander he despised as "Russian."

Kalm, defiant, went south, instead. To hell with Löfström!

The day before Kalm's fit of pique, a German bicycle battallion had stormed Lahti, largely unopposed, and had taken it. Now, they linked up with Kalm just north of the city and began to search for Reds in hiding. One of the Germans found Rabbit instead, cooking supper for himself in an abandoned house by the railway station.

"*Identifizieren Sie sich selbst!*" the German soldier yelled as he came upon Rabbit, standing by the stove, pot in hand.

It was perfectly clear to Rabbit what he meant. "Ivor Solbakken," he said, then quickly added, "White."

"*Weiss?*"

"*Ja, ja, weiss,*" Rabbit said earnestly. "Soldier."

"*Soldat? Weiss soldat?*"

"Yes," Rabbit said. "I am a white soldier, but I was a prisoner of the Reds. They brought me here to kill me, I think. But then you came, and they all ran away. I'm very grateful."

"*Weiss,*" the German said, ignoring everything that he could not understand. "*Komm mit mir.*" He used his rifle instead of his arm to show that he wanted Rabbit to accompany him.

"Okay," Rabbit said. "But would you like some soup, first?"

"*Wir haben zuerst die Suppe?*"

"*Ja,*" Rabbit said, hoping that was the correct answer to a question

111

that seemed to boil down to soup. He pulled out a chair from the kitchen table, and the German sat down.

An hour later, having been brought to the White camp, Rabbit was interrogated by one of Kalm's non-commissioned officers.

"I've been told that you claim to be Ivor Solbakken, a White soldier, but you have no papers," the officer began. "How do you explain this?"

"When I was about to be captured by the Reds, sir, I got rid of anything that would identify me as White. And I pretended to be deaf, sir."

"I see. Who was your commanding officer?"

"Lieutenant Östlander, sir."

The NCO tapped the pad on which he had been writing. "A tough commander, I hear," he said.

Rabbit kept his tone noncommittal. "Yes, sir."

"If I contact him, will he be able to identify you?"

"I don't know, sir."

"Who would?"

"I have a brother, Anders Solbakken. He is a Jäger. If you contact him, he will be able to identify me. Or you can contact my other brother, Karl. He's in Tampere."

"And Anders is where?"

"I am not sure, sir."

After a pause, the NCO said, "Ivor, how old are you?"

"Eighteen, sir."

"How old really?"

"Fifteen, sir."

"Well, that explains quite a lot." The NCO sat thinking for a moment. "Östlander has you listed as dead," he said at last.

Rabbit tried to keep his emotions in check. "I'm not dead," he said.

"No, you're not." The NCO put his pen down and transferred the pad on which he had been writing into an attaché case. "But we're going to keep you listed as dead for a while. And I'm going to give you a new name. What shall it be?"

"A new last name?"

"Yes."

"Can it be Mantere?"

"If you wish."

"Why do I need a new name, sir?"

"Sometimes, soldier, you need to trust those who are of higher rank than you. You need a new name, and I'm giving you one. When we get new documents for you, I'll arrange a transfer for you to Lieutenant-Colonel Sihvo's forces at Ahvola in Karelia. Do you know where Karelia is?"

"Almost in Russia, just above Petrograd."

"Yes," the NCO said. Then quietly, "Best to keep you as far away from Östlander as possible."

"Thank you, sir," Rabbit said. "And sir?"

"Yes?" the NCO said hesitantly.

"One of the Germans found me. He had a bicycle, and I don't understand...."

The NCO laughed. He had been expecting another question entirely. "Horses have to be fed," he said. "Bicycles don't. Brandenstein, the German general, landed at Lovisa a few days ago. He commands a whole battalion of those guys. Cavalry. Modern cavalry." He shook his head ruefully.

#

Jussi and his father, now part of Colonel Eduard Ausfeld's forces, were stuck, bogged down, stymied. The order to advance had been given the previous day, but the warmer weather in Karelia had made it impossible for the nearly starving horses to pull their loads through the melting snow, and the artillery could not keep up with the infantry. The sleds were lightened by having the men carry as much as they could, but still they lagged behind the advancing troops.

"You'd think that somebody would have remembered that in April, the snow melts," Jussi's father said. He transferred his bundle from his left shoulder to his right. "I don't even know what I'm carrying," he complained.

"Dead guy," Jussi said. "Very short, small, good dresser, though."

"Smells like gun oil and rags with some heavy cylindrical things mixed in."

"He wasn't much for cologne, but quite a lawn bowler. English, you know. Might be his balls are rattling."

"Any idea where we're going?"

"I don't have any idea where we *are*," Jussi said. "But if Major-

General Wilkman is going to lead the attack on Viipuri, my guess is that our job will be to hold off the Russians and blow up some railway track. We're pretty far east of Viipuri, maybe close to the Russian border."

"The Russians aren't coming," his father said. "If I were Russian, I wouldn't get involved." He shifted his bundle once more. "What are *you* carrying? Why aren't you complaining like a *real* man?"

"Feathers," Jussi said. "I'm the pillow-porter. Generals have to sleep well, you know, to keep sharp."

"Some of your pillows are clanking like my Englishman."

"Some of the generals are a little hard-headed."

"And stiff-necked."

Ahead of them, one of the sleds bogged down for the hundredth time. And for the hundredth time that day came the order: "You six men on the poles to pry, you four to shovel snow under the runners. Let's go."

Jussi and his father put down their bundles. It wasn't their turn to get the horses moving; it was their turn to rest.

#

In Antrea, a little east of the village of Ahvola but on the far side of the Vuoksi River, Lieutenant-Colonel Sihvo surveyed the map laid out before him. He had four thousand men, now, with more on the way, and Mannerheim's order was clear: engage the Reds at Ahvola, and prepare to attack Viipuri from the north.

In Ahvola, the day was passing in the same way it had passed for three months now, with the Reds and the Whites entangled in a protracted war of attrition.

Each day at seven o'clock in the morning, they went to war as civilians might go to work. They received their allotment of cartridges—three hundred and fifty for the day. Then at nine o'clock, they began shooting at each other from depressions that had been dug into the snow and lined with stones, back when the war was new-born. Now, as the weather warmed, they were bona fide trenches dug into the thawing ground and lined with timbers.

From these trenches, aiming was considered unnecessary and dangerous since it exposed the shooter to enemy fire. One peek too many over the edge of the pit, and a man would lose his face. Let the bullets go where they want, the men said. It's just to keep the bad guys from attacking anyway.

Most days about a dozen men died from stray bullets on each side; some days a few more, some days a few less. The dead were replaced when the next shift of men arrived at seven o'clock in the morning and again when the day shift was replaced by the night shift twelve hours later. The long walk to and from "home" made for a fifteen-hour work day.

In the middle of March, by which time the Whites had become bored by the drudgery of the war, the soldiers had started having competitions. Two men would ride their horses up a nearby hill where the Reds could clearly see them, and let the Reds have some target practice. The winner was the man who got to the top of the hill first.

After a while, when the enemy grew more accurate, and when they began to use machine guns and artillery to fire at the riders, enthusiasm for the competitions diminished.

A favourite pastime—though not nearly as exciting as the races, of course—was smoking, and a few human skulls had been transformed into ashtrays. They would make good souvenirs when the war was over, the men said.

Some days, the Reds sent an armoured train north along the tracks that lay a few kilometres east of the battlefield to shoot things up a bit. Other days, the Whites called upon their own train, *The Saviour of Karelia,* to come south and shoot back.

Verdun, the men called Ahvola. We have died and gone to *Verdun,* they said.

The rats that lived with them in the pits and trenches agreed.

9 • APRIL 25 AND 26, 1918

WHEN HE HAD ARRIVED at Ahvola, Rabbit, for all his insistence that he was a cook, had been given a rifle and assigned a place to sleep in a farmhouse a few kilometres from the trenches. Now, at seven a.m. he was ensconced in a hole in the ground with three other men.

"It's very quiet," one of them said.

"Yes." Rabbit added, since he could think of nothing else to say, "Very." Because he was uncomfortable with the silence, he tried again. "I am Ivor...Mantere," he said.

The only person he knew, the man who had brought him to his quarters the previous night, looked up and shook his head in mock remorse.

One of the men laughed. "Having some trouble remembering your name, boy?"

"I'm nervous," Rabbit said. "I have never been in a battle before. I'm a cook."

The third man took pity on him. "Elmer Törngren," he said. He shook Rabbit's hand. "And this son of a bitch," he added, "is Elias Forström and—" he pointed at Rabbit's guide.

"I already know Jonas," Rabbit said. "Jonas Björkgard."

"Do you know what happens today, Ivor?" Törngren asked.

"We attack?"

"I hate General Foch," Jonas said.

Törngren frowned. "Foch? The French guy? What has General Foch got to do with anything?"

"The battle at Marne," Jonas said. "Foch's troops are being beaten back in the centre, retreating on the right, so he says, 'Situation excellent. I am attacking.' He attacks and wins."

"Bullshit," Törngren said. "He wouldn't say something like that."

"It doesn't matter," Jonas said. "That's what people believe—the generals, especially. All they want to do now is attack. It makes them

116

look good, like Foch. And you know what? This goddamned little war of ours is next to nothing compared to what's going on in the rest of the world. More soldiers have been killed already in the big one down south than the entire population of half a dozen Finlands. Nobody's going to even know that this little war of ours ever happened. It's too small to mention, too tiny to bother remembering."

"If we have to attack, what happens first?" Rabbit asked.

Jonas shook his head in dismay, then he said, "There will be an artillery barrage aimed at Hauhia—that's the village just behind the enemy line—and when the barrage stops, we charge. The barrage will begin in a few minutes. Whatever you do, don't shoot the men in front of you—they're ours, after all. Don't even try to shoot over their heads. Wait until you can get a clear shot at the Reds."

"I don't like this," Forström interrupted. "There's no sound from the Reds. I think maybe *they're* getting ready to attack *us*."

"It's—" Björkgard began, but the first volley of cannon fire had begun, and there was no point in trying to say anything more. It continued for half an hour, volley after volley. Björkgard left his sentence unfinished.

When it was over, Rabbit was the first out of the trench. He ran downhill toward the enemy lines. Ahead of him, men were erupting out of trenches and foxholes and from behind trees. Rabbit remembered to hold his fire.

The first wave of men swept over the line of fortifications and disappeared behind them. The gunfire stopped.

"What the hell?" Törngren's voice behind Rabbit. "Don't shoot!" he yelled. "Don't shoot!"

Rabbit had reached the fortifications—a line of piles of rock and timber-framed holes. He clambered over the rock pile in front of him. Before and below him, the leading group of men were unsure what to do. They peered into foxholes, looked up and down the trench works, but there was nobody there. The Reds had left.

Rabbit turned around on the top of the pile and began to wave his arms and shout. "Don't shoot! Don't shoot! Nobody home!" He yelled as loudly as he could. "Nobody home!"

#

When the news reached Lieutenant-Colonel Sihvo that the Reds had abandoned Ahvola and were now retreating swiftly toward Viipuri, he did not accept the facts with grace. His orders from Mannerheim had not addressed this possibility.

And now everyone, even Mannerheim, had heard the story of Rabbit shouting "Nobody home!"

It was now up to Sihvo to block the eastern exits from Viipuri. Even with the addition of the Red Ahvola troops, the garrison at Viipuri would fall. People would try to escape the city as it fell. They would flee like rats from a flooded sewer.

Some, Sihvo thought, might try to head north and west to join their comrades in central Finland at Kymi. He ordered his troops to advance to the town of Juustila to cut off the northern route at the bridge over the Saimaa Canal, and to Tienhaara to block the railway.

It was very early the next day, Friday April 26th, when the group that included Rabbit reached the bridge over the canal. The sun would not rise for some hours.

Without warning, they found themselves under heavy fire in the darkness. No one in their group was in military uniform—they were not, after all, Jägers—but they knew how to fight, and they didn't want to die, and they began to fire back.

Forström was the first to fall, then two more of the Ahvola men went down in quick succession. Rabbit moved forward to take Forström's place, and the firefight continued.

Across the bridge, the leader of the Reds yelled. "I want two men on each side of the bank to watch the water. They may try to flank us."

It was the voice of a Finland-Swede, a voice Rabbit recognized.

"Anders!" Rabbit shouted. "Anders! It's me, Rabbit!"

Heavy gunfire from both sides made it impossible for him to be heard.

"Stop shooting!" he yelled back at the men from Ahvola. "They're not Reds! They're our guys. My brother's with them!"

Some of the men, but not all, held their fire.

"Anders!" Rabbit shouted. "Anders, it's me! We are Sihvo's men! Sihvo's!"

"Cease fire! Cease fire!" Anders commanded, and the gunfire stuttered and then stopped. "Rabbit? Is it you?"

"I'm with Sihvo's men!" Rabbit called out. "Who are you with?"

"Wilkman. We were sent to guard the bridge."

"So were we. Dammit, Anders, we have casualties. We have casualties." Rabbit dropped his rifle and ran across the bridge. When he saw Anders he ran to him and threw his arms around him.

"My brother," Anders said to the men who could hear him. "He's a cook."

#

On April 24th, two days before the firefight at the bridge, the Reds had discovered that the railway in and out of Viipuri was now in the hands of the Whites. No escape by rail would be possible. Kullervo Manner, the Red dictator, had decided that he, the People's Commissaries, the general staff, and their families, needed to get out of Viipuri. Only one escape route seemed possible—the sea.

The planning had begun five days earlier, when a Finnish Red Guard Naval Staff was set up to make sure that a ship, armed with naval guns and machine guns, was always available to the leadership. At midnight on the 24th, the Red command decided to leave. During the night of the 25th, three ships sailed for Petrograd. Only one of the leaders, Dr. Edvard Gylling, chose to remain behind with the people in Viipuri.

At noon on the 26th, Gylling approached the White Colonel von Coler with a plea to allow the Reds to negotiate a surrender, not just of the troops at Viipuri, but of all the Reds in Finland.

Von Coler told him that only unconditional surrender would be acceptable since the Reds had only Viipuri left.

Gylling went back into the city with no option but to fight on, and to bet everything on the possibility of a breakout.

By the evening of the 26th, the story of the Red leaders' desertion was spreading like a wildfire through all of Finland.

"They have decided to save themselves! They have left us to die!" the people cried.

Far fewer and much softer were the voices who said, "If the revolution is to go on, they *have* to go. They have to survive to lead us forth again! The revolution is a *process*, never ending until the final victory." It was an argument without weight.

The Reds, disheartened and disillusioned, had only two options— fight to the death or try to escape the city. Fight and die, run and live.

Two thousand of them managed to escape to the south. Some were captured; some headed out to sea while others took routes that zig-zagged through swamps and forest. Some made it to Russia.

#

Shortly after noon on the 26th, Rabbit said good-bye to Anders. The Jägers would remain to guard the bridge; Sihvo's men would go south to Naulasaari where a roadblock was being set up to prevent a breakout to the west from Viipuri.

"The war will be over soon," Anders said, hugging Rabbit once more. "Every war ends. This one will, too."

"I know," Rabbit said. "Stay alive." He broke off the hug and went to rejoin his comrades.

10 • APRIL 28, 1918

VIBORG UNDER THE SWEDES. *Vyborg* under the Russians. *Viipuri* now because it was hard for the Finns who were in the majority there to pronounce *b* and *g*.

At midnight the White artillery opened up on the town, the guns shouting its name in cannon fire.

Jussi and his father, exhausted, kept the rhythm of loading and firing going for the full forty-five minutes of the bombardment.

"We're done," Jussi's father said in the silence that followed the last shot. He and Jussi sat down on the ground, their backs against the wheels of the field gun's carriage.

"I don't ever want to shoot anything, not even a rifle, ever again."

His father nodded in the darkness.

They were close enough to hear the noise of the assault as it began a minute or two later. "Jernström's men are going in," Jussi said.

"From the south. The first part should be easy—they'll work their way through the suburbs. But then, I think, the Reds will start to retreat up Patterinmäki hill and toward the citadel. That's when the real resistance will begin."

"Will we take the town tonight?" Jussi asked.

"Maybe. If not tonight, then tomorrow."

"And the war will be over?"

"Maybe not over enough to hold a parade, yet, but over enough for almost everyone to recognize that it's over."

"Almost everyone?"

His father shrugged.

The sound of the fighting grew louder. The pop-pop-pop of rifle fire began to include the clatter of machine guns, the explosions of hand grenades, the cries of men being eviscerated by shrapnel, and men first astonished that they were suddenly missing a hand, an arm, a jaw, and then overwhelmed by the pain of their wounds.

In the middle of the din, an animal's cry, a pig in pain.

"I hate it when the horses die," Jussi said. "It's not often that they make any sound—maybe groan a little, that's all. They just fall and lie there. This is not their war."

#

As dawn broke on the 27th, the fighting in Viipuri intensified, and the end began to seem inevitable, even to the most hardened of the Reds.

One group, knowing that the city would soon be lost, broke into Viipuri prison where White prisoners were being held along with common criminals. If the war was to be lost, the men reasoned, they would take their revenge now. At Viipuri castle, farther away, there were only White prisoners, and they were under Edvard Gylling's protection and, therefore, not to be touched.

But at Viipuri prison this was not the case, so the Reds, worried that they might unknowingly kill Red convicts along with White combatants, separated the prisoners into two groups by dress—those in prison uniform and those without. The men who wore street clothing were assumed to be Whites, not regular convicts, and were ordered shot. Though some escaped, more than two dozen of them died, among them a teenaged boy and some convicts who had been unlucky enough to not have been issued their prison clothes yet.

In late afternoon, several thousand Red Guards and their wives and children tried to escape the city by heading west along the road that led to Naulasaari.

Colonel Sihvo had positioned two battalions in the area. At the crossroads, there were a hundred men, and behind them a little farther along the road at a place called Rasalahti, there were more.

Rabbit was in the latter group.

As darkness began to fall, Rabbit could hear the noise of battle in Naulassari.

"The Reds have broken through," one of the men close to Rabbit said to another.

"Dammit," the other said. "I hope those guys got their ammunition in time."

"What do you mean?" Rabbit asked.

"When the transports that brought us here headed back, the ammunition transports went with them by mistake. Somebody screwed up. We've got enough, but I don't know about the fellows up ahead." He pointed up the road.

Rabbit heard machine guns.

"Well, they've got some ammunition at least," the man closest to Rabbit said. In a few minutes, however, the rattle of the machine guns stopped.

"Maybe the Reds have surrendered," Rabbit offered.

"Maybe," the one who had talked about ammunition replied. "But I don't think so."

"If they got through," Rabbit said, "then what?"

"To get by us, they've got to come across the open fields in front. We have machine guns left and right and in the centre. As soon as the gunners open fire, the Reds will have to surrender. If they don't, they'll die."

A few minutes later, a man on horseback, a courier, appeared on the road. "They've broken through!" he yelled. "They've broken through! Get ready!"

"How many?" someone yelled back.

"Jesus Christ! Too many! Five thousand, six thousand, I don't know. Some with rifles, but most have nothing. They took on our guys at Naulassari with bayonets, knives, and clubs."

The courier wheeled his horse and headed for one of the peripheral machine gun emplacements, passed on his message, and then rode to one on the other side of the field.

At dusk, less than half an hour later, the column of Reds approached. Left and right of them were the fields of Rasalahti. When the refugees saw the machine gun emplacements, they slowed, stopped, and went silent.

Someone, a woman among them, cried, *"Rohkeutta! Eteenpäin!"* her voice carrying across the open fields to the White lines.

"What does that mean? Who knows Finnish?" Rabbit's anxiety compelled an answer.

"Courage," someone said from behind him. "And *forward.* They can see our guns, but they're going to attack."

"Hyökkäykseen!" the voice cried.

"Attack," the man said, translating. "Here they come!"

It was still just light enough for Rabbit to see the mass of attackers.

In the front there were not just men, but women and children as well, all of them now running at the Whites. The machine guns opened up in front and from the sides, and the Reds began to fall.

At first, the people behind them ran around the bodies that started to litter the farmers' fields, then as more and more died, they began to climb over the piles of bodies, and still they did not stop.

Darkness fell on the battlefield and still the shooting and the hand-to-hand fighting continued.

Rabbit began to fire his rifle mechanically, his index finger pulling on the trigger of its own accord. Time and time again he reloaded, as a man trapped in a nightmare would repeat the same scene.

He shot at the men coming toward him, and he shot at the women and children. He shot at those with weapons and those without.

Sometime during the attack, when gunfire alone illuminated the battlefield, he heard his own voice screaming as he fired again and again.

And when the Reds at last surrendered, his voice did not stop, and his finger kept moving as if there were still cartridges in the rifle.

The man who had translated the Finnish words grabbed Rabbit and put the boy's head in a headlock, the thickness of the man's coat sleeve muffling the screaming.

At last, as if it had decided on its own that it should scream no longer, Rabbit's voice turned to sobs, and the headlock was released.

"This one can't fight anymore," the man said. "He's broken."

"I am a cook," Rabbit said.

11 • MAY 16, 1918
VICTORY PARADE

RABBIT GOT OFF THE TRAIN in Gamlaby and headed straight for Svensson's store. As he walked along the street, he felt that everyone was looking at him. There were eyes at every window. Sometimes a man would light a cigarette so that behind cupped hands he could whisper to the person he was with that Rabbit was back.

As he walked, Rabbit rehearsed what he was going to say. His mother would be in the store, and he would speak in private with her. He would tell her what had happened and....

Always at this point the narrative died. He would tell her—what? Would he say, "Mother, I am damned!"?

No, he would start by telling her that Anders had paid for the train ticket.

No, he would tell her first that Anders was all right, that he would be home as soon as he could arrange to be furloughed.

At the steps of the store, he stopped.

His mother, who had watched all morning at the window, rushed outside.

"Oh, Rabbit." She wrapped her arms around him and held him to her.

Rabbit heard himself begin to cry and, from a distance, wondered if it was in sorrow or relief.

"Come along, Rabbit," his mother said. "Let's go home."

#

In Helsinki, the sun was shining. Mannerheim had ordered that significant numbers of troops, representing all the units of his army, be transported to Helsinki to take part in a victory parade. If possible,

125

army uniforms were to be worn; men without uniforms would march wearing appropriate headgear and their armbands, at the very least. German soldiers were not to participate. Now, at the head of the troops, Mannerheim rode his horse, and the thousands of people lining the streets cheered.

Far back, Jussi and his father marched side by side. The spectators waved and shouted, children yawned and pointed, families tried to spot husbands and sons among the troops as they got into position.

"Have you thought about what you'll do now that the war is over?" Jussi's father asked.

"Work on the farm," Jussi said. He did not feel like saying more.

"Then what?" his father persisted. "Marry, settle down, have children?"

Jussi decided to tell the truth. "Finland doesn't feel like my country anymore," he said. "I can't get Tampere out of my mind. When I have enough money I think I'll go to America, make a new life."

His father was quiet. "Did you know," he said at last, "that to get into Helsinki a few years ago, you had to have a passport? It was so that the capital would be free of anarchists and socialists and Jews and, of course, beggars." He fell silent again.

"What about you?" Jussi asked after a time. He knew his father was waiting for the question.

"Your mother is gone. There's not much call for tar-makers these days. But I think I'm still good for many more years. I'll make do. A man who can handle animals still has value. But if things don't work out...." He let the thought hang.

"Anders Solbakken is marching with the Jägers. I saw him as we were just starting to form up."

"You think he'll stay in the military?"

"I'm sure of it," Jussi said. Then he laughed. "If anyone was ever born to be told what to do, it's Anders."

\#

At the front of the line, Mannerheim reined in his horse, dismounted, and entered Government House. The long line of soldiers continued to organize itself outside. Mannerheim bristled when he was told by an official that the government wanted to speak only to him and his entourage was to remain outside.

Instead of deferring to the official, Mannerheim signaled for his men to come in, and then he proceeded to lecture Svinhufvud, the Prime Minister, and the other ministers of the government on what they owed the army, and they should realize how *dependent* the government was on its continued support.

When he was done, he and the official representatives of the people went to church, and when they came out there was a roar of appreciation from the crowd, and from every window and balcony people threw white flowers. No one knew until later what he had said to the government. All the people knew was that they loved him.

Jussi and his father had waited patiently in line for the parade to begin. There seemed to Jussi to be no connection between the parade and the war. "The people that are cheering us—they weren't really in the war. Do you ever feel like that?"

"Sometimes," his father said. "They weren't in much danger, except for the ones that were directly helping us—the gun runners and the spies."

"We weren't in much danger, either," Jussi said. "Every once in a while an armoured train shot at us, or one of the Reds lobbed a shell over our heads, or shot too short, or off to the side. We were artillery—it was in everyone's best interest to protect us, to keep us away from the front lines."

"Except for the Reds," his father said. "They didn't like us one damn bit."

They began to move forward at last.

"This parade," Jussi said. "That's the part of the story that they're going to tell their children or grandchildren."

"That's what our side will tell about. The Reds, well...."

"Our grandchildren won't care, no matter what story they hear," Jussi said. The noise of the cheering got louder. "Except when they're very young. Children love a parade."

#

"The last time I saw Karl," Rabbit said, "was when I was leaving Vilppula for Ruovesi. They promised me that I would be a cook. And, for a while, I did get to cook. I learned a lot."

Rabbit sat at the table. His mother kept her hands busy in the kitchen. He paused to redirect his story.

"But there was a Jäger officer, Lindenvall—he wasn't a good man, nothing like Anders. When we got to Tampere and conquered it, he made me and my friend, Benjamin, and some other guys, all of us young—"

Rabbit looked around the store as if he was inside no store at all, but somewhere else entirely.

"He took us into a warehouse next to the railway station and he said, 'I have a special job for you boys to do.'"

"Rabbit?" Ellen said. "If this is something you don't want to tell me, you don't have to. If you're not ready, we can just let it be. I can make you something to eat. You look like—"

"I have to tell you," Rabbit said. "I have to tell you, *now*. Please."

Ellen felt cold. "You can tell me," she said. "I'm going to make us a fire while you talk. Is that all right?"

"Yes, a fire. I'm cold. He had guns in the warehouse, and he gave us each a gun, a rifle—mine was an Enfield—and he said, 'Come outside. You boys are going to send some Reds to hell,' and I said, 'Kill them?' I had never killed anyone, mother. I had never shot at anyone, even. Not really."

Ellen raised the cover of the wood box, took out some kindling and then opened the feed door of the pot-bellied stove.

"I told him—I told him I would not do it. And then he said, 'Anyone else refuse to shoot?' and Benjamin put up his hand. Lindenvall had a pistol, and he raised it, and he shot Benjamin. He shot him in the head, and Benjamin dropped like a stone onto the floor."

Ellen tried to put the kindling into the stove, but some of it fell out of her hands. Instead of picking it up, she leaned on the cold stove so that her hands would stop shaking. Rabbit did not seem to notice. He was, she knew, in the warehouse beside the railway tracks in Tampere.

"Then Lindenvall had us march outside. Another Jäger—I don't know who—went into another part of the warehouse and brought out six prisoners. One of them was a woman. One was a girl. He made me be the one who would shoot the girl. And he said, 'Ready, aim, fire!'"

Rabbit stood sighting along the barrel of an imaginary gun. "And my finger pulled the trigger. He said, 'Fire!' and I couldn't stop my finger from shooting the girl. It shot her, *I* shot her...in the heart."

"Oh, Rabbit," Ellen said. She let the rest of the kindling fall to the floor, and put her arms around her son.

"There were people," Rabbit said as if his mother's arms were not around him at all, "people standing on an overpass outside. It went across the railway tracks, and they were standing on it and watching. They had come out to watch the executions as if they were at the theatre, and we were all part of the show.

"And after that day, every day Lindenvall had us execute people. At Kalevankangas cemetery even. They walked the prisoners from the Russian barracks, walked them straight to the cemetery and we shot them there beside the pits where they would be buried.

"One day I ran away. I walked with the Reds. They were heading east, away from the Whites and the Germans, and I went with them."

Ellen held him hard now, as if by holding on tightly she could protect him, keep him as safe as he had been when he used to play under the kitchen table. Her body shook with sobs, and tears ran down her face, but she did not let herself make a sound.

"I ended up in Ahvola," Rabbit said after a while. "I met Anders at a bridge south of there. Did you know that?"

"Anders wrote me," was all Ellen could say.

"I was part of Sihvo's group, then. It was at night and some of Anders' soldiers shot at us. They thought we were Reds who had escaped from Viipuri. I didn't mind being killed, you know, but nobody killed me—not there."

"Rabbit," Ellen started to say, but her son would not let her continue.

"Our group was sent to Rasalahti. We were supposed to be the backup for another group that was at the crossroads at Naulasaari, but the Reds who were fleeing Viipuri overwhelmed them and came at us."

Rabbit broke away from his mother and turned to face her. He looked at her, and his eyes were filled with horror. "It was very dark, but I could see that some of the people in the front rank were ones I had killed. Then all of them were. And—"

Rabbit suddenly laughed, but his eyes did not change.

"I died," he said. "I think I died. The girl from Tampere killed me. Benjamin was with her."

PART IV

WATER

Time, like an ever rolling stream,
Bears all its sons away;
They fly, forgotten, as a dream
Dies at the opening day.

~ Isaac Watts

1 • PORT ARTHUR
THE SUMMER OF 1955

FROM THE ATTIC WINDOW of his bedroom, Jimmy Mantere could look down on Montgomery Street, the street that everyone in the world who went out to the creek had to take.

To Jimmy, the creek was neither Three Mile Creek nor the McIntyre River—it had no name; it was the water that composed it, and the forest it ran through. He was almost ten, and when someone had told him that the bush—the forest—was actually a park, and that the city owned it and had recently named it George Burke Park after a city jeweller, he did not believe it. Had anyone told him that the Finns who had built the park's outdoor theatre and running track called it *Nahjus*, meaning slob or slowpoke, he would have laughed, and not just because of the name. No one, he believed, could own the creek, any more than anyone could own anything that wasn't theirs. And no one had the right to give it a name. The creek was the creek.

His mother's room was in the attic as well, but on the south side of the house, and it was nowhere as fine as his own. It had no window. His mother didn't live in her room—she just slept in it and, sometimes, read in it. She couldn't watch friends and strangers walk by on Montgomery Street heading for the creek or returning from it.

No one ever stood outside below her window and called her name like they called his.

"Jiii-meee!" his friends would call. "Jiii-meee!"

He would run down the stairs, through the living room, into the hall, out the door to the porch, out the porch door, and down the front steps to where his friends waited.

His room had a desk in front of the window, with bookshelves to either side. The wood floorboards creaked under his feet, but he was careful to avoid the really noisy spots. At night, when the single overhead light was off, he kept his door open so that he could listen to his grandparents talking in the rooms below. No one—not even one of the rich kids—had a room as great as his.

This morning as he sat at the desk looking out over the street, he saw Uncle Ivor coming along, heading for the creek. As always, Jimmy had wound his father's Waltham pocket watch before going to bed, and it hung from its chain on a hook beside the window. Jimmy looked: *8:30* it said. The calendar, hanging on the wall on the other side of the window, reminded him that it was Saturday morning.

Ivor looked up at the window and waved. Uncle Ivor was going fishing. At noon he would stop in for lunch. When his uncle was too far along the street for Jimmy to see him, he went downstairs. His grandmother was cleaning up the breakfast dishes.

"Uncle Ivor's on his way to the creek," Jimmy said.

"Was he carrying anything?" his grandmother asked. "I couldn't tell from here." She had seen Ivor from the kitchen window, but since it faced west, she had caught only a glimpse of him on Montgomery Street.

"No." Jimmy knew that his grandmother was asking if his uncle was carrying a bottle. "He's probably going fishing. He had his creel, but not his rod. Most of his stuff's at the shack now, I guess."

Viktoria wondered if Ivor had spent the night on the street. Thursday had been end-of-month, the last day of June, and Ivor's spot at the rooming house might have been given to someone else if he hadn't paid since the first of June. Today was Saturday, so where had Ivor slept last night? She could ask him at noon.

"*Creel?* What is that?" she asked.

"That wicker basket with straps. He wears it when he goes fishing. It's got a hole in the top so that he can drop the fish in. It looked heavy, so I think he had his books in it."

"*Ja,* I understand," Viktoria said.

After almost forty years of living in Canada, she still preferred *ja* to *yes*. When she spoke to her English-speaking friends, the Swedish accent almost disappeared, but traces of it still lingered at the edges of her voice and in her refusal to use contractions. A person should always say *what is* instead of *what's*.

"*Creel*," she said. "I have to remember that." And she would.

"May I make some toast?" Jimmy asked. He was careful not to say *can*. He went to the part of the kitchen counter where the old electric toaster stood.

"Certainly," Viktoria said. She wiped her hands on the towel that dangled from the handle of a counter drawer, and then got the bread out of the breadbox. "You remember how to do this?" she asked, then smiled.

"Open the two doors, put the bread in, close the doors, plug in the toaster," Jimmy recited, "wait three minutes—less if there's smoke—then open the doors to let the bread slide down, close the doors to flip the bread, wait two minutes, unplug the toaster, open the doors and take out the toast."

"And?"

"Be careful," Jimmy said in his best imitation of his grandmother, then he made a sour face and laughed. Every time he made toast, they went through the same routine.

When the toast (slightly burned) was ready, Jimmy put it on a plate and sat down at the kitchen table to eat. He buttered the toast carefully. Some of his friends' mothers let them stand around with food in their hands—some of them even let their children drink pop at a meal—but not his grandmother.

Viktoria took a glass from the cupboard, put it on the table beside his plate, and got a bottle of milk from the Frigidaire. "I don't miss the icebox one bit," she said.

Jimmy took a bite of his toast. When he had swallowed, but not before, he said, "*Farmor*, how come Uncle Ivor can be my uncle when he's not related to us?"

"Not *how come*," Viktoria said. "Say *How can Uncle Ivor be*."

"How can he, then?"

Viktoria smiled at Jimmy's attempt to spar. "I have told you this before. He was the brother of my first husband."

"The one who died in the war."

"Yes."

She didn't say *ja*, Jimmy noticed. She was being careful of language. "Do you miss him?"

"Yes, I miss him."

"When did Uncle Ivor come to Canada?"

"In 1925," Viktoria said. "*Farfar* came in 1920 and I came in 1921.

I have told you this. Remember?"

"Why did he wait so long? Uncle Ivor, I mean."

"He was not well for a long time, and his mother had to look after him. But when she died, he emigrated to Canada and came to live with us. He worked with *Farfar* for a few years when Jussi was just starting the contracting business." *Just* emerged as *yust*.

From outside, "Jiii-mee! Jiii-mee!"

Thank God, Victoria thought.

Jimmy drank the last of his milk quickly. "Can I go?" he asked.

"*May*," Viktoria said. "And yes. But do not be late for lunch. And if you see Uncle Ivor, invite him. He'll show up regardless, but invite him anyway. And take your jacket with you—it is going to rain."

"Okay. Bye." Jimmy was out the door, jacket in hand, before the boys called again.

When the door closed, Viktoria sat down at the table.

"*Gud*," she said. "God."

She sat for a moment, then took the dishes to the sink, washed them and put them away. There were tears in her eyes now. She remembered seeing Karl's name on the list of the dead. She remembered *everything* about that day.

She shook her head, wiped her eyes, then got a cup and saucer from the cupboard and poured herself some coffee. From the sugar canister, she got a sugar lump—a square of very hard sugar the size of four regular cubes—and, from the kitchen drawer, she took out the sugar cutter. Jussi had asked a blacksmith to make it for her the year they were married.

Viktoria placed the sugar lump between the jaws of the cutter and made two quick cuts to create four cubes. Three of these she put in the sugar bowl. The fourth she put in her mouth. Carefully she poured some of the coffee into the saucer, lifted the saucer to her mouth and sipped the coffee through the cube.

She forbade her hands to shake. She thought about Karl sitting beside her in the Solbakken house, Rabbit playing with people's shoelaces under the table. And, because she knew no one would see her, she let the tears come again.

#

Montgomery Street changed from an oiled road to a dirt road at

Mrs. Toivonen's potato field. There was no longer a Mrs. Toivonen, or a potato field, but there was an open area where the potato field had been. It was overgrown now with grass. Jimmy's grandmother once told him that Mrs. Toivonen had lived on Montgomery Street close to their house, and she had kept chickens in her back yard. But because the yard was small, she had "borrowed" some land that the cemetery wasn't using, and planted potatoes there.

The cemetery property began where Montgomery Street turned into a dirt road, and went all the way to the creek. The cemetery ran south to Oliver Road, but since only a few acres along Oliver Road were in use, the north end remained bush—except for the potato field where the neighbourhood kids played baseball.

They played their own version—one team, and the players rotated through all the positions. If there were a dozen fielders, so what? And it didn't matter how many boys and girls turned out to play because everyone still knew who the best players were, and nobody (unlike at school) ended up on a losing team.

Jimmy's grandmother had told him that during the Depression, some of the Finnish men who had emigrated to Canada found themselves out of work and with no place to live, so they had built shacks in the bush beyond the creek. If the shacks were past the power line that cut through the bush, they were beyond the city limits. That meant that neither the police nor the tax collector would show up, and no landlord would knock on the door to ask for the month's rent. And once in a while, if a man were hungry enough, he could steal a chicken or just some eggs from Mrs. Toivonen, then dig up a potato or two at the field. Mrs. Toivonen turned a blind eye to the eggs and potatoes, but the chickens were another matter.

Uncle Ivor had built his shack out there, one of four in a little clearing half a mile out. When the autumn came, he would find work, install himself in a rooming house somewhere near downtown, then move his belongings—books, mostly—out of the shack. He'd sweep the shack's floor, board up the only window, and make sure the door was closed. And that would be that until spring.

Jimmy and the three other boys were at the end of Montgomery Street, past the oval running track, standing on the high bank where the creek changed its direction to flow west instead of south. From where they stood, the ground sloped gently downwards ahead of them, but on the right it dropped precipitously. Someone had driven his car past the end of the street and down the bank to the rock flats where the river once again turned south. He was washing his car in the river.

"I wish he wouldn't do that," Jimmy said.

"Your uncle's not going to like it if he's fishing downstream," said Charles, whose thick London accent gave every sentence weight, though it also advertised his recent immigration. More than once he had needed defending in the schoolyard. "There will be soap bubbles."

"Does he ever catch anything?" Tony Four-eyes wanted to know. Tony, a year younger than everyone else, had a voice that headed for soprano whenever he became excited. Fishing—successful fishing—excited him a lot, as did hunting. The best book he'd ever read was about bears, he'd told them. That he'd ever read a book at all was surprising to the others. Even when he read a comic book he seemed to read only the pictures, not the words. The words just slowed things down.

"Yup. He fillets and cooks them at the shack," Jimmy said.

"You ever been to the shack?" Charles wanted to know.

"Nope." Jimmy felt a twinge of guilt. *Yup* is not a word, and *Nope* is slang, his grandmother would have pointed out. "My mother and, for sure, my grandmother don't let me go there. They're afraid of the old Finlanders. My grandfather always tells her there's nothing to be afraid of, but he loses the vote every time."

George, who was almost a year older than everyone else and could claim that he was two years older than Tony Four-eyes, had lost interest in the conversation, but not the car. "That's this year's Plymouth," he said, pointing. "Let's go talk to the guy, have a look."

Jimmy shrugged his agreement. Of the four, he was the leader—George was older, stronger, a better athlete, but Jimmy always had ideas about what would be fun to do. It was Jimmy's approval that broke or sealed any deal.

The four started down the slope. It wasn't unusual to see someone washing a car in the creek. It was unusual, however, to see a *new* car being washed there.

"Nice car," said George, who was born without shyness.

"Like it?" the man said. He was at least twenty-one, maybe way older than the age of majority—twenty-five, even. He looked like a grain elevator worker, muscled, lean, and wiry. "You wanna give me a hand?"

"Sure," George said immediately. "Is it souped up?"

"Nope. Everything's standard. But it's got the Hy-Fire V8, four-barrel carb, dual exhausts and...come look at this. Wait. Take your shoes off, first, and roll up your pants." He waited until George was beside him in the water then said, "What do you think that is?" He leaned over and pointed at the dash.

George put his face up to the window. "That little lever? I don't know."

"Car's got auto. That's the shift. See the prindle markings beside it?"

"Wow."

"Got a friend says he's heard they're gonna replace that with pushbuttons next year."

"Wow."

"All right, guys," the owner said, waving the remaining three to come down. "If you wanna join in....Two buckets—big one's got the soap mix, smaller one's for rinsing. Washcloth's for windows, brush is for wheels. Get to work. I'm gonna have a cig. When you're done, I'll back it up and let the sun do the drying."

He waded out of the water and walked gingerly up the slope, then sat down on the grass.

Good luck drying the car in the sun, Jimmy thought. *When* Farmor *says it's going to rain, it rains.*

#

At noon, just as the rain began, Ivor showed up for lunch. Jussi arrived a couple of minutes later and sat down at the head of the table, opposite Ivor. Jimmy took the chair by the wall so that his grandmother could move easily between table and counter.

"Ivor brought us two fish," Viktoria said to Jussi. "I wrapped them in wax paper and put them in the Frigidaire so that we can have them tomorrow. And a young fellow out at the creek let Jimmy and his friends wash his car."

"Ahh," Ivor said. Jimmy hoped he wouldn't say anything about the soap. "I have a book you might like, Jimmy." *Jimmy* he pronounced as *Yimmy,* just for the hell of it. "It's called *Tom Sawyer,*" he said as Viktoria glared at him.

"Very funny," Jimmy said. "We weren't asked to *paint* the car."

When the meal was over, Viktoria sent Jimmy out to find his friends. After he had gone, she shifted from English to Swedish and said, "Ivor, sit a while. I'll put more coffee on, and we can talk. It's Saturday and Jussi doesn't have to work this afternoon. And we haven't seen you in a while."

Jussi nodded in agreement.

"Okay," Ivor said, "but my life's not that interesting, you know."

"You've moved into the cabin for the summer?" Viktoria asked. While Ivor considered his reply, she emptied the dregs from the coffee pot into the garbage can, then rinsed out the pot.

"Yes," Ivor said at last. "I could have stayed at the rooming house, but you know...."

"The place is too dark," Jussi said, anticipating where Ivor was going.

"The only window faces the wall of the Hemmet," Ivor said, referring to the Scandinavian restaurant next door to the rooming house. The Scandinavian Home Society owned both buildings. The Society was proud of the restaurant, but ashamed of the rooming house. "I never get to see the sun. I could have stayed there if I'd wanted, but...." He shrugged. They knew the story.

"Are the nightmares back?" Viktoria asked. Since they had all switched to Swedish now, she could be direct without being impolite.

"Yes," Ivor said. "They wake the others up."

"The walls are thin," Jussi said.

"The other tenants have complained?" Viktoria's tone was of one who would like to beat Ivor's tormentors with a stick. Ivor was a gentle man; the others were not.

"Some," Ivor said. "One fellow likes to take his belt off once in a while and make it snap like a gunshot when he thinks things are too quiet. He knows I can't stand that."

Viktoria filled the pot with water, added the coffee, and put it on the stove to boil.

Ivor went on, "If he's not there in September, I'll move back. If he is, I'll find another place."

"What about meals?" Viktoria asked. "You like eating at the Hemmet and talking Swedish with your friends."

"I can still walk there from the creek," Ivor said. "And I can go to the Hoito, too, and eat with the Finns. I can even speak a little

Finnish now, you know."

"You can?" Jussi asked. "You don't learn a word of it in Finland, then you come to Canada and start learning?" He laughed. "Well, better late than never."

"The days can be long," Ivor said. "I have a Finnish-Swedish dictionary and a child's grammar book that I got from that bookstore on Bay Street. The guys that live in the other shacks are all Finns. One of them was in the war." He did not need to explain which war.

"Does he know...?" *That you fought for the Whites* went unspoken.

"Yes, but like most of the others he pretends he doesn't. We don't talk about it."

The kitchen filled with silence. After a while, Viktoria said, "Mannerheim was right, you know. It is best to leave some things alone."

2 • IMMANUEL

SUNDAY WAS CHURCH. Every Sunday Jussi, Viktoria, Jimmy, and Jimmy's mother Marilyn would get in the car, and Jussi would drive them to Immanuel Lutheran Church at the corner of Pearl Street and Banning for the ten o'clock service. Jussi would let them off, and then he would drive back home to read yesterday's paper and have a smoke. At eleven he would return to pick them up.

Jimmy seldom thought to ask why things were as they were. For instance, Jussi, his *farfar*, didn't go to church because Jussi just didn't go to church. A lot of men didn't. Some did, of course, but the visible congregation was mostly women. Of the men who went to church, very few sang, and at least half of those who did couldn't find the right notes. Most of them just moved their lips to the hymns and prayed with their heads bowed but their eyes open—something Jimmy had found out last year when, for the first time, he had risked not closing his eyes.

The service was always held in the church basement because there was no main floor. The oldest people in the congregation remembered Immanuel's founding in 1906: the purchase of the lot, and then after six years of saving money, the building of the church basement. The plan had been to hold services in the basement for a couple of years until there was enough money to put up the church proper. Now, forty-three years later, the congregation had almost enough cash to start construction once more...but not quite. Next year, perhaps.

Every time Jussi saw Immanuel, he thought of the shattered Russian Orthodox church in Tampere, the holes in the roof, the plaster on the floor. It had taken the church's congregation many years to rebuild it, but not forty-three.

The old-country Scandinavians were a patient and conservative bunch. Immanuel's full name, as spelled out in its constitution, was the Swedish Immanuel Evangelical Lutheran Church, and for over a quarter of a century, the congregation had worshipped in Swedish—a language their children did not bother learning. At least a dozen of the fourteen ministers, ignoring the possibility that someone else might have had the idea too, had delivered a sermon on the fact that Immanuel meant "God with us." No one, of course, ever mentioned this to the pastor of the moment.

English had intruded in 1940, to the dismay of those who believed their children would learn Swedish if it remained the language of worship, and to the relief of others who knew better. What stayed constant was that Immanuel remained a church for people of Scandinavian heritage—and the more Swedish and White, the better. The exclusivity wasn't because (as one of its many pastors had suggested) the congregation needed to "guard against lowering the standard of admittance." It was because the church teemed with people who, comfortable in the presence of familiar faces, were shy in the company of strangers. Every Sunday each member sat in the same place in the same row of old chairs. Where would the new members sit? At the front? There wasn't much room, you know.

All this had no bearing on why Jussi didn't go to church. *That* he kept to himself.

Viktoria believed in going to church, but she never spoke on God's behalf. That would have been *högmodig*—haughty, arrogant, full of one's self. For a while she had attended the Finnish Evangelical Lutheran Church, but there were too many Finns in it, and not enough Finland-Swedes. So she had switched to Immanuel.

"James," Jimmy's mother called from the kitchen. "Are you ready?"

Clean shirt, good shoes, church pants, combed hair, fresh handkerchief. "Yes, mom!" he yelled back.

"Then get down here. We're leaving. Your grandfather's at the car already."

The drive from home to God's house was just a little over a mile. When his grandfather drove them to church, the route was always the same—down John Street to Banning, then up Banning to where it met Pearl Street. It would take them five minutes to get there, and they'd be twenty minutes early.

They filed out to the driveway. Jimmy and his mother got in the back seat, Viktoria in the front beside her husband. Jussi started the car, then immediately turned the engine off.

"What did you forget?" Viktoria asked.

"Nothing. It's Ivor," Jussi said. He used his thumb to point behind him, then rolled down his window.

In a few seconds Ivor stood beside the car. He bent over to talk to Jussi. "Is it okay if I go with you?" he asked in Swedish.

Jussi leaned back from the window, trying to create a little more space between himself and Ivor. "You've been drinking," he said in English. "I thought you were going to cut back."

"Can I ride with you to church? I won't go in. I just need to talk to you about something." He noticed that Marilyn, who spoke no Swedish, was in the car. "Sorry," he said to her in English.

"Ivor," Jussi began.

Viktoria cut him off. "Get in the car, Ivor," she said, indicating the back seat. "You can sit beside Jimmy."

Ivor opened the door and got in.

Marilyn said, "Jesus, you smell like a brewery."

"Winery," Ivor countered. "But I'm through with liquor. I quit."

"You quit."

"Yes. Just now," Ivor said. "And I won't say another word until Jussi and I are alone. I have an important thing to say."

"Important," Marilyn said, doubt and disgust in her voice. "That'll be the day."

Ivor touched thumb to forefinger and closed an imaginary zipper across his mouth. Marilyn shook her head dismissively and settled back in the seat as Jussi started the car once more and put it into reverse and backed out of the driveway.

Only fourteen minutes early—for which Jimmy was grateful—Jussi turned from Banning onto Pearl Street and stopped the car. Jimmy followed the two women down the steps and into the church basement. Jussi put the car back in gear and drove down the Pearl Street hill.

The car was almost at Secord Street when Jussi asked in Swedish. "Well, Rabbit, what's on your mind?"

"I have to show you," Ivor said. "You know the shoemaker's place at the corner of Hill and Oliver? Find a place to park somewhere. Close, but not in front."

"Drunk or sober, you love your mysteries, Rabbit."

"Not this one," Ivor said.

A few minutes later, they were parked.

"Well?" Jussi said. He put his hand on the door handle. "Shoemaker?"

"I have to tell you something first," Ivor said. Jussi took his hand off the door handle and waited. "Sometimes I walk this way when I need something from Kangas's store—bread, cigarettes."

"Yes?"

"Someone's been watching me. Someone who knows us."

"Who? How do you know?"

Ivor got out of the car without answering, and Jussi followed. "I have to show you," Ivor said. Somewhat unsteadily he led Jussi to the shoemaker's storefront. Because it was Sunday, the shop was not open.

"Look in the window," he said, pointing to the small display of various boots and shoes that were on a shelf just behind the window.

"Jesus Christ!" Jussi said.

In the window was a pair of mismatched footgear—a shoe and a boot. The shoe Jussi recognized immediately. It was like the one that had been lost by one of the Reds who had killed Fredric Svensson at his store in Gamlaby. Of this, Jussi was certain. He had taken its mate to every shoemaker and store in Jacobstad and Nykarleby to try to find the man who had made it.

The boot, on the other hand, was certainly Karl Solbakken's, and had been taken by the person who had shot his corpse in the back in the Kalevankangas cemetery. In the bedroom closet at home, Jussi had the match to both the shoe and the boot.

"He's here," Ivor said. "He's in Port Arthur."

"The shop will be open tomorrow," Jussi said. "I will speak to the shoemaker. You will say nothing of this to Viktoria, or to anyone else."

"Do you think he lives nearby—the killer, I mean?"

Jussi had not considered this yet. "Yes," he said finally. "He may have chosen this shop because he can see the shop window. We should go now. It may not be a good idea for him to see us."

Ivor nodded, then he said, "I think he watches me walk past the place. I think he knows who I am."

In less than a minute they were back in the car and driving home.

"Marilyn thinks I am a drunk," Ivor said.

145

"Yes, she does." Jussi said nothing more until they were close to home. "I can drive you to the creek," he offered.

"You are a good man, Jussi," Ivor said. "I should not have shown you the display. This will bring you trouble. When I drink I do foolish things."

"It wasn't foolish."

"You don't need to take me to the creek. It will look better if I walk." At the house Ivor opened the door and got out. Then he started up the street.

Jussi went inside and, out of habit, looked for Saturday's paper. He always saved something in the paper to read on a Sunday morning. This morning, however, though he found the newspaper, he did not open it. He left it alone, lit a cigarette instead, and waited for the clock to tell him it was time to go back to the church and fetch his family.

At eleven o'clock, the door of the church opened and the competitors began to stream out of the basement. Viktoria was first, Marilyn not far behind, then Jimmy, all three squinting like creatures of the night dazzled by sudden sunlight.

The slower members of the congregation, slow to rise from their pews, slow to make it to the steps, slower still to climb them, at last slowed to a standstill as soon as they were out in the sunlight. Then, blinking like owls, they clumped together in a bunch and talked and gossiped and traded stories—stories, like money, were a form of currency. Some spent it lavishly while others hoarded it or used it to bargain.

In the past, Viktoria had been a little too slow out of her chair once too often, and had found herself tangled up in the clump just outside the door. Now the last note of the final *Amen* was to her a shot from a starter's pistol. She was the first up the steps, the first to reach the car.

"What did Ivor want?" Viktoria asked as soon as she had closed the door.

Jussi waited for the rest of the family to get in before he answered. "He wanted my opinion about getting a new place to stay in the fall."

"He was drunk," Marilyn said.

"A little. But he has a lot on his mind, too. He's getting older, and it's not so easy for him to find work and a safe place to hang his hat."

"You're making excuses for him," Marilyn said. "He's a grown man, not a child."

"Mom," Jimmy said, and she knew she had gone too far.

"I'm sorry," she said. "It's just...." She leaned back against the seat.

"Uncle Ivor has a lot of friends," Jimmy said.

His mother nodded in agreement. "I know he does, but he's...." She let the sentence die.

Just before the corner of John Street and Oliver Road, Jussi said, "I always go the same way. Time for something different," and turned up Oliver Road instead of taking the John Street hill.

As they passed the shoemaker's shop, he stole a glance at the window display. A few minutes later they were home.

3 • THE SHOEMAKER

ON MONDAY, JUSSI went to the McLeod house to make sure the crew knew how to remove the house's skirting. Then he gave them instructions for digging away the dirt from the four corners of the basement and preparing the forms for the concrete pads on which the jacks and timbers would sit. Jacking up a house so that a dugout basement could become a concrete block structure was never easy, but he could leave his men alone now for at least half an hour.

It took ten minutes to drive to the shoemaker's shop. Jussi parked the car some distance away, then took a paper grocery bag from the passenger seat, and got out.

A bell above the door rang as he entered the shop. The interior smelled of leather and polish. A counter ran almost the whole length of the narrow room. Near the window there was an old National cash register. Behind the counter were shelves and cubbies that held shoes, each pair tagged with the name of the owner.

At the back of the room, behind another counter, the shoemaker used a foot treadle to operate a sturdy but ancient walking-foot sewing machine. As he worked, he slowly rotated the shoe on the machine's narrow arm. The stitching stayed even and straight; the machine clattered loudly.

"You are the shoemaker?" Jussi asked after a moment.

The man took his foot off the treadle. He looked around as if searching for someone else who might be the shoemaker, then he smiled.

"No, actually," he said, "I'm not. A shoe *maker* is called a *cordwainer*—I only *repair* shoes. I am a *cobbler*. Just a cobbler." He pointed to a machine set against the wall beside him. "I also sharpen skates," he said.

"And what does sharpening skates make you?" Jussi smiled too.

"Tired. I have to stand to do the sharpening. I can sit to fix the shoes."

"You own the shop?"

"I do. At least until the bank wants it back. What can I do for you?"

"You have a boot and a shoe on display in your window. I want to know who gave them to you—unless, of course, they are yours."

"Not mine."

Jussi reached into the paper bag he had brought from the car. He pulled out a shoe—the one that Karl had taken from the man who had murdered Fredric Svensson more than thirty years before. He set it down on the counter. Then he reached into the bag again and retrieved Karl's boot, the one that Olavi Karppinen had given him.

"Ah," said the cobbler. "Mates. He said you had these. Now we each have a shoe and a boot." He came out from behind his machine and went to the window, then came back with the two items that formed the display and put them on the counter.

"May I have a look?" He reached out for the shoe that had belonged to one of Svensson's killers, and Jussi allowed him to pick it up. He turned it over carefully in his hands, then picked up the shoe that had been on display. "Both shoes were made by the same man. Stitching is like a fingerprint, you know—unique."

He handed the shoe back to Jussi, then picked up the boot and examined it. "This one, too," he said, "same technique, same machine, same man as the other boot. But the shoes were made by one man, and the boots by another."

"Who gave you these?" Jussi asked.

"A man. A Finn, like you...not quite as old, not quite as tall, thin as a rake. Better dressed. Better shoes, but not handmade. He gave me twenty dollars to put the items in my window. I don't make that much money in a week, sometimes."

"Why did he want you to put them on display?"

"He didn't say. Did he steal them from you?" The cobbler handed the shoe and the boot back to Jussi, raised his glasses so that they rode on his forehead, and examined Jussi carefully.

Jussi shook his head. "No. If he comes by again, tell him I want to talk to him."

"And you are...?"

"He will know." For a moment Jussi considered. "Put the shoe

149

and the boot back on the window ledge as they were. When you have given him the message, turn their toes the other way. I will keep tabs on them, and come by again to hear what he says to you." Jussi leaned over the counter. "Do you understand?"

"Yes," the cobbler said. "But, you know, he gave me twenty dollars."

"I am not the bank," Jussi said. "And I will give you no money for this. But if you do *not* do this, I will...foreclose."

He stared at the cobbler for a brief moment, then put Karl's boot and the killer's shoe back into his bag and left. The door's bell rang softly behind him.

The cobbler sat without moving for a few moments, then he went back to work. *This is not my affair*, he thought, but he would do as the customer had asked.

#

Just before seven o'clock each weekday evening, Jussi turned on the television set so that they could watch *Tabloid* for the news, interviews, and weather. Jimmy's job was to stabilize the picture as the set's tubes warmed up. He used the vertical control knob to stop the picture from rolling, then the horizontal to stop it from flipping sideways. He had to do the job twice—once just after the set was turned on, and again when the set was at normal operating temperature.

When Percy Saltzman, the TV weather man, finished the weather forecast at his chalkboard, he would flip his piece of chalk into the air and try to catch it behind his back. If he caught it, the family cheered. If he missed, they said "Ahhhh" in disappointed unison.

When *Tabloid* ended, Jimmy went up to his room, read comics for a while, then at nine o'clock, he went to bed. His mother came up the stairs at ten, looked in his room to make sure that everything was okay, then went to bed herself. By ten-thirty, all the lights in the house were off.

Just past midnight, Jussi, unable to sleep, broke the family's routine. He got out of bed and went into the kitchen, sat down at the table, lit a cigarette, and thought about the shoemaker. *Why had the shoemaker agreed to be the go-between? Twenty dollars? Fear?*

4 • NAMES

TUESDAY SEEMED TO BE a good day to go to the creek. The weather forecast was for a high in the eighties.

By one-thirty, the boys were at the end of Montgomery Street, where the road became a path that was just wide enough for a car to drive down into the water. The water there wasn't deep enough for swimming, but if you had goggles you could go upstream a few hundred feet and hunt the crayfish that hid under the rocks.

When crayfish got spooked, they used their tails to scoot backwards, so it was easy to trap them in a glass jar. You just needed to put the jar behind the crayfish and then touch the whiskers. After that, you could bring your crayfish to shore, pour it out of the jar, and pick it up, being careful to keep your fingers out of range of its pincers.

When you got tired of just looking at it, there could be crayfish races, crayfish fights, wars, whatever.

And when boredom set in, the crayfish could be returned to the river. Every crayfish that was released into the water re-entered it newly baptized. "Wounded" had only one pincer; "Rocky" was small but aggressive. Like people, no two crayfish were exactly alike.

Today, though, the boys followed a trail that ran downstream to a spot where the water was deep enough so that, with a little engineering, a rock dam was possible. Maybe, Jimmy thought, they could make their own swimming hole. Since the cemetery was right beside the creek at that point, it was unlikely that someone would destroy their dam.

"How do we start?" Charles wanted to know.

"A line of big rocks," Jimmy said, "the biggest you can find. We'll string them across the bottom of the creek. Start with the ones that are in the water upstream of where the dam is going."

"They'll be heavy," Four-eyes said.

"Not if you keep them underwater when you move them," Jimmy

151

said.

"And if you can't move it," George said, "I'll move it for you. Me Tarzan." He flexed his muscles, like Johnny Weismuller.

Later in the day, the sun had slipped far enough west so that the river was in the shade of the spruce trees and the balsams that grew along its west side. The water began to feel cooler. One line of rocks had become two, then three, and a second tier had begun to rise from the creek bottom. At four-thirty, the boys picked up their clothes and started the walk home. No one needed a watch to know the time.

"What are we going to name the place when it's finished?" Four-eyes asked on the way back.

"Spider Dam," Jimmy said. "Did you see all the water spiders rowing in the shady spots?"

"Spider Dam," Four-eyes repeated. He picked up a stick and, walking backwards, waved it like a magician's wand. "I christen thee Spider Dam. There! That's one less thing to worry about," he said, his voice an echo of his mother's.

#

At supper Jimmy was still thinking about the day at the creek.

"*Farfar,*" he asked Jussi, "in Finland did you have crayfish?"

"Oh, yes," Jussi said. "They are not exactly the same as the ones that are here, but they are crayfish. Crayfish are *kräfta* in Swedish and *rapu* in Finnish. And in both languages the word for crayfish means Cancer, the constellation."

"What about cancer, the disease? Can crayfish give you cancer? Or do you have to smoke them?" The merest hint of a smile showed in his face.

Jussi laughed. "You think that cigarettes give you cancer?"

"The *Reader's Digest* says they do. Mom told me," Jimmy said. "She read an article on it called *Cancer by the Carton.*"

Marilyn looked up, caught Jussi's eye and looked at him evenly.

"If cigarettes give people cancer," Jussi said, "why do doctors have favourite cigarettes, and why do they smoke?"

Viktoria gave Jussi the look that meant "stop talking."

Jussi said, "Has anyone seen Uncle Ivor today?"

There was a knock at the front door. Jussi got up to see who it was. As he opened the door and saw Ivor he said, "Thank God.

Someone who doesn't pick on me all the time. Come in, come in."

"I had a thought," Ivor said coming into the front porch, but going no farther.

"Hold on to it," Viktoria said from the kitchen. "It's time for dessert. I have pie."

"Thank you, but no, I need to get back soon or—" He moved to where he could see Marilyn and, his voice now a stage whisper, "they'll start drinking without me."

Marilyn laughed. "I deserve that, I think."

"Let's sit outside on the steps then," Jussi said a little too loudly, "so I can have a cigarette."

They went outside and sat on the steps.

"Was it a whole thought, or just half a thought?" Jussi asked Ivor. He opened the pack of Player's, then took out a cigarette and tapped it to push some of the tobacco back from one end. He made sure that he was downwind from Ivor, then put the tapped end in his mouth and lit the cigarette. In the past, smoke had triggered Ivor's worst memories. Recently, it seemed to be better. Ivor had begun smoking occasionally himself. Still, Jussi wasn't taking any chances.

"I'm not sure," Ivor said. "I've been thinking about all the people that I knew by name in the war. One or two of them could easily have been part of the gang that killed your mother or Fredric Svensson or might even be the person who shot my brother in the back and maybe stole his boot at Tampere. But 1920, remember? A lot of them would have changed their names when the government passed that law that everyone had to have a surname. And even those who didn't have to change it—like you and me, for instance—could have picked a new name when they came into Canada."

"Yes," Jussi said. "So where has this thought led you?"

"It's impossible to find him," Ivor said. "The advantage is all his. He could stay hidden forever, if he wanted to. But, instead, he's put a notice in the shoemaker's window. He's let us know that he's in Port Arthur—that he lives within spitting distance of you."

"So?"

"So he wants us to find him. He's setting up a meeting with you. I know it sounds crazy, but it's the only thing that makes sense."

5 • THE DAM

AFTER LUNCH THE NEXT DAY, Jimmy and his friends began work on the dam once more. They had to wait an hour, however, because his grandmother said that he might get a cramp and drown. The depth of the water where they were now working was not part of the equation. No matter that his knees were completely out of the water and that he was walking, not swimming. He could get a cramp, double over with pain, topple head-first onto a rock, get knocked unconscious, and then float face-down, unable to breathe, and die. And that would be that.

All of which seemed preferable to death by horsefly. The horseflies tore little chunks of meat out of the back of the neck but, since humans were neither horses nor deer and had flexible arms and dexterous hands, the flies paid for some bites with their lives.

The black flies, on the other hand, were more skilled at torment than were the horseflies. Black flies came in clouds of silent attackers, rather than singly or in pairs. They were tiny biters and rapid suckers of human blood—lovers of all places wet, especially around eyes and behind ears. When they were slapped to death, their bodies squished into a brush stroke of black and red on the skin, and when they were flicked into the creek they took the victim's blood with them into the water. If all creeks eventually end up flowing into the sea, Jimmy thought, river mouths must run red by the end of the summer.

The topmost rocks of the dam were now visible above the creek, and the shoreline had begun to recede as the water level rose. The sun had positioned itself behind the trees as the afternoon's heat began to wane. In the west, clouds formed and started to advance upon the city, promising the thunder of an evening shower. The boys added a few more rocks to their project and then got ready to head for home.

From deep in the underbrush on the far side of the creek, Ivor watched them leave. Then he, too, started back to his own place.

#

Jussi had left work a little early. His men, he knew, would not let themselves get lazy. Each of them depended on the others to work safely, to do the expected, to work seriously and carefully.

At the cobbler's shop the boot and shoe were still arranged in the window as before.

When Jussi entered, the cobbler was speaking with a customer, a man about the age that Jussi's son, Raimo, would have been had he lived.

"It will rain soon," the cobbler said, "I can feel it in my hands. Rheumatism." He turned to get a pair of boots from the second shelf, then put them on the counter in front of the customer.

"The Winnipeg Goldeyes are playing the Superior Blues at the Stadium tonight," the customer said. Then, before the cobbler could comment, the customer tacked on, "What do I owe you?"

"On the house, Mr. Millbridge. You're a regular, and it was just a small repair."

"How's your son these days?" Millbridge asked.

"Passed this year. Plans to go on."

"Take him to the game with you." He put two dollars on the counter. "Buck and a quarter for you, seventy-five cents for the kid, right?"

"Yes, sir." The cobbler swept the dollar bills off the counter and pocketed them.

Millbridge picked up his boots, touched the brim of his hat in farewell, and left.

"Is he—" Jussi began.

"The one? No. The man you want is at least thirty years older. And a Finn. Mr. Millbridge is much younger. Thirty-five, maybe?"

"I need to know everything you know about the man who had you put the boots in the window—and Mr. Millbridge, too," Jussi said.

There was something familiar about the man, and it was nagging him.

"Everything," Jussi repeated. "I have made a list to help you." He handed the cobbler a piece of paper. "Learn it and use it. I will be back in a few days."

The cobbler glanced at the list, folded it up and put it in the breast pocket of his shirt.

"No problem," he said as casually as he could. After Jussi was gone, the cobbler took the list out of his pocket and read it closely.

#

Ivor walked the path back to the clearing and went into his shacks. It was still hot, but with luck, an afternoon shower would cool things off. The heat sat behind his eyes, and his head throbbed. He took down the towel that hung from wire strung between the rafters of the low roof, then went to the table and poured a little water from a pitcher into the porcelain basin, put the towel into the water, wrung it out, applied it to the back of his neck. He let the water drip on the table.

He did not close his eyes. He was afraid that he would start to see the rapids that ran beside the Kalevankangas cemetery again—the bodies that had washed up on the riverbank, the red foam, the white snow....

"No," he said aloud, and with the towel still on his neck, he went outside. He stared up through the trees, made himself look at the clouds drifting slowly past and thought about rain. After a while he felt a few drops on his face.

I will keep the boys safe, he thought. *No one will harm them.* The thoughts were in Rabbit's voice—the voice of a fifteen-year-old boy, still a child.

#

Just before six o'clock, Jimmy's mother got off the bus at the McBean Street stop, walked a block along Montgomery Street, and arrived home in time for supper. She took off her shoes at the door.

"Long day?" Viktoria asked.

"Long as they come," Marilyn said. "At least there were no customers around after noon. We took inventory, put the new gowns out, did the cleaning. Betty thinks we're going to have to stay open all day Wednesdays pretty soon."

"She's the boss," Viktoria said. "Everybody come sit. Supper's ready."

Marilyn, in stocking feet, sat in her usual chair. "Where's Ivor?"

"Probably at the shack," Jussi said.

"What about you, Marilyn?" Viktoria asked. "Still planning on going to the dance at the Finn Hall?"

"Not tonight," Marilyn said. "My feet have been dancing all day. Maybe next Wednesday. Fifty cents is fifty cents." Since she didn't want to be quizzed again about the dances at the Finn Hall, she changed the subject. "I put the newspaper on the couch in the living room, Dad."

She turned to Jimmy, already at his place at the table. "Did you see your uncle at the creek today?" she asked.

"Nope," Jimmy said, and then quickly, "I mean no." He glanced at Viktoria, who nodded her head just once to let him know he had done the right thing. "We went home early, though, because it started to look like rain."

"Why is Big Day Bridal going to stay open on Wednesdays?" Jussi asked Marilyn.

"Because Simpsons-Sears is open all day. Betty says all the stores are going to have to stay open soon, just to compete."

"Speaking of competing," Jussi said, "I picked up two tickets at Gussi's Garage for the stock car races at the Exhibition Grounds tonight. Anyone want to go?"

"Yes!" Jimmy said.

#

Around nine that evening, Ivor went for a walk. The headache was gone. Inside him, the part that was Rabbit had gone quiet.

He noticed the dam. *They have done well*, he thought in English. *Enough water gets through so the dam does not break.* He felt calmer now, more in control of his thoughts. He wished he were back in Finland—in *before* and at *home* with only Swedish in his brain. But he wasn't.

He shrugged and started back to the shack. From the Exhibition Grounds two miles away, he could hear the muted roar of the cars and the crowd. And every once in a while, from the Port Arthur Stadium, which was a little closer, the sound of the announcer's voice—the sentences broken of meaning, their syntax lost in the trees.

6 • THE CIRCUS IS COMING

THE NEXT DAY, after Jussi had finished reading the evening paper, Jimmy read the comics—all except for *Martha Wayne,* which was always full of romance. And too full of his own life, too—Martha Wayne's husband had been killed in the war, and she was trying to start a new life with her son, Billy, in someplace called Centerville. *Blondie* (though everyone called it *Dagwood*) was much better, but the best was *Mandrake the Magician.* Mandrake could hypnotize anyone just by gesturing hypnotically!

Jimmy preferred comics with interesting people in them—Alley Oop had a dinosaur called Dinny that he rode. Vic Flint solved crimes in a city full of gangsters and sleazy nightclubs. Mutt and Jeff always got into trouble.

But Martha and Billy just lived in a little city like Port Arthur. *Poor Billy*, he thought, *having to live in a city where nothing much happens. And having a mother who always sounds like a teacher.*

When he finished the comics, he flipped through the rest of the paper.

"Mom," he said when he saw the ad, "the circus is coming Monday, August eighth. And the matinee grandstand show on Friday is going to have Davy Crockett with Uncle Jim as the master of ceremonies!"

"That's interesting," Jussi said. "Show me the ad."

Jimmy passed his grandfather the paper. "Well," Jussi said after he'd finished looking at it. "August eighth."

Viktoria glanced at him.

Later, after Jimmy had been sent upstairs to bed, Viktoria asked Jussi, "What was wrong with the ad?"

"Davy was spelled with an *ey*," Jussi said quietly. "It's not going to be the *real* Davy Crockett, the one on television." He shook his head sadly.

"Should we tell him?"

"No," Jussi said, "this is something he must find out on his own. It's better that way."

Viktoria glanced at Marilyn, who shrugged. "He's right," Marilyn said.

#

Friday evening, Marilyn found the story of the Sleeping Giant on the editorial page of the newspaper. After she had read it, she passed the paper to Jimmy. He knew he was supposed to read the story, so he did.

"What's *Abitibi Magazine*?" he asked when he was finished.

"Let's see," Marilyn said. She took the paper from him. "It's where the story was first published, I think." She looked at Viktoria, who nodded.

"Is it a true story?"

"No."

"Then why is it in the paper?"

Marilyn looked to Jussi for help.

"Sometimes," he said, "the legends—the stories we tell ourselves—are just as important as the real news."

"Why?"

"Because...." Jussi caught Viktoria's eye. *Rescue me,* his expression pleaded.

"They are not just about what people believe," Viktoria said. "They show what people *want* to believe. What they want to believe tells us what they are like."

"I want to believe that Mandrake is real," Jimmy said. He gave the paper back to his mother. "What does that tell you?" he asked Viktoria.

"That you are normal," she said.

Later, when Jussi, Viktoria, and Marilyn had gone to the kitchen for coffee and coffee bread—*pulla*—Jimmy got the paper from the magazine rack and began to look through it again.

When his mother came to tell him it was time to go to bed, Jimmy said, "Can I ask *Farfar* something first?"

"Sure," Jussi said from the kitchen. "What do you want to know? I know everything."

"What's Yucca Flats?" Jimmy asked.

159

#

Saturday evening, when Jussi came back from having a cigarette outside, Viktoria was already in bed. The sun had set at ten o'clock, but Jussi had waited half an hour more before he went inside. He undressed and got into bed beside her, but lay staring up at the ceiling, his hands cradling his neck.

"Something wrong?" Viktoria asked.

"Jimmy's getting older," Jussi said. "He's reading more of the paper now."

"That is good, is it not? He cannot stay a boy forever."

Jussi was silent for a while, then he said, "That article about the atom bomb test in Nevada that he asked me about...." Jussi didn't continue.

"What about it?" Viktoria asked at last.

"It was about a presentation to the Fort William civil defense workers. A lawyer showed colour pictures of the blast. The city Treasurer chaired the meeting—he's the Civil Defense Director. Jimmy read the article. That's why he asked about Yucca Flats."

"Oh," Viktoria said. "Do you think Jimmy should not have read it?"

"No, he needs to get to know the world. But...."

Viktoria waited but eventually had to say, "But what?"

"There's a shoe store on Arthur Street and it's got a fluoroscope in it."

"Not *got*. It *has*. A fluoroscope?"

"It looks like a fancy cabinet, but it's for fitting shoes. There's a platform that you stand on, and you're supposed to put your feet through holes that are cut into the cabinet. At the top there are three viewing holes. They look a lot like the face mask a diver might wear. One is for the person who is going to buy shoes, one is for the salesman, and one is for...I don't know...maybe the mother who is buying shoes for her kid."

"Do not say *kid*. A kid is a baby goat."

"For her *child*, then. When the salesman flips a switch, there's a thing, an electrical tube of some kind, that turns on, and if you're looking though the viewer you can see the bones in the feet of the person who's standing on the platform. It uses x-rays."

"I do not understand."

"It's like atomic radiation. Ivor says that when some of the customers get older, they're going to have cancer. He says that the machines are going to be illegal soon. But they aren't yet. They're dangerous, and the sales people know that, but they use them anyway because people—kids especially—like to come into the store to see what it looks like when they wiggle their toes."

Viktoria did not correct his use of *kids*.

"The whole world is dangerous now," Jussi continued, "and the dangers are so hard for people to understand. There's a movie playing now, *This Island Earth*. It's about aliens who come to Earth to get advice about how to make war. And there's another one, *Three Years to Victory*. It's an old war movie—from 1940, I think. And tonight in the paper there was an article about the Fire Marshall giving a speech in Fort William about how the Lakehead would not be safe from atom bombers even if they were shot and about to crash, because the bombers would dump their loads before they hit the ground. He also said that Fort William would be in better shape than Port Arthur after a nuclear attack because Fort William sits on muskeg and Port Arthur sits on rock.

"Day after day that kind of stuff is in the paper. It's as if the clowns, the scary kind, have decided they're in charge of the world. Remember when you told Jimmy that what we want to believe shows us what we're really like?"

"It shows *other* people what we are like."

"Jimmy is going to think that we'll be going to war soon, and that the war will be an atomic war, and we will all die because we live on top of rock."

For some time, Viktoria said nothing. Then, "He wants to believe in Mandrake, Jussi. And he thinks that is who *you* are. And he believes you will always keep him safe, no matter what. And he is right. You will, and I will, and Marilyn will, and Rabbit will, too."

"And if I can't?" He didn't mention Raimo, their son, lost to war.

"Jussi, sometimes you have too much of the *sad* Finn in you." She was quiet for a moment. "Oh, I forgot. I think Marilyn has found someone she is interested in."

"A man?"

"Yes, a man." Viktoria laughed lightly. "At a dance at the Finn Hall. She told me she hopes he is there the next time she goes. Good dancer. And I am sure he does not work in a shoe store. Now go to sleep. Things will look better in the morning when I make you some bacon and eggs."

"We have bacon?"

"I'll even scramble the eggs. Go to sleep."

And he did.

#

Jussi woke Sunday morning from a dream of muskeg. He had fallen through the floating mass of vegetation on a lake, and his father was trying to pull him up, but his father couldn't find a solid place to stand. The Reds were firing at them from the cover of the trees.

Viktoria was not in the bed. He could hear her preparing breakfast for Marilyn and Jimmy. Jussi didn't want to risk more sleep. He got up, dressed, and went into the kitchen where Viktoria was making bacon and eggs as promised. Later, he drove the family to church, then went past the shoemaker's shop, but nothing had changed.

7 • ORANGEMEN AND IRON LUNGS

"*FARFAR*," JIMMY ASKED after church and after lunch, "what are the orange men? Are they like the bread man?"

"Oh," Viktoria said. She got up from the kitchen table and went to the front porch.

"She forgot to put the bread card in the window," Jussi said to Jimmy in his loud voice, the one he saved for teasing Viktoria. "Again." He laughed. "No," he said in his normal voice. "It's an organization—Orangemen. Where did you hear about them?"

"George. He said he went to see their parade. There was a guy on a white horse, and he was dressed like a king."

"Ah."

"What are they?"

Viktoria came back from the porch and went to the sink. "While you gentlemen talk," she said, "I'll do the dishes. One of you gentlemen—the young one, perhaps—is welcome to join me when it's time to dry them."

Marilyn looked at Jimmy to make sure that he was going to offer to help.

"I'll do it, *Farmor*," he said. "And *gladly* because you are such a fine, *fine* cook."

"You'll make some lucky woman a good husband," Viktoria said.

"The Orangemen," Jussi began again, "were supporters of the king of England when the English were fighting the Irish in...sometime in the 1600s. The king's colour was orange, so they were called Orangemen. They were Irish, but they were supporters of the king, and were mostly Protestants. The Irish on the other side were mostly Catholics."

"George said there might be Orangemen at church today."

"Not at Immanuel," Jussi said. "Orangemen are usually Presbyterians, so they wouldn't be at our church."

"Oh." Jimmy was quiet for a moment. "Who won the war?"

"The British sort of won," Jussi said, "but the Irish on the other side didn't all give up. The fighting has been going on for over three hundred years now, mostly in Northern Ireland. There are really two Irelands, one in the north that is part of the United Kingdom, and one in the south that isn't. So in the north you find Orangemen and Catholics still at each other's throats, and in the south the Orangemen keep their mouths shut. Most wars end that way, with everyone muttering and holding onto their grievances, and nobody talking. And I'm going outside for a smoke."

Viktoria waited until Jussi was outside before she spoke. "How is Tony's friend?" she asked Jimmy.

"Tony says Frank still can't walk and he's really weak and he's still in the hospital."

"Do you know how he caught the polio?"

"His parents think it was from swimming in Boulevard Lake."

"That is possible. But you do not need to worry about getting polio. You had the shot—in May, yes?"

"Everyone did. They wanted everyone vaccinated before school ended. Some *children* passed out."

"But not you."

"I'm not queasy." He took his place at Viktoria's side and began to dry the dishes she had put in the dish rack. A minute or two later he said, "I think Uncle Ivor's here. *Farfar* is talking to someone outside."

#

"You've been drinking," Jussi said without sounding accusatory.

"Not enough. But enough so that I don't want to go inside and get that look from You-Know-Who. I'm not drunk now, but maybe I'll go get drunk later."

"What's the problem?"

"The boot and shoe have been switched around," Ivor said. "And between them there's an envelope."

"Is there a name on the envelope? Could you see?"

"*Viktoria.*"

Jussi stubbed out his cigarette on the front steps, then immediately lit another one. "It's from the man who shot Karl, then." He thought for a moment. "So he's here. But why is it addressed to Viktoria?

164

Why is it not addressed to me?"

"Does Viktoria know about the boot?"

"No. She knows only that Karl was without boots when he was found. That's the story she was told. I asked the man who found Karl's body to spread it around. She doesn't know that someone shot him in the back after he was dead, and she doesn't know about the boots. All she knows is that the Reds often took the boots from corpses because their own were worn out. She doesn't know that I have one of Karl's."

"These are things you have to tell her. The letter *is* addressed to her. Are you...." He couldn't finish the question.

"Going to read it first?" Jussi took another drag on his cigarette. "No. You're right. It is addressed to her. She must read it first."

"And then will you tell her all the rest?"

"It depends on what the letter says." He was quiet for a moment, then he said, "Come in, Ivor. Have coffee with us. And don't worry about what Marilyn will say. Her tongue is sharp, but her heart is soft."

8 • A LETTER

AT NOON ON MONDAY, Jussi left work at the McLeod's place and went to see the shoemaker.

As soon as he entered the shop, the shoemaker said, "You're very prompt. He said you would be in today."

"He left a letter for my wife," Jussi said.

The shoemaker let his sewing machine coast to a stop. "Here's what I can tell you about him. He's younger than you—five or six years, maybe—but it's hard to tell for sure. He probably worked with his hands for much of his life. His fingers are strong and thick still, but not rough. I think his working days are long past. Oh, and he probably plays the violin."

"How do you know that?" Jussi asked.

"The fingertips of his left hand, even the little finger, have callused tips. You don't get those unless you play a stringed instrument. His right thumb doesn't have a callus, though, like some guitar players get."

"You're a regular Sherlock Holmes, aren't you?"

"I see people's hands every day," the shoemaker said. "Their hands tell me things about their feet. But other things, too. You, for instance, smoke too much, and you strike the match with your right thumbnail."

Jussi laughed. "Well done. Does our mysterious stranger smoke?"

"Not now, but he used to. I can hear it in his voice."

"Do you have his name?"

"No. Maybe it's in the letter."

"When he came to the shop, did you see what direction he was coming from?"

"No, but when he left, he turned up High Street and started up the hill."

"Fancy houses up there," Jussi said. "Was he wearing nice clothes?"

"Not brand new, but not old. Clean. Very good shoes. He had a pocket watch on a chain."

"How about his accent? Does he speak English better or worse than I do?"

"Worse," the shoemaker said. "But his vocabulary is good, and he doesn't use those old Finland expressions that some of them do."

"Maybe he has children. Children teach you how to speak English."

"Maybe. One more thing. He said you were to keep the boot and shoe if you want them."

Jussi thought for a moment. "I think I will leave them with you," he said. "Let the display stay as it is."

He went to the window, picked up the letter, and headed back to the work site.

#

A little after five, Jussi came into the house, carrying the letter. Viktoria had already started supper—a pot of stew was simmering on one of the back elements of the stove.

"I have something you must read," he said quietly.

Viktoria turned from her cooking and looked at him. He had spoken in the same tone he had used when they learned that their son Raimo was dead in Belgium, a tone for serious things, things that change one's life.

"After supper," he said. "Later tonight when Marilyn and Jimmy have gone to bed."

Viktoria nodded.

#

They had put their pillows up as backrests and leaned against them.

"Well," Viktoria said quietly in Swedish, "you wanted to say something before I read this." She indicated the letter, the envelope still unopened.

"Do you remember the day that Fredric Svensson was killed?"

"Yes."

"You remember that Karl managed to grab a shoe that one of the killers was wearing."

"The shoe that you took to every shoemaker you could think of, but no one recognized it."

"Yes." Jussi waited a moment and then said, "I still have it. And Viktoria, there is something I have to tell you about the day Karl was killed at Tampere. Karl's squad leader, Olavi Karppinen, found his body. One of Karl's boots was missing."

Jussi paused again, a little too long.

"Both boots were missing," Viktoria said.

"No. Olavi gave me the remaining one," Jussi said. "I kept it because...I don't know why I kept it. I couldn't throw it away, and I couldn't give it to you because—"

"Because I would know that someone had stolen something from Karl when he was dead." Tears welled up in Viktoria's eyes. "To tell me this—it is the right thing to do, Jussi, but why?"

"Last week Rabbit was walking past the shoemaker's shop on Oliver Road and there were two items on display in the window. One was a match to the shoe that Karl had taken from Svensson's store the day Fredric was killed, and the other was a match to the boot that Karl's squad leader gave me the day Karl died."

"I don't understand."

"It was the boot that had been stolen in the graveyard. It was a message meant for me—or, perhaps, for anyone who knows the story, like Rabbit, for instance. Rabbit saw it in the window first, and he told me. The shoemaker and I struck a deal. I asked him to reverse the display if the fellow returned. Rabbit's been my lookout. He told me that yesterday the display had been reversed."

"And the letter?"

"Was tucked between the footgear. It's probably from the man who stole Karl's boot in Kalevankangas Cemetery—a man who was probably part of the crew that killed Svensson."

"But why is it addressed to me?"

"He must know that you and Karl were married. Perhaps he knows more. If you don't want to open the letter, don't do it. I have no idea what it says. If you think that this is something we should just let go by, then that's what we'll do."

Viktoria stared at the envelope for a moment, then opened it and read it silently.

Dear Mrs. Lassila Solbakken Mantere:

The penmanship was like her mother's—Old-World, each letter carefully formed, yet not smooth. The lines, though, were exactly parallel to the top of the page.

Please forgive my bad English. I do not write well in English. When I need to write I have my son do it for me but this one I have to write it myself. I was with the men who killed Fredric Svensson and I also took your husband's boot at Tampere. Somebody else killed him but I shot your husband in the back when he was dead. I was lentävä osasto. *I do not ask for your forgiveness, but I am sorry for what I did. I took your husband's boot because for each boot or shoe I was paid. Your present husband, I was also part of the group that killed his mother, but I was not there when she was killed. To kill a woman is wrong.*

There was no signature. When Viktoria had finished reading the letter, she passed it to Jussi. He read it quickly, then gave it back to her.

"What does *lentävä osasto* mean?" Viktoria asked.

"It means *flying detachment*. We had them, too. They were small cavalry units—men on horseback who made raids behind the lines. There might be half a dozen or as many as several dozen men in each. They were terrorists."

"Like the ones who killed your mother—the butchers?"

Jussi nodded.

"Why did you take Karl's boot?"

"I took it because I did not want you to know that someone had taken just the one boot. Better for you to believe that the thief had needed winter boots, that his own were falling apart. I...I didn't want you to feel that someone had done this just to be disrespectful, to mock Karl...I should have told you this long ago."

He told her more about Olavi Karppinen, and the fighting in Kalevankangas cemetery.

When he had finished, Viktoria asked, "Why have you never told me this before?"

"I was afraid the story would be too much for you. It would eat at you."

"But I had a *right* to know."

"And I had a *duty* to keep you from being hurt. That's what I thought at the time. It was a young man's foolishness, and I was wrong."

Viktoria considered before she spoke. "You still have Karl's boot?"

"Yes."

"Will you let me see it tomorrow?"

"Yes. I still have the shoe from Fredric Svensson's killer as well. The one that Karl took."

"The letter writer's shoe?"

"No. It likely belonged to one of his brothers. I will explain everything tomorrow. I promise."

Upstairs in his bedroom, Jimmy was still awake. He had been listening to Jussi and Viktoria, but the two had kept their voices so soft that he couldn't hear most of what they said, and because they were speaking in Swedish, he understood very little. He tried to concentrate, but their voices carried the sounds of worry more clearly than they carried the words.

Something about shoes and boots, he thought, his thoughts drifting. Soon, he knew, *Farfar* would ask him what he wanted for his birthday. And then he was asleep.

9 • DINKY TOYS

WEDNESDAY, IT WAS TOO COOL to go swimming, so Jimmy and his friends went to the potato field in the afternoon to play war with their Dinky toys. Jimmy had an armoured car that looked like a small tank with wheels instead of tracks. George and Four-eyes had planes, both silver-grey. George's had British markings on its wings; Four-eyes' had the American ones. Charles had brought his Alvis Saracen Armoured Personnel Carrier, about which he knew nothing, but which he had seen advertised in *The Meccano Magazine* and which, naturally, his parents had immediately bought for his birthday. The cannon on Jimmy's armoured car was bigger than the one on the personnel carrier.

The boys had prepared the village they were all going to attack. Streets had been marked out in the sand, buildings created of rocks and sticks, small trenches dug with an old spoon. George and Four-eyes fought the Nazis in the air while Jimmy and Charles attacked the German village. Mid-battle, Jimmy noticed that his Uncle Ivor was standing on the road, watching them. Battle ceased, and Jimmy stood up and waved. Ivor walked over.

"What are you playing?" Ivor asked.

"War," Jimmy said. He hoped Ivor would not ask if they were pretending it was a specific battle. George's father had been in battles in Italy and George always wanted to tell them about troop movements and how attacks went and how many men were lost.

And that made Jimmy think about things he didn't like to—his father, whom he'd never known, dying in Belgium. Things that made his mother cry, and *Farfar* go out into the back yard to smoke and look at the ground, and *Farmor* fold her lips together and scrub hard at her kitchen counter.

Ivor pointed at Jimmy's armoured car. "Do you know what that is?" It was Rabbit who asked, Rabbit who always forced himself to examine war, who kept himself alive by doing so.

171

"Armoured car."

"Not just any armoured car," Rabbit said. "That's the Daimler Mark Two. Those are still in use. They seem to outlast their replacements."

"I have a Saracen armoured personnel carrier," Charles interrupted.

"Yes," Rabbit said, "a fine vehicle, and Tony, you have a Gloster Meteor. That's the plane they used in World War II to shoot down flying bombs over London. Four cannons in the front, engines at mid-wing. It was very hard to fly—sluggish. That's why they gave it the job of shooting down the flying bombs, the V1s. It couldn't take on the much-faster German aircraft."

"What's my plane called?" George asked.

"It's a Lockheed P-80 Shooting Star. It's the trainer version of the fighter."

"No guns?"

"No guns."

"Darn."

"It could be a spy plane, perhaps?"

"Yes!" George said. "A spy plane."

Rabbit started to walk away.

"Uncle Ivor," Jimmy said, and Rabbit stopped and turned around. "How do you know so much about the war?"

"It is something I am interested in." Ivor was surprised that Rabbit was so insistent on speaking for him today.

"Were you in the war?" Jimmy thought he knew the answer to the question before he asked it. Uncle Ivor was old—too old to have been in the war, maybe. In 1939 he would have been...thirty-six or so.

"Not the Second World War," Rabbit said. "I was in another one. A small one. It was in Finland."

"There was a war in Finland? Was it the First World War?" Jimmy persisted, but he knew the question was foolish. Uncle Ivor was old but not that old.

"No," Rabbit answered. "It was another one." Then he added, "Jimmy, isn't your birthday on Saturday?"

"Yes," Jimmy said.

"Will there be cake?"

"There's always cake."

"Good. Enjoy your war. I have to be going."

"See you later," Jimmy said.

Ivor, who had successfully put Rabbit back in the hat, chuckled, then started down the road. No "Goodbye, Uncle Ivor" from Jimmy. He had said *See you later*, like a real Canadian. The boy was growing up. *Yes*, Rabbit agreed. *And we must keep him safe.*

"Where's he going?" George asked, watching Ivor walk away.

"Bay Street, down by the Hoito and the Hemmet. His friends all live around there. On Saturday morning he'll go to the Port Arthur Steam Bath—it's just half a block from where he used to live—and get all cleaned up for my birthday. He'll be sober, too."

"Sure he will," George said, and Jimmy gunned him down with a blast from his armoured car.

#

On the way to Bay Street, Ivor detoured past the shoemaker's shop. The mismatched pair were positioned as he had first seen them, but there was an envelope tucked between them so that it stood on its end. He was tempted to go in and pretend to look around, but there was danger in that. He would stop by Jussi's house and tell him about the new envelope on his way home.

"Don't bother," Rabbit said. *"It's likely not the mystery man's letter."*

On Oliver Road, five blocks from the shoemaker's shop, Ivor saw Jussi's car approaching. As Jussi got closer, Ivor began to wave his arms and then point down the street toward the shop. Jussi drove by, acknowledging Ivor only by shaking his head.

"He's been to the shop already," Rabbit said. *"Let it be, Ivor. There's no new letter. It's Jussi's reply."*

#

Just after two o'clock, Jussi pulled into the driveway.

"You're home early," Viktoria said. "Is something the matter?"

"No. The men have the house up on timbers and girders," Jussi said. "The footings are in, and they've started the concrete block work. They don't need me to hang around and criticize."

"You dropped the letter off?"

"Yes."

"What will he do?"

"He'll read it and make his decision."
"You asked him to meet with you?"
"Yes."

#

Later in the evening Marilyn left to go dancing at the Finnish Labour Temple. Al Jason and the Melody Ranch Boys were playing; Buddy Duval, the man who had recorded *Are You Mine?* with Myrna Lorrie, was the vocalist. Marilyn spotted Laura, the girl who worked part-time with her at Big Day Bridal.

Laura gave a little laugh as Marilyn approached. "I see you've caught someone's eye," she said.

"Oh?"

"Good-looking. Watched you walk over here. Nice clothes, nice hair, good shoes, good taste."

Marilyn glanced in the direction that Laura was looking.

"So who is he?" Laura asked.

"Owen," Marilyn said as casually as she could. "Millbridge, I think. I met him a couple of weeks ago."

"Millbridge." Laura considered the name. "Might be a keeper." She winked at Marilyn. "I'd like to find one of those, myself. But right now looks like a good time to get myself something to drink." She walked away.

Millbridge, seeing her leave, came over. "Dance?" he asked.

"Sure," Marilyn said. She made herself leave the dance a little early, however, and was home by midnight.

10 • THE REPLY

ON THURSDAY, WHAT CAUGHT JIMMY'S EYE in the newspaper was the short piece about Davy Crockett. He was coming to Port Arthur—three weeks before the circus on August 8th, even, and was going to be present at a local gas station!

Friday's paper brought more details: Davy Crockett would be at McEwen's service station all day Saturday, and the pony rides would be on real Davy Crockett ponies. When Jussi asked Jimmy what he wanted for his birthday, the answer was easy.

On Saturday Jussi and Jimmy left early, but they were back home well before supper.

"How was it?" Viktoria asked, noticing Jussi's warning glance too late.

"It was all fake," Jimmy said. "It wasn't Davy Crockett, just some guy dressed up to look like him."

Viktoria did not reprove him for saying *guy*. "Did you get to ride a pony?"

"The ponies were for little kids. There was a man who lifted the kids up and other guys held onto the reins and led the ponies in a circle. I would have looked stupid."

"We had ice-cream, though," Jussi said. "And there were a lot of people there."

"May I go up to my room before supper?" Jimmy asked.

"Certainly. Supper is in an hour. After supper, when your mother can be with us, you can open your present. She has something special for you."

"Thanks," Jimmy said, and he headed for his room. Once there, he went to his bookshelf and fetched *The Biggest Bear*. He loved the book because Johnny Orchard, the hero, finds a bear cub and keeps it until it becomes fully grown.

And more importantly, it was large enough for him to hide his 3-D glasses in. He took out the cardboard glasses with their red and green plastic lenses, then dug down into his pile of comics until he found *Three Dimensional Tales from the Crypt of Terror*. Part of the fun of reading the comic was that his mother did not know that he had it—that he had, in fact, traded a lot of his older comics for it.

Lately it had become impossible to find horror comics of any kind—no werewolves, no vampires, no zombies, no nothing. Comics that had the stamp of the Comics Code Authority in the upper right corner, Jimmy had discovered, were not much fun to read.

Downstairs, Viktoria said to Jussi, "Ivor will be here for supper, too." She had switched automatically to Swedish since Jimmy was not with them now. "He has a present for Jimmy."

"Good. He always comes up with something interesting. That Davy Crockett show was awful. I wish Jimmy had asked for a chemistry set instead, like last year. He's old enough for it this year."

Viktoria nodded. "Your letter—has the man picked it up?"

"Yes, but there's no reply. I asked for a face-to-face meeting. We have to wait and see what happens."

#

Ivor, as promised, showed up at the house just in time for supper. He was clean and sober. After supper, after the dishes had been washed and put away, the family went into the living room so that Jimmy could receive his presents.

Ivor had put his gift in a brown paper bag. Jimmy knew that it would be something that his uncle had made, but when Ivor took out the empty plastic bottle of Elmer's Glue-All, Jimmy was more than puzzled.

"Marilyn," Ivor asked, "do you have a sheet of writing paper and a pair of scissors?"

She went upstairs and in a minute returned with the items.

"Thank you," Ivor said. From his pants pocket he took out a scotch tape dispenser. "Please, this will take some time, give Jimmy his present."

Jimmy's mother handed him a box wrapped in blue birthday paper. She had taped a card to the top of the box.

Jimmy opened it first and read the message aloud. "Ten! No more single numbers! Happy Birthday."

There was a drawing of a man in a black tuxedo scooping

numbers out of his hat. Jimmy carefully unwrapped the box so that the paper could be reused.

"It's a Kodak Brownie Hawkeye camera!" he said when he had unwrapped enough to see what it was. "With flash bulbs and everything! Oh, thank you!" he said.

"Jussi," Viktoria said, "go get the film and show Jimmy how to put it in."

While Ivor was busily cutting up the writing paper, Jussi showed Jimmy how to put the film in the camera.

Ivor rolled a strip of the paper into a slim funnel with no opening at the tip. He made sure the wide end of the funnel fit perfectly over the tip of the squeeze bottle, and then used the scotch tape to hold the funnel together.

"What are you making?" Jimmy asked.

"You'll see." The unused paper was cut and folded into two triangles—a large one and a smaller one. The large one was attached to the wide end of the funnel, the small one to its tip, making two delta wings. Ivor folded the wings up at their tips, then handed the object to Jimmy.

"It's a rocket plane," Ivor said. "Put it carefully but tightly on the end of the squeeze bottle. Now point it at the kitchen doorway, and give the bottle a good fast squeeze."

The rocket plane flew across the room and through the doorway.

"It works!" Jimmy said.

"Of course it does," Viktoria said. She smiled broadly. "When your uncle makes something, it always works."

"Now you can take a picture of it," Marilyn said.

#

On Sunday as Jussi returned home after dropping the family—except for Ivor—at church, he drove past the shoemaker's shop. In the window he saw a reply to his letter.

177

11 • HISTORY LESSONS

AT SUPPER ON MONDAY, Marilyn noticed that both Jussi and Viktoria were unusually quiet. Even Jimmy seemed to feel that something was not quite right. However, Marilyn held her peace.

It was Jussi who broke the silence. "So, Marilyn, are you going dancing on Wednesday night?"

"No," Marilyn said. "Maybe next week. I asked Laura if she wanted to go, but she says she can't."

"Laura is the girl who works part-time at Big Day with you?"

"That's the one."

"Why can't she go?"

Marilyn laughed. "Her mother won't let her." She raised both eyebrows, looked straight at Jussi and waited for him to ask for an explanation.

Jussi couldn't resist. "She's what, thirty years old? And her mother won't let her?"

"Too many Finn boys," Marilyn said. She was enjoying this as much as Jussi was. "Her mother lets her go to the Sons of England Hall, but not to the Finn Hall. Her mother's heard about the drunks and the fights."

Jussi shook his head in dismay. "People always remember what they've been hoping to hear. But nobody fights at the Finn Hall anymore." He sighed then winked at Marilyn. "They go to the John Street gravel pit, instead, or the Community Hall. That's where the Friday night fights are."

Viktoria looked at Jimmy. "Do not you go there—ever." Then she shifted her steel-gray eyes to Jussi. "And you! We are at the table. This is not the way we talk at supper."

#

Later, when they had gone to bed, Jussi said, "I got the reply to

178

the letter today." The language of the supper table was English; the language of the bedroom was Swedish.

"What did he say?" Viktoria asked. "Is he willing to meet you?"

"He said *Not yet.* But there was more." Jussi reached over to the night table, turned on the light and opened its drawer. "I will read it to you." He switched to English and was careful to read very softly.

Dear Mr. Mantere,

Forgive please my bad handwriting. I have Parkinson's. I also have cancer in my stomach. The doctor says that I am going to die. Not right away but not too long.

Before I die I need to tell you about what I did. I do not ask you for forgiveness. What I have done I have done and that is that. Tulee mitä tulee.

"Whatever will be, will be," Jussi translated. There was more.

Even my family does not know what I was so long ago. It would make them shame if they find out.

Perhaps some time we can meet, but not yet. I would like to hear from you, but if you do not want to write back, I understand. I know about Ivor Solbakken, but I promise you that whatever your decision is, Ivor's story I will not tell.

Jussi put the letter back into the envelope, then put the envelope back into the drawer. "There's no signature," he said.

"He knows that Ivor changed his name," Viktoria said. "That it wasn't originally *Mantere.* And what does he mean, Ivor's story?"

For a long time, Jussi remained silent. At last, he said, "I can't tell you. It is Rabbit's to tell, and I will not ask him to. When and if he wants to tell it, he will."

"His mother, Ellen, did she know?"

"Yes."

"Did Karl?"

"No."

Silence filled the bedroom until it was full of little else.

Finally, Viktoria spoke. "Are you going to write back?" she asked.

"I don't know. Some things should be left alone. Perhaps this is one of them."

"Sleep now," Viktoria said. "You have to work tomorrow. This will wait. You can decide when you have had more time to think."

In the bedroom above Jussi and Viktoria, Marilyn had been listening. She had heard, just barely, the contents of the letter. Of the conversation between Jussi and Viktoria, she understood nothing but the names—Ivor, Rabbit, Ellen, Karl. Ellen had died in 1925. Whatever they were talking about had happened before then.

In his bedroom, opposite his mother's, Jimmy had been listening as well. He understood a little Swedish, but not enough to make sense of what he had heard. *Brev,* he knew, was *letter,* and the letter was probably in English because *Farfar* had read it too quietly for him to hear.

It was hot in his bedroom, and he lay awake for a long time. When finally he fell asleep, he dreamed of driving the Daimler Mark Two. It was hot and stuffy inside the armoured car. The dream, as if afraid of disappointing him, morphed into a dream of piloting a rocket.

#

Tuesday dawned cold and cloudy—more like fall than summer. Marilyn had already left for work, as had Jussi, by the time Jimmy went downstairs.

Viktoria made him cinnamon toast for breakfast. "A treat," she said, "for *Farmor's* favourite grandson."

"The only one," Jimmy said.

"The one and only," Viktoria responded. She got a small plate from the cupboard, put two pieces of toast on it, dusting each one carefully with cinnamon, then put the plate on the table before him.

"*Farmor,* what did you want to be when you grew up?"

"A teacher," Viktoria said immediately. "I wanted to be like Mr. Berg, my teacher in Gamlaby. I wanted to learn everything and tell everyone all sorts of wonderful things the way Mr. Berg did. Even math."

"Why didn't you become one?"

"The war started and when it was over there was nothing but hard times for a while. So I stayed in Finland for as long as I could, and then I came to Canada."

"By yourself?"

"There was another girl with me, someone I knew from school. She and I came over on the *Nordam* together."

"Did she come to Port Arthur, too?"

"No. She was going to Toronto, instead. After we got off the boat in Halifax I never saw her again."

"Why didn't you become a teacher here? You could have taught me."

"I do that already, you just do not know it." Viktoria smiled at him and took a sip of coffee. "I could not be a teacher here, because I did not know any English then. And I did not have the right education. So I worked as a housekeeper. I stayed with my uncle for a while, then I got a room of my own."

"But *Farfar* was here."

"I did not know where he was staying, though. For a while he was working in the bush in British Columbia, but he got laid off and came to Port Arthur. And then one day I ran into him at the Hemmet."

"And you got married."

"It was not quite that quick." Viktoria laughed. "We got married in 1924, and a year later your father was born. He was named after *Farfar's* father, who died in 1919. Your great-grandfather would be *Farfarsfar*. He was not even fifty, but he had worked most of his life with tar, and he got stomach cancer. He was such a good man, but a lot of men died young in those days. The year after he died, *Farfar* left Finland."

"Do you ever want to go back to Finland for a visit?"

"I think about it, and maybe sometime I will go, but not now."

"Why not now?"

"There is really no one there that I am close to now. My parents are not alive, most of my old friends have moved away. If I went back home, I would have to travel back in time. Home is not just a place, you know. And I would have to drag *Farfar* kicking and screaming. He does not want to ever go back."

"Why not?"

"It would make him feel sad."

"Did *Farfar* get a letter yesterday?"

The question came too suddenly, and Viktoria hesitated a second too long before answering. She could not lie—one does not lie to children.

"Yes," she said, the word forced out of her by the need to be truthful, "but I am not supposed to tell you what it was about."

"Could I have another piece of toast?" he asked.

"Certainly," Viktoria said, capitulating. They both knew it was a bribe.

#

Ivor showed up for lunch. He had two small fish wrapped in newspaper. "I caught these this morning," he said. "I'll trade you for five loaves."

"I do not have five loaves," Viktoria said, "but I have enough bread for lunch."

"Done," Ivor said. "John the Baptist isn't coming anyway."

Viktoria stopped laying out the plates to look at him. "That is not a good joke," she said sternly. "It is not appropriate."

"Sorry." Ivor waited a moment. "Where's Jimmy?"

"At the potato field, playing with the Dinky toys, I think. He took the rocket ship with him. He will be here in a couple of minutes."

"Does he have a pocket watch?"

"He has his father's, but he never winds it. He just keeps it in his room. His body tells him the time."

Two minutes later, Jimmy arrived. He took off his shoes, washed his hands in the bathroom, then came into the kitchen.

"What are you doing today?" Ivor asked.

"Nothing much," Jimmy said. "It might rain, so I don't know if the guys are going to come over after lunch."

"Ah," Ivor said. "How would you like to go fishing, then? Fish love days like today."

"Yes!" Jimmy said.

12 • FORBIDDEN

JIMMY ATE LUNCH QUICKLY. Ivor lingered over the meal, but as soon as he had finished he said to Jimmy, "Come on, then. We'll borrow *Farfar's* rods and tackle." Ivor turned to Viktoria. "Is it all still in the shed?"

"Yes," Viktoria said, to Jimmy's surprise. He had often been sent to get something from the shed, but had never seen any fishing gear.

They went into the back yard, and Ivor opened the door of the shed.

"*Farfar* is a very clever man," Ivor said. "When he was a boy he used this trick to fool the Russians."

He reached down and put his finger into a knothole that was near the bottom of the right side of the shed. When he pulled, part of the wall swung toward him. Behind it a set of racks and hooks held gardening tools, as well as three fishing rods.

Ivor said, "The rod with the steel line is for trolling for lake trout. We'll take the others." He passed them to Jimmy, who stood just outside.

"Now for some tackle." Ivor closed the wall, then bent down, put his finger through a hole in the shed's floor and pulled upward, and there under the floor was the tackle box. Ivor passed the box to Jimmy, then came out of the shed.

"Is the other wall fake, too?" Jimmy asked.

"I think so," Ivor said. *You tell him too much,* Rabbit warned. "There's no obvious handle, but there are screws in four places where there should be nails. People who break into sheds don't normally carry screwdrivers. Anyway, let's see what hooks and such we can borrow."

"*Farfar* wanted to hide things from some Russians?" Jimmy asked.

"It's a long story," Ivor said, "and I'm not the one who should tell it. *Farfar* will tell you the story when he's ready to tell it—but you're not to ask him about it. It's his to tell, not yours to request.

Understand?"

"Yes." Jimmy was quiet for a moment. "I'm going to build a shed someday, and it'll have a secret compartment, too—for things I don't want people to steal."

"Like your 3-D comic book?"

"You know about that?"

"Of course. But no one else does. Now, let's see what's in the tackle box. After that, you can go get your rubber boots."

#

Ivor and Jimmy didn't begin the actual fishing until they had gone a few hundred feet south of Spider Dam to a point on the McIntyre River where there was a short stretch of rapids. The trail they'd been following ended at the rapids in a tangle of fallen trees and brush. Jimmy had never gone past the end of the trail. From the look of things, almost no one had.

"Keep your boots on, but roll up your pants," Ivor said. "We're going wading. The water will be higher than your boots in some places, but the walking will be easy even if they're filled with water."

"How far?" Jimmy asked. "I mean, how far are we going?"

"Just past the end of the rapids. The creek turns east toward town and then swings back west. There's a pool at the bend. We'll start fishing just below the rapids and work our way to the pool. Walk carefully when we're in the water. There are some slippery parts. Always get a good footing before you take the next step. Understand?"

"Yes. How deep will it be?"

"Roll your pants up to your knees."

As they started into the water Ivor said, "Did you know that to catch fish you have to learn how fish fish?"

"What do you mean?"

"Fish eat food that comes to them in the water. At the riffle— fishermen call the rapids a riffle when the rapids are small—the river narrows, and the bugs and the other good stuff bunch together. The narrowing makes the river like a funnel. Little fish hang around the mouth of the riffle and do their fishing there, but they're easy prey for gulls and kingfishers and hawks in the shallows. A lot of the little guys get gobbled up. They're easy for us to catch there, too.

"But the bigger fish need deeper water, so they do their hunting in the slower-moving part of the river—that's called the run. In the run, the bigger fish have more protection from their predators. And where there is a pool, that's where you find the biggest fish of all. But there aren't many of them left at the end of the summer, and the ones that are alive are smart. They don't fall for most fishermen's tricks."

"Fish are smart?"

"In their own way. Your *Farfar* is the best fisherman that I know. He *thinks* like a fish when he's holding the rod."

They had reached the top of the riffle and began to work their way down. Ivor carried the tackle box. Where the riffle ended and the run began, they rolled their pant legs up a little higher.

"Blackflies fish too," Jimmy said looking at the bite marks on his legs.

"Horse flies are the worst," Ivor said. "They sneak up on you from behind and bite you on the neck like Lilliputian vampires." He knew that Jimmy had read *Gulliver's Travels*. "When I first came to Canada, I worked in the bush with a man who used to catch dragonflies and tie one onto his hat with a couple of feet of fishing line. He said that horse flies never came near him."

"Are you making that up?" Jimmy asked.

"Maybe," Ivor said. A minute passed before he spoke again. "Your *Farfar* once owned a horse he called *Perho*, which means *fly* in Finnish."

"No, he didn't." Jimmy was sure that Ivor was setting him up for a joke of some kind.

"He did. Ask him." Ivor reached into his creel and brought out a glass jar containing a bit of soil and some dew worms.

"We need a couple of bobbers," he said, pointing at the tackle box, "and two of the smaller single hooks. And then," he imitated Boris Karloff," I will show you how to put the verm on de hoook."

#

At four-thirty Ivor decided it was time to take Jimmy home. Each had managed to catch two small trout that Ivor had pronounced "keepers." Three others had gone back into the water "to be fattened up."

"Is it okay if I come here with some of my friends?" Jimmy asked as Ivor dropped the last fish through the hole in the creel.

Ivor considered the question. *You cannot tell him,* Rabbit said.

"I think that would be all right," Ivor said, "but you have to tell your mother or *Farmor* exactly where you are going."

"I will."

"And you have to promise me something—this is important. You and your friends must never go farther downstream than the pool."

"Why?"

Don't tell him, Rabbit warned again. *He can't know about the tree.* "Because I say so. Promise."

"I promise," Jimmy said.

They were home by five.

"Well?" Viktoria asked. "Did you catch anything?"

"I have two fish to trade for five loaves," Jimmy said. "And John the Baptist isn't coming."

Viktoria, instead of laughing, gave Ivor *the look.*

"Go wash your hands for supper," Viktoria said to Jimmy. She went to the sink and filled the coffee pot. After he disappeared, she asked Ivor, "How far did you go?"

"Just to the pool."

"You told him he cannot go farther?"

"Yes."

#

After supper, after the table had been cleared and the dishes put away, after Ivor had left, after the newspaper had been read and Jussi had mocked the editor's support for the crazy idea of having seatbelts in cars, Jimmy went up to his room. He read for a while, then went to sleep.

It was almost midnight when he woke to voices in the kitchen. *Farfar* and *Farmor* were talking in Swedish. Most of the words were easy, and Jimmy's Swedish was just good enough to follow some of their conversation.

"When the time comes, you will tell him what he wants to know, but only that," Jimmy's grandmother said. "He is young; he will not know what questions to ask."

"Perhaps," his grandfather said.

"Raimo never asked you about it."

"No. That is true. But Jimmy is not Raimo. Young people are more curious now."

There was a pause in the conversation, and in the pause Jimmy fell asleep once more.

#

On Wednesday, Marilyn put in her half day at work, spent an hour or two on inventory and bookkeeping, and then went home.

"Did you have lunch?" Viktoria asked as Marilyn came into the kitchen.

"Didn't have time, Mom."

"I will make you a sandwich. And we have some soup I could warm up."

"I'd like that."

"Milk or coffee? We have both."

"I'll get some milk." She poured herself a glass from the cupboard and went to sit at the table. "I'm tired," she said.

Viktoria laughed. "Too tired to go to the Finn Hall tonight?" She got the bread from the bread box and used the bread knife to cut two perfect slices.

Marilyn waited until Viktoria had put the knife down before she answered. "No," she said. "Laura and I are still going. She's decided that it's time to be a grown-up and just go, whatever her mother thinks."

"Good for her," Viktoria said. "Will...."

"Owen," Marilyn said. "Yes, he'll be there. He's got a friend, too, that he's invited."

"Oh. And how did all this get arranged?"

"Owen stopped by the store today."

"Well," Viktoria said. "He must really be interested in you. Most men have a natural fear of going into Big Day. Someone might see them."

She winked at Marilyn. She brought out ham slices, in their butcher paper wrapping, from the refrigerator. She buttered the bread, added the ham, cut the sandwich diagonally to make two perfect triangles. Then she fetched a small plate from the cupboard and put the sandwich on it.

Marilyn smiled. Viktoria always thought about the consequences of every action in her kitchen. She anticipated, she planned, she never hurried. She ran a calm kitchen.

Viktoria handed over the plate. "His first name is Owen, but what is his last name?"

"Millbridge."

"English?"

"Canadian," Marilyn said.

"Ah," Viktoria said. She took a small pot from the refrigerator and put it on the stove. "There isn't much soup. It will not take long."

"I'll eat slowly," Marilyn said.

After Marilyn had finished eating and had put the dishes in the sink, Viktoria came to sit with her at the table.

"Can I ask you something?" Marilyn said.

"Of course you *may*."

"Was Dad in the first war, World War I?"

Viktoria did not answer immediately. "This is something you have never asked me," she said finally.

"Jimmy said that Ivor knows a lot about military stuff. He would have been too young for the war, but Dad wouldn't have."

"Jussi was in a war, yes," Viktoria said, "but it wasn't really the world war. It was in Finland."

"In Finland? When?"

"Early in 1918."

"The first world war was still going, then."

"Yes," Viktoria said. "It is complicated."

"Is this why Dad was so upset when Raimo went overseas?"

"Yes," Viktoria said. She tried to collect her thoughts.

"Marilyn," she said at last, "this is something you must not speak about with Jimmy. It is a thing he does not need to know. You can ask Jussi about it, but I am not going to talk about it any more."

"I don't understand. Why?"

"We do not speak of this. Jussi will tell you what he is willing to tell you, but I do not want you to...badger. Is that the word? You must not badger him. And you must not speak to Ivor about it, either. Ivor, especially."

"Okay," Marilyn said. "I don't understand, but okay."

"Thank you," Viktoria said. "Now tell me about Owen. How did you meet him?"

13 • MEMORY

THE FOURTH WEEK OF JULY had begun hot, and hot it continued. During the day the temperature rose into the low 90s; at night it dropped to the 60s. Thursday brought rain, but not enough to cool the house; it only added humidity to the heat. On Friday, the temperature rose into the 90s once more.

Marilyn was exhausted when she arrived home from work. She went upstairs immediately and changed her clothes. When she came down to the kitchen, Viktoria put a glass of water on the table for her, then checked the potatoes, which were boiling on the stove.

Marilyn took a sip, put the glass down, then immediately picked it up again and drank it all. "Where's Jimmy?" she asked when she had finished.

"He and Jussi are in the back yard. Jussi came home early today. The McLeod house is done, so he let the crew have the afternoon off."

"He paid them for the whole day, I bet," Marilyn said.

Viktoria smiled. "Yes. He has a good heart."

"And a soft head," Marilyn said. She went to the sink and filled her glass once more. "I've been thinking about Ivor," she said, returning to the table. "Could he have been in the war? At fifteen?"

"Let it go." Viktoria kept her voice soft. The door to the back yard opened and Jussi and Jimmy came in.

"Did you know that Uncle Ivor is learning Finnish?" Jimmy said.

"Really?" Marilyn said. "Why is he doing that?"

"The guys in the shacks are teaching him," Jussi said. "He says they enjoy it—especially when he makes mistakes." He laughed.

"Good for him," Viktoria said.

"But why is he bothering?" Marilyn persisted.

"He's like that," Jussi said. "Ever since he was a kid he's wanted to know everything."

"He can cook, for instance," Viktoria said. "He is better at it than

189

I am. He can find ways of cooking turnips and peas and yellow beans and potatoes—anything we have in the garden, including dandelions—and it will taste better than anything you can buy at the Hemmet."

"He learned this in Finland?"

"After the war," Jussi said. "Anyway, Jimmy, did you see that yesterday's paper had an ad for the circus? It's starting August 8th."

"I saw it," Jimmy said. A second later, he added, "Was Uncle Ivor in the war?"

"Yes," Jussi said, because one does not lie to children. Viktoria glared at him nonetheless.

"Was he a soldier?"

"For a while," Jussi said. "But now we are going to have supper. I will tell you about it tomorrow. It's time to eat."

"One more question," Jimmy said. "Did you have a horse in Finland?"

"Two horses. One was called Viola, and the other I named *Perho*."

"*Fly*," Jimmy said. "Uncle Ivor has been teaching me a little Finnish."

#

After supper, after Viktoria had finished the dishes, and Jimmy had gone upstairs to his room, Marilyn came to sit at the kitchen table with Jussi. She folded her hands in her lap.

"Dad," Marilyn said, "I want to know what you're going to talk about with Jimmy tomorrow."

For a moment, Jussi did not reply. Then, he said slowly, "I will talk to him about Rabbit and the war, but not all of it. There are things he is too young to hear. These things I will tell you after I have talked to him, and when he is older you may tell him the rest. But not now."

"Thank you," Marilyn said, and she meant it.

#

The heat wave broke on Saturday, and after Jussi returned from work at noon and had lunch he asked Jimmy if he felt like taking a ride.

"Sure," Jimmy said. "Where are we going?"

"Someplace I don't think you've ever been," Jussi said.

The ride didn't last long. They drove the route they usually took on Sundays, but Jussi parked the car on Banning Street on the north side of the church.

"I've been to church," Jimmy said elfishly.

Jussi laughed. "It's okay, you're safe. We're not going to church today. We're going to school."

"What?"

"Okay, we're not going to school, either. We're going to the lookout."

"What lookout?"

"The one beside the Collegiate. At the top of Waverly Street."

"Where the cannons are?"

"Have you been there?"

"I walk past it when I go to the show with my friends."

"This time you'll get to really look at it."

They walked up Banning Street a short way, then crossed Waverly Street and began the long climb up the sidewalk to the lookout.

"I've never gone this way," Jimmy said. He was panting after a few minutes.

"The boys who like cross-country running do their training here," Jussi said. "They run all the way up the hill, walk down, then run up again. Many times."

Jimmy saved his breath for the top of the hill. At the base of the lookout, they went up a set of concrete steps that ran from the base past a thick wooden door and then up along the lower wall before turning right to take them up another flight. There was no railing on the stairs, so Jimmy kept touching the stone wall as they climbed.

The lookout, a semicircle of low stone wall with a concrete floor, was bigger than Jimmy had expected.

"I guess you don't remember when this place had a roof," Jussi said. His voice was steady and untroubled by the climb up the hill. "The roof was round and made the building look like half a flying saucer. It was a beautiful place. When the roof started to deteriorate, the city took it down—four years ago, I think—along with the stone pillars that supported it. This used to be a popular spot once, before everyone started taking the bus instead of walking, and before all the cars, of course. People used to bring blankets and sandwiches and have a picnic up here on the grass. Now, nobody even stops here to look. The trees have grown so much that it's hard to see the lake."

Jimmy nodded.

"It used to have lights at night. Raydiant made them, I think. You can see where they repaired the cement after they took them out." He pointed to the patched sections of the stone enclosure. "To get to the wiring, the workmen would go down the outside stairs and through the doors into the basement."

"Were you ever down there?"

"Just once. Lots of mold. Very dark. There's a story that during the Second World War some prisoners of war were kept in the lookout's basement for a while. I don't know if that's true or not. I don't see why they'd do that. There was a prisoner of war camp at Boulevard Lake, though, at the end of the war. Maybe it had something to do with that."

Jimmy said nothing for a while. He was, Jussi knew, imagining what it would have been like to be locked up in the windowless dungeon below them.

"Lots of churches," Jimmy said at last, "all around the park."

From prison to church, Jussi thought. *The boy is quick.*

"I'll say. You can't see them very well from here because the high school is in the way, but on the left across from the park there's a Pentecostal church for those who like some emotion in the service, and a Baptist church—but I don't know if they're the no-drinking, no-dancing Baptists or the friendlier kind. There's the Catholics on the other side of Algoma Street, and on this side of the park there's Trinity United which used to be Methodist, and St. Paul's United which used to be Presbyterian. Those two didn't want to share one building, so they just bought new hymn books, glued their parishioners to their pews, and told them to sit still."

Jimmy laughed.

Jussi pointed. "The armoury is behind and between the two of them so that things don't get out of hand. And our church is tucked away over there on Pearl Street where it doesn't have to get involved in the squabbles of the others."

"Why are there so many different kinds?"

"People like to bicker more than they like to worship."

"There's a monument in the park," Jimmy said. "I've seen it from the bus."

"It's the cenotaph. They put it up the year your father was born. It was supposed to honour the soldiers who died in 'the war to end all wars,' but then the Second World War came, and then Korea, and they had to add more dates."

"Does it have the soldiers' names on it?"

"No, it's much too small." They stood quietly for a moment.

"My dad's grave is in Belgium," Jimmy said after a while.

"Yes," Jussi said.

"Was Uncle Ivor in the war? Mom thinks he wasn't."

The question, so long in coming, had been asked.

Jussi took a deep breath. "Yes."

"But Mom says he was too young to be in the war."

"He was," Jussi said, "but they let him be in it anyway. They needed everyone. He and your uncle Karl, Ivor's brother, joined up together. Your uncle Anders had joined a couple of years earlier."

"Was Karl my real uncle?"

"No," Jussi said. "But Anders was like a brother to me, and if he had been my real brother, Karl would have been your real uncle, and Ivor, too."

"Okay," Jimmy said.

"What made you ask about Uncle Ivor?"

"He knows a lot about war." Jimmy paused. "And he's a little...funny. You know? Noises bother him. And sometimes...it's like he's not really all there. Like he's away someplace, and he's looking at you from a distance."

"He was shell-shocked in the war," Jussi said. "He was only fifteen, and the war was too much for him."

"Did bombs go off too near him?"

"Yes," Jussi said. It was close enough to the truth to be true. "Sometimes the world doesn't seem real to him still."

"Did his mother know he wasn't okay?"

"Mothers know. The boy she watched go off to war was not the boy who came back, but she loved them both. She took care of him, taught him to cook—how to *really* cook—and slowly he got better. Not completely, not fixed, but able to *pretend* to be better. That's probably as close as he'll get. And in 1925 he came to Canada."

"When Dad was born."

"Just a few days before, in fact. *Farmor* used to say that she was racing the boat, but the boat won. Uncle Ivor got here before the baby did." Jussi smiled at the memory. "She had been in the country for four years, long enough to learn English, and she taught both her 'babies' how to speak the language."

Jimmy laughed. "She still doesn't let Uncle Ivor speak slang," he said.

"No, nor me," Jussi said. He pointed to the high school. "Is this where you plan to go to school?" he asked.

Jimmy knew *Farfar* was asking if he thought he'd be taking up a trade or going to university. The Technical Institute, perched on High Street a few blocks behind them, was where students went to study business or the trades. The Collegiate, just left of them, was for those who wished to be doctors, teachers, or lawyers.

"Yes," he said, "and then I can join the Air Cadets and learn how to fly."

"Ah," Jussi said. "Time to go home."

14 • MARILYN

ON SUNDAY AFTER LUNCH, Marilyn and Jussi sat in the back yard on the wood-and-canvas lawn chairs. The sun had slid behind the birch tree in the southwest corner of the yard, and they enjoyed the comforting shade. Jimmy and his friends had gone to the creek to catch crayfish at their dam.

Marilyn took a sip of water, then put the glass down on the small round table beside Jussi's. "You had your talk with Jimmy?" she asked. She knew that the two of them had taken a drive to the lookout.

Jussi nodded. "He's a smart boy," he said. "He asked about Ivor."

"And?"

"I told him a little about Ivor being in the war," Jussi said. "But just a little."

"Ivor was really in the war? At fifteen?"

"Yes. Lots of boys who were too young lied about their age and signed up. Not many were turned away."

"He signed up?"

"With Karl. For a short time they were stationed together at Vilppula—that's about fifty miles north-west of Tampere, where Karl died—and then Rabbit was sent to Ruovesi about fifteen miles east of Vilppula. It doesn't sound very far, but it was winter and travel was hard. He had been told he was going to be a cook. A day or two after he got to Rouvesi, though, he was raped by one of the officers."

"Oh my God!" Marilyn said.

"This is something you will never say to anyone," Jussi said. "Not to Viktoria, not to anyone. Not ever. I tell you this because I want you to know Rabbit's story and why he is like he is. Even Viktoria knows only some parts of the story. You will not talk to her of any of this. It is not gossip. You will keep silent."

Marilyn nodded. She looked down at the grass. She could not look at Jussi. Her eyes filled with tears.

195

"The Whites started to move south toward Tampere. The force that included Karl and me was on the west side of Lake Näsijärvi. Tampere is at the south end of the lake. Rabbit's group was on the east side. The idea was that the two groups would push the Reds south.

"When we got to Tampere, the fighting was awful. Karl died in the battle at Tampere's cemetery just before Easter. The fighting was from gravestone to gravestone.

"When Rabbit arrived in Tampere, thousands of Reds had been captured, and executions began. The Red soldiers—there were women soldiers, too—were taken to the railway yard, lined up against the wall of a warehouse, and shot. People watched from a walkway over the railway tracks, and they cheered when the shots were fired."

Jussi suddenly could not continue. He sat for a minute, then took a drink of his water. "This, too, you will not speak of," he said when he had composed himself as best he could. "Rabbit was forced to be part of one of the execution squads."

"Oh, no," Marilyn said. The tears flooded her eyes and ran down her cheeks. "No."

"Rabbit had made a friend on the way south from Ruovesi, a boy his own age named Benjamin. When Rabbit refused to shoot the prisoners, the officer in command of the squad killed Benjamin, then pointed his gun at Rabbit, and Rabbit shot his first prisoner—a girl, a teenager, who had been fighting for the Reds."

Marilyn's knuckles were white as she held onto the arms of her chair. She could not speak.

"After that, he shot many more. Then, one day he saw a chance to run away, and he deserted."

"He went home?" There was no accusation in her voice. She wanted Jussi's story to end with Rabbit safe in his mother's arms.

"That was not possible. All the routes north were blocked with White troops. If they caught him, he thought, they would find out who he was, and they would kill him. So he went east and joined a caravan of Reds—men, women, children, all fleeing with their belongings to what they had been told by their leaders was safety. Most were Finns; a few were Finland-Swedes.

"By this time, though, the Germans had landed in Finland and were sweeping north and east. Rabbit had to leave the Reds and strike out on his own. The Germans caught him in Lahti." Jussi smiled at the thought.

To Marilyn, the smile was bewildering.

"Rabbit is not stupid," Jussi said. "And he was not yet broken. He passed himself off as a soldier who had lost his papers, and was sent to Ahvola in Karelia to fight on the eastern front. Karelia was part of Finland, then. It was lost to Russia during the Second World War.

"Anyway, at Ahvola the Whites had been bogged down in trench warfare for three months, but shortly after Rabbit's arrival the Reds abandoned their lines. It had become obvious that they were needed to defend Viipuri close to the Russian border. They fled south. The Whites followed, Rabbit with them, and along the way Rabbit ran into his brother, Anders, my friend from Gamlaby."

Jussi took a moment to marshal his thoughts. "It was at a bridge and at night. Anders' men and the troop that Rabbit was with got into a firefight. Each thought the other was the enemy. A few were killed. All by mistake.

"Rabbit's group, sometime in the next days, was sent north to prevent the escape of any Reds that managed to survive the siege of Viipuri. Viipuri was their last stronghold."

"Did the Reds escape?" Marilyn asked.

Jussi took a drink before he answered. "It wasn't like that." He was silent for a moment. "There wasn't a Red army anymore. There were just men and their families. My father and I were there, part of the artillery. We surrounded and flattened the city. The living left their dead in the streets and fled with their families, or tried to. They headed off in all directions, getting killed wherever they went. A large group of them headed north to a crossroads where Rabbit and two small companies of our men had orders to stop them, but there were so many of them. The Reds overran the first company, then tried to get past the one that Rabbit was in. It was late in the evening by this time.

"I think Rabbit might have been okay except for that last battle. He was strong—he still is, in his own way—and he was young then. The young can stand almost anything. But the Reds had few weapons. They had run out of most of their ammunition and had armed themselves with knives, clubs, stones, bayonets. Waves of men, women, children, came running through the open fields into the rifle fire and the machineguns of Rabbit's company. Most of the battle was fought in the dark. Toward the end, the attackers were climbing over hills of flesh, long waves of bodies made of the dead and the dying.

"Sometime in the battle Rabbit broke. He thought one of the girls that was running toward him was the one that he had killed at Tampere, and he killed her again."

Beside him, Marilyn was weeping. Her body shook with grief and with the effort of keeping her voice silent.

"They sent Rabbit home. I know the story only because he told his mother, and she told me. Ivor never speaks of it. After his mother, Ellen, died in 1925, Rabbit wrote to me asking what I thought of him coming to Canada. He worked for me for a while, but...." Jussi let the sentence die. He waited a moment before he continued.

"Rabbit is what he is. He holds himself together by force of will. Jimmy says that Rabbit knows a lot about war. He does. He makes himself read everything about war that he can get his hands on, and every day he stares his demons down. And when it becomes too much for him, he goes fishing, or he gets drunk."

"I am such a *fool*," Marilyn said. She wiped her eyes with her hands.

"No, you are not. This is something you could not know. It is part of a silence that we keep in our family. And that you will keep," he added.

"Yes," Marilyn said. It was an oath. "Jimmy," she said, but did not finish the sentence.

"Knows nothing of this. And he is not fifteen, not Rabbit." Jussi said. "And his Uncle Ivor watches over him. You do not need to worry when he is out of sight."

"Mom?"

"She knows almost everything, but not this, not the rape. And she may know things about the war I do not know. She probably does, in fact."

"Do you talk about the war?"

"No. Viktoria feels the shame of it still, the guilt that comes with having been on the White side, the *winning* side. So what Jimmy hears from his *Farmor* about Finland is all good. It is not true, perhaps, but it is useful. She keeps it a country of good manners and good people who are honest and fair and who work hard and treat each other with respect."

"You do that too."

"Yes," Jussi said. "And so does Ivor. And so, for the most part, do the men who live in the shacks beside him. It is a useful fiction. It keeps us kind. It keeps the past separate from the present."

Marilyn kept her voice soft. "So the war, the actual fighting, lasted just a few months. But what horrible consequences." She thought again of Viktoria, her clean-scrubbed kitchen, her concern for proper speech and politeness, her careful ways. Always making order from chaos.

Jussi considered. "The war didn't end just because the fighting was over. Some prisoners of the war were held for years in awful conditions. But yes, the shooting war lasted just one winter and a few weeks into spring. The one in Rabbit's mind doesn't end."

#

Jimmy came home well before supper. Shortly after Jimmy, Ivor showed up.

"No fish?" Viktoria asked as he came into the kitchen.

"I gave them to Vilho," Ivor said. "He's the one who's teaching me Finnish. He hasn't had much luck getting work, so I figured he could use them."

Marilyn got up suddenly from her chair and went upstairs.

"What's wrong with her?" Ivor asked.

"Oh, who knows. *Vimmen.*" Jussi exaggerated his accent and shook his head in mock-perplexity, but still, Viktoria shot him a look.

15 • WINNERS AND LOSERS

ON MONDAY, JUSSI CAME HOME EARLY. "Trouble?" Viktoria said when she heard him come into the house through the side door.

"No," Jussi said. He began to get out of his work clothes, hanging up his hat first, then taking off his boots and putting them on the rubber mat by the wall. "We're just starting on the new place, and the boys know what to do." He walked up the steps from the entry and came into the kitchen. "Where's supper?"

Viktoria laughed. "In my mind," she said. "Go wash."

A few minutes later he was back from washing up. He had on a clean shirt and pants, fresh socks, and smelled of aftershave.

"So you are the good-smelling handsome one I hear so much about," Viktoria said. She set a cup of coffee on the table for him. "Marilyn has a boyfriend, now, but not as handsome as the one I have."

"Owen? Is that his name?"

"Do not pretend that you have not bothered to learn his name," Viktoria said.

"Millbridge," Jussi said, then winked.

"He is taking her to that dance place on the highway—the Mid-Canada Dance Pavilion."

"Ah," Jussi said. "That's good. He has a car. Does he have a job?"

"I do not know," Viktoria said. "He must have a job, though, if he has a car. And if he is serious about Marilyn, even if he has a car and no job, she will just make him sell the car and go to work."

"Yes," Jussi said. "She just might." After a moment he added, "I know something about Owen Millbridge that you don't know."

"What is that?"

"He takes good care of his shoes."

"Oh?"

"He has them fixed at the place on Oliver Road."

200

"He is not—"

"No," Jussi said. "The shoemaker says the man who wrote the letters is an old Finn. Not a Canadian."

#

After supper, after dishes, after Jimmy had gone to bed, there was a light knock at the side door of the house. Jussi had been reading the paper, but he got up and went to the door. It was Ivor, smelling of drink, his face bloodied.

"What happened?" Jussi led Ivor up the stairs and into the kitchen. As soon as she saw him, Viktoria headed for the bathroom for bandages and disinfectant.

"Vilho," Ivor said. "He called me a goddamned *ruotsalainen*, and I called him a *kirottu* hun." Ivor leaned heavily on Jussi. "He didn't know what a hun was, so I called him a Cossack, just to help him out, and he hit me. Here." Ivor tried to point at his forehead which was crusted with blood, but his hand shook too much to hit the mark. "I don't think you should hit a teacher, do you?"

"Sit him at the table," Viktoria said as she came out of the bathroom.

"I know a hun is not a Cossack," Ivor said, "but a hun is *like* a Cossack."

Viktoria started to clean away the blood. "This will hurt," she said matter-of-factly.

"Vilho is still my friend, isn't he?" Ivor asked Viktoria. "We just got a little too drunk."

"I am sure he is still your friend," Viktoria said, "but you have got to give up the drink."

"Can I sleep on your floor?"

Marilyn came down from her bedroom. "Jesus, Ivor," she said.

"I'm not Christ, but I damn near got crucified tonight. Crucified." Ivor started to laugh, then suddenly stopped. "It hurts when I laugh. I wrinkle my face too much," he said.

"Is Vilho okay?" Jussi asked.

"Vilho," said Ivor, "Vilho is a bear. He's a *karhu*. And he snores like a *karhu*, too. I can hear him from my cabin. He's too tough to hurt. That's why he's such a good teacher."

He closed his eyes, and Viktoria began to attach the gauze with strips of tape that she tore off the roll with her teeth.

"I'll get the cot," Jussi said. He headed down the stairs to the basement.

"Jussi is a good man," Ivor said. He looked at Marilyn. "He was a good father to Raimo. Jussi learned how to be good from his father. Did you know his father was called Raimo, too? And he learned how to hunt from his mother before she was killed. She was a good hunter. She killed—" He broke the thought before any more words came out.

Marilyn turned quickly to Viktoria. *Drunk,* her expression said. Viktoria nodded her head and put a finger to her lips.

"Oops," Ivor said. "I'm drunk. Sorry, Marilyn."

Jussi came up the stairs with the army-style cot.

"Set it up in the front porch," Viktoria said. "And *you,*" she said to Ivor, "if you have to throw up, you make sure you are in the bathroom first."

"I don't feel well," Ivor said.

#

On Wednesday afternoon, Marilyn came home early. Jussi was sitting in the back yard on a lawn chair.

"Is Jimmy in the house?"

"Creek," Jussi said.

"And Mom?" Marilyn asked. Ivor, she knew, had made himself scarce on Tuesday morning. And she knew that it was because he did not want Jimmy to know that he had been drinking and had got into a fight. But Jimmy knew, of course. He just pretended he didn't.

"She went to get some groceries."

"Walking, I'll bet."

"She says she likes it. She'll take the bus back, though. It's almost two miles to the People's Co-op on Bay."

"And a hard walk up the John Street hill on the way back." Marilyn got a lawn chair from the shed and unfolded it beside Jussi. She sank into it. "Ahh, it feels good to sit."

"You have to practice, though. I'm getting very good at it."

Marilyn laughed. She closed her eyes for a moment. When she opened them again, she said, "Dad, you never talk about what it was like in Finland before you emigrated. Why is that?"

It was a long time before Jussi answered. "Things happened after the war," he said finally.

Marilyn knew that she was supposed to let her question die, but she couldn't. "What things?" she asked.

"Things," Jussi said.

"Dad, please." She said it the way an adult would. She was asking, not whining, not begging.

Jussi leaned back in the lawn chair. "The war," he began, "didn't end when it was over. The White side—*my* side—went crazy. The Red soldiers gave up and we started to hold trials—some real ones, some not—and execute the guilty, the near-guilty, and the innocent...by the thousands. Five thousand, six thousand, I don't know how many, were killed, then buried in unmarked graves in the forests, or left in roadside ditches or in mass graves in the cemeteries."

"Did Ivor—?"

"No, he was safely home. I was, too. I didn't see this, but I heard about it." He stopped to let the story come back to him. "There was a forest close to a place called Mustakallio—about twenty miles northwest of Helsinki. A hundred women and girls were executed there because they had been part of a women's contingent of Red soldiers—'skirt Russians.' Some of the girls were as young as thirteen.

"In the prisons right after the war there were tens of thousands of prisoners, maybe eighty thousand at one time or another. Four or five thousand of them were women. And in 1918 the Spanish flu swept through the prisons. Twelve thousand died because they were starving, weak, crowded together. There were almost no doctors, few nurses.

"White farmers, even when they had lots of grain to spare, refused to provide it to the prisoners. They said they needed everything for seed grain for the coming winter. Some farmers, of course, weren't like that, and sent food, but a lot of the food 'disappeared' along the way. And got sold in markets.

"After the war, there were maybe twenty thousand orphan children whose fathers and mothers had fought for the Reds. Many were taken from what was left of their families and sent to orphanages or given to White families who wanted children. Some were so young that after a while they forgot who their parents were or if they had brothers or sisters even. All they knew was what they were told, and that was that their mothers had been monsters.

"And the White children made life hell for them, of course, because that's what kids do with anyone who is different. Over six hundred of them were sent to Ostrobothnia—that's the province Gamlaby is in—for 'a decent upbringing.'"

Jussi stopped speaking for a while, and Marilyn let him sit in silence until he could continue.

"Some of them never learned what their names had been before the war, or what part of the country they had come from. They had no way of finding out anything about themselves. They had turned *ruotsolaisiksi*—into Swedes."

Jussi was quiet again. Then at last, he looked straight at Marilyn. "Finland stopped being my country. My father and I had gone back to the farm, but someone had burned both the house and the barn. Raiders, I guess, *lentävä osasto*. The words mean 'department of flying,' but the men were just on horseback."

Jussi leaned to the side to pick up a blade of grass from the lawn, crushed it between his fingers, and let it blow away.

"My father said, 'There is nothing for us here,' and went to work for Inga Svensson in Gamlaby at Svensson's general store. Inga and Ellen Solbakken and Viktoria had kept it going during the war with a little help from Harald Berg, the schoolteacher. My father and Inga would have gotten married, I think—Ellen and Harald did, finally— but he died within the year, had a heart attack. In those days, lots of men died young. My father was forty-nine.

"Anyway, I tried to start over, bring the farm back to life, but my heart was not in it." Jussi looked across the lawn to the flower bed in front of the fence.

Marilyn knew he was seeing the farm in Finland, trying to figure out once again how to start anew.

He took out a cigarette and lit it, took a couple of quick puffs, then let the cigarette rest between thumb and finger.

"The country church had been burned. Some of the gravestones had been defaced; some had just been pushed over. Right after the war, some of the people I knew started to return—first, the ones who had fought for the Whites, but not many of them. The others, the Reds, came back more slowly, and there weren't many of them, either. The country had lost half a generation of young men. My old neighbours wouldn't—couldn't—talk to me. Some of the guys who had fought had been wounded so badly that they couldn't do anything for themselves. Others were filled to the brim with hate—Reds and Whites."

Jussi took a breath. "Hate, real hate, doesn't *burn* in a man, you know—it *freezes* him, makes him despise warmth." He shook his head.

"The ghosts, the men who had spent months starving in prison, started to return the following year, gaunt, weak, sick. Someone who had been thought dead would suddenly show up alive, and stories would fly into the air and seed themselves all over Gamlaby and the countryside."

Jussi leaned over and plucked another blade of grass. Marilyn stayed silent, hoping he'd continue.

"This one said that he had been in prison in the Suomenlinna camp, and the men there were so hungry that they had eaten all the plants that grew in the yards of the prison."

He threw the blade away and plucked another.

"That one said that guards threw a live grenade into a prisoner's cell one night and killed the guy, just for fun."

He blew the grass from his hand once more.

"It was impossible to tell if the stories were true or false. There were hundreds of stories, thousands of stories. You could believe whatever you wanted.

"For a while, no Red could be buried with any sort of ceremony. No clergy could preside over a Red funeral, the Church saw to that. No marker could be erected, no flowers could be placed on the grave. Some women protested by hanging their husbands' bullet-riddled clothing on their laundry lines for all to see."

Jussi raised his cigarette to his lips, but didn't smoke it. He stubbed the cigarette out, then threw it on the lawn.

"So in 1920 I got my papers in order and left."

Marilyn said, "And Mom?"

"At the end of the war she was just twenty-two. Karl had been killed in Tampere; her parents had died in Helsinki. I was a friend, but no more than that. She'd say hello if I stopped by the store in Gamlaby, but she wasn't sure of me. I had been to war, and nobody knew if the person who went to war would be the same person who returned.

"She tried to stay in Finland, but there was no future for her there, either, so in 1921 she got in touch with her uncle who was in Port Arthur. He had a job in the shipyard. He wrote her to say that if she came to Port Arthur he knew of a job she could get as a housemaid, so she came to Canada. Lots of girls did that. They would try to find another girl to travel with so that nothing bad would happen to them on the boat, then they'd pack a suitcase and leave. She didn't even know that I was in Port Arthur until a few weeks after she got here. A year or so later we were married."

"And a year after that, Raimo was born."

"Yes. I had been working in a logging camp, and when he was born I decided to go into business so that I could stay in town. When the Depression came in '29 I did well. I knew how to fix things, keep things running. I didn't make much money, but I always made enough."

"Dad...." Marilyn had started, but she didn't know how to continue.

"Yes?"

"I miss Raimo."

"I know."

"And I've met someone."

"The young man who likes dancing."

Marilyn smiled. "That's the one." She grew serious. "But I feel guilty. What should I do?"

"Live," Jussi said. "You should live your life as fully as you can."

"But Jimmy. What about him? He's always asking about his father."

"Jimmy is ten. At ten, summer is a whole year long. Every day he learns a thousand things and wants to learn a thousand more. He will be fine. Live your life. He will adjust. He loves you and he trusts you, and I do, too."

Marilyn exhaled. She hadn't even known she'd been holding her breath.

16 • MEDICINE

ON SATURDAY, in the early afternoon, Ivor showed up sober. He had removed the bandage, but his forehead was still creased with a jagged scar.

"It doesn't bleed, so I took the bandage off," he explained when Viktoria opened the door. "You could be a doctor," he said.

"A veterinarian, maybe," Viktoria said. "Come in. Jussi is home, and I have put the coffee on."

"No, no," Ivor said. "I just need to see Jussi for a minute."

Victoria knew that it must be something about the letters, but she also knew that it was best not to ask.

By this time Jussi had come to the door. "How's the Finnish coming?" he asked. "Are you and Vilho on speaking terms again?"

"We apologized and agreed that we'd stop drinking. Well, maybe not that last part, but we apologized. Can I talk to you for a minute?"

Jussi stepped out of the house. "What's happened?" He closed the door behind him.

"This morning I walked past the shoemaker's shop, and there was a man on the other side of the street. He looked like he was watching the shop."

"The letter-writer?"

"I don't know. He was old, but not really old—mid-fifties, sixty at the most. He looked like a Finn, though—very fair skin, round face but not round like the Slavs, small nose with a thin bridge, high forehead, thin eyebrows, pretty bald, not someone you'd expect to have hair on his back."

Jussi began to laugh. "Rabbit, with an eye for detail like yours, you should have been a painter."

"Something else," Ivor said, ignoring him. "He looks like someone I met...*before*."

Before was what Ivor always called the time before he left Vilppula for Ruovesi. Everything before Ruovesi was the first part of his life—when he was young. Everything after was *after*.

"That's a long time ago," Jussi said.

"Yes," Ivor said. He considered. "Maybe it was after. I don't know."

Jussi shifted the subject. "Was he watching you? Was he paying attention to you?"

"No, I think he was just looking at the window of the shop. I didn't stare at him, though. I just kept walking. After a minute I turned back, and he was walking up the High Street hill. He doesn't walk well. He's unsteady."

"The shoemaker said the letter-writer was an *old* Finn," Jussi said.

"Everyone looks old to someone who is even just a little younger."

"What about the window?"

"No change," Ivor said. "But when I think about it, maybe the Finn had an envelope in his hand."

"It wouldn't be mine," Jussi said. "I haven't written anything yet."

"His?"

"Maybe. Are you sure he was carrying an envelope?"

"No," Ivor said. "I...I don't know. I was afraid to look for too long."

"Jesus," Jussi said, but he was looking past Ivor and toward Fort William. "Look!"

Ivor turned around. A black cloud rose into the sky.

Viktoria opened the door and came out. "The Mission mill, the sawmill, is burning!" she said. "It is on the radio."

Jussi glanced at Ivor, then quickly put his hand on Ivor's shoulder. Ivor was shaking.

"It's the mill, Rabbit," Jussi said. "It's just the mill. Now come inside and Viktoria will make you a sandwich."

"Thank you," Ivor said, and Jussi knew that he was going to be all right.

The sandwich turned into an afternoon of talk—about the mill, the church picnic that Immanuel was holding at Chippewa Park on Sunday, Marilyn Bell's attempt to swim across Lake Ontario, the fact that The King and His Court were coming to play softball at McKellar Park on Wednesday, Disneyland, what the Canadian Lakehead Exhibition would be like this year.

Jussi kept the conversation light.

At five o'clock, Jimmy came home from the creek, and he and Ivor started to talk about fishing. Marilyn, who had gone straight from work to spend part of the afternoon shopping at Simpsons-Sears, was home fifteen minutes later. After supper, Ivor sat and talked awhile and then made his excuses and got up to go back to his place past the creek. Jussi went outside with him.

"Rabbit," Jussi said when they were outside, "this man you saw—how was he dressed?"

"Nice clothes, good shoes. He's not a working man. He walked very slowly up High Street, as if the hill was hard for him."

"I don't want you asking around about him, especially your Finnish friends. Word might get back."

"I understand," Ivor said.

"Now, home with you, and play nice with Vilho."

Ivor laughed and headed home.

#

Later that evening Jussi and Viktoria sat in the back yard cooling off from the warmth of the day. Rain clouds hung low in the sky now, and the temperature had fallen to near seventy. The smoke from the Mission Mill fire had finally disappeared.

Though there was no chance that they would be heard by either Jimmy or Marilyn, Jussi and Viktoria were careful to keep their voices soft.

"He never gets better, does he?" Viktoria asked.

"Rabbit? He's a lot calmer than he used to be. But no, this is probably as good as he'll get. The war is still in him. He's worried now that he won't be able to handle the fireworks or the noise at the CLE. Remember last year when he stayed away from the midway because of that booth where people shoot at metal cutouts of ducks? He couldn't walk past it—we had to take the long way around."

"Jimmy wants to try his hand at it this year," Viktoria said.

"The shooting?"

"Yes."

"I could ask Rabbit to come to see the animals in the barns," Jussi said. "Jimmy doesn't like the smell there, so you and Marilyn could take Jimmy to the midway."

"That is a good idea."

They were quiet for a few moments. Then Viktoria asked, "Have you thought about the letter?"

"Ivor said he saw a man near the shoemaker's yesterday. He thought he had an envelope in his hand."

"Do you think...?"

"I don't know." Jussi longed for a cigarette. "Rabbit said the man reminded him of someone, but he didn't know who."

"Someone in Canada or someone in Finland?"

"Finland."

For a long time there was silence. "I think I will go inside now," Viktoria said at last. "It is almost time for bed. Are you coming? I could make some tea if you want to stay up for a while."

Jussi looked at his watch. It was close to ten o'clock, and the sun had already set. Twilight was giving in to darkness; July would soon be giving way to August.

"In a while," Jussi said, "after I have a smoke. Put the tea on."

17 • THE CIRCUS

THE WEEK BEFORE the start of the Canadian Lakehead Exhibition, both Port Arthur and Fort William were full of news, as usual. It went door to door like the milkman, the breadman, the earnest young fellow who sold spices, the man who sharpened scissors and knives; it traveled as gossip, as speculation, as voices in bars and barbershops and beauty parlours.

How about that Marilyn Bell girl, swimming across Lake Ontario! A Lutheran pastor in the States is on trial for heresy—behind closed doors, of course. What's heresy? Barbara Ann Scott's gotten engaged. Good skater, that one. The anniversary of the bombing of Hiroshima is going to be marked on Saturday. You ever see a picture of that church or something that was at ground zero? It wasn't a church—it was some kind of an exhibition hall. Now they've charged a second pastor with heresy. The midway's going to be a mile long this year. Can you imagine? The polio vaccine is working, they say, but not as well as the scientists expected. Kids might need a second dose. Royalite Oil and Can-American Oil Sands Development have come up with a plan for getting oil out of the Athabaska bituminous sands. That's never going to happen—you can't get blood out of a turnip. You can buy Orange Crush now in king-size bottles. Did you hear? The Port Arthur Board of Education got 130 applications for the jobs of those 44 teachers who resigned. Television viewers might have to get a licence soon, they say. Next thing you know, you'll have to get a licence to fish. The government is going to start up the Chalk River atomic reactor next year; the paper had a diagram showing how it works. Dean Martin is sure sore that Jerry Lewis is getting the bigger parts. Well of course he is—Jerry's funny and Dean isn't. Did you hear that actors have gone on strike because they don't get paid for re-runs? Why the hell should they get paid for something they're not doing? Saw a picture, too, of how a satellite could be put into orbit. Damnest thing. What the hell are they thinking we'll need satellites for? To take pictures of us?

The week had begun hot and stayed hot, even with Wednesday's rain, and then began to cool. The circus, the Ex, the CLE—people had many names for it—was coming. No one could remember a year when it hadn't rained at some point during circus week. It was time for mothers with cute children to think about whether they should take the children to Children's Day, and for fathers to plan whether the family should go on Monday when the Ford was being given away in the draw, or on Tuesday when the prize was a Chevy.

Jimmy went to the circus twice. He and his friends spent Wednesday afternoon at the midway. Thursday evening he went with his family. His grandfather, it seemed, wanted the Dodge—not Wednesday's Nash, not Friday's Studebaker, and not Saturday's Pontiac, which he dismissed as "a Chevy in high heels and an evening dress."

Just inside the main gate stood the Co-op Dairy's Bottle—an ice-cream stand in the shape of a gigantic glass milk bottle. "Meet me at" sloped up the neck, and "THE BOTTLE," in giant bold lettering below, completed the slogan. Above the two concession windows it said "Co-op Dairy" and "Milk-Bar."

"Remember...." Viktoria said to Jimmy as the family came through the gates. She pointed at the slogan.

"If I get sick or I can't find you, go to the Bottle," Jimmy said mechanically.

"That thing's got to be three stories tall," Jussi said. "The man that built it, he's the one who had the skating rink made out of milk. Remember that?"

Victoria nodded.

"Skating rink?" Jimmy said. "Nobody makes a skating rink out of milk."

"Your grandfather and I used to skate on it," Viktoria said, and Jimmy knew it had to be the truth. "The fellow—he was Danish, I think—was the boss of the dairy, and instead of throwing away the skim milk that the dairy couldn't sell, he used it to make a skating rink. This was right at the end of the Depression. It was on the lake side of Memorial Avenue between Queen Street and Lisgar Street. Do you know where they are?"

Jimmy nodded. "What happened to it?" he asked.

"People liked it in the winter. There was even a shack where you could put on your skates. But in the spring the milk melted and started to stink, and people made a fuss, so after a couple of years he stopped dumping the milk there."

"Your grandmother could skate like the wind," Ivor said.

"And I could fall like the snow," Jussi added. "So where do you want to start?" he asked Viktoria.

"Crafts," she said. "There is a new building."

"Doilies, here we come," Marilyn said. "It's ladies first, gentlemen." They started walking south. Behind them the games booths, the freak shows, and the rides stretched north—over and past the bridge that crossed the Neebing River—all the way to where the creek, here officially called the McIntyre River, ran east into Lake Superior.

Jussi, Ivor, and Jimmy put up with the various crafts buildings for some time. But when Marilyn and Viktoria announced that they were going to hang around for the demonstration on how to cook frozen TV dinners, the men quickly excused themselves and went to the Coliseum building to look at the more interesting displays. Half an hour later, Marilyn and Viktoria came to fetch them.

"Thank God," Jussi said. "We've seen everything in here about five times."

"I have an idea," Viktoria said. "You and Ivor can go look in the animal barns while Jimmy and Marilyn and I try some of the rides on the midway. Jimmy does not like the barns, and you and Ivor do."

"Good idea," Jussi said. He and Ivor headed for the barns. There were seven barns filled with animals—and with men whose wives stayed in the fresh air and waited for them to come out.

Ivor and Jussi had been in the cattle barn for just a few minutes when Ivor suddenly stopped talking.

"In Finland," Ivor had been saying, "we would not have treated the animals so badly. We would...." And he had stopped.

Jussi turned to look at him. Ivor was staring at the entrance to the barn, and suddenly, in mid-sentence, he began to run toward it.

"He's here!" Ivor yelled to Jussi over his shoulder.

Jussi took off at a run to catch up, but Ivor was already outside, past the little children's rides, heading north toward the main midway.

"Ivor, stop!" Jussi yelled. People turned to look as he ran past them. "Who's here? Where are you going?"

Ivor slowed just enough for Jussi to catch up. "The man who was watching me when I was near the shoemaker's last week," he panted. "He's here!"

"Where?" Jussi said.

"Up there," Ivor said, pointing past the concession buildings where the churches and lodges and sports organizations sold food. "He's heading up the midway. He saw me, and he's trying to get away! I got a good look at him, Jussi. I got a good look!"

"Rabbit, stop! Just stop!" Ivor stopped running and stood still. Jussi caught up. "We can't just chase him up the midway. Did he seem to be with anyone?"

The question seemed to keep Ivor in check.

Jussi went on, "If he's with someone, he can't suddenly leave. If he's not, we've lost him already. Let's just walk up the midway, and you can keep your eyes open."

"All right," Ivor said, but his eyes were nervous now, and the sounds of the midway were beginning to bother him—loudspeakers competed for attention; people screamed on the rides; and wheels clattered and squealed as carriages dipped and spun, plunging down steep steel hills and flying around impossible corners.

God, I hate the midway, Jussi thought. Far ahead of them, a neatly dressed man handed his ticket to a concessionaire and entered the tent of the World's Smallest Horse.

18 • GONE

JUSSI AND IVOR walked the length of the midway, but their quarry had disappeared. No customers, thankfully, had been waiting for their chance at the shooting gallery. They turned back and began to work their way south. They had passed the Ferris wheel and were beside the shooting gallery once more when Viktoria, Marilyn, and Jimmy came walking toward them.

Viktoria looked quizzically at Jussi as she came up. She could see that Ivor was upset about something.

Jussi said only, "We had a look at the midway."

Half a mile from them, along the spur of the CN railway line that lay to the west of the fairgrounds, a locomotive slipped into position behind the last of a line of iron ore cars from the Steep Rock mine. It started to shove the line forward, toward the trestle at the iron ore dock, and the couplings between the cars engaged with a sound like machine gun fire that swept the length of the train as the locomotive slowly accelerated.

Ivor put his hands to his ears. From right beside him came three quick unexpected shots from the shooting gallery.

Viktoria saw Ivor mouth the word *No!* but couldn't hear it above the noise of the midway.

Ivor broke into a run and headed south.

Jussi did not go after him. "Jimmy," he said calmly, "you know what to do. When you catch him, just talk to him. Ask him to show you the barns or something."

"Is it safe?" Marilyn asked.

"Yes," Jussi said. "Go, Jimmy. We'll meet you at the Bottle."

Jimmy ran after Ivor.

"He'll be all right," Jussi said to Marilyn. "Jimmy is a child— Rabbit will need to protect him."

"It is okay," Viktoria added. "Jimmy is a child, yes, but he is a smart child. He will know what to do."

It took them several minutes to work their way through the crowds. When they got to the Bottle, Jimmy and Ivor were not around.

"Where are they?" Marilyn said.

Jussi considered. "Jimmy will ask Ivor to show him the sheep barn, I think."

"Why?" Marilyn asked.

"Because there are lambs."

"Jimmy hates the smell of the barns."

"But he loves his Uncle Ivor," Jussi said. "We'll wait here. They won't be long. You and Viktoria go sit at one of the picnic tables. I will buy ice cream."

Twenty minutes later, Ivor and Jimmy showed up. Jussi said calmly, "Jimmy, get two ice-creams—one for you and one for your uncle. I give you a dollar. You make sure to count the change."

Jimmy took the dollar bill and headed off. Ivor sat down beside Jussi at the table.

"I am sorry," Ivor said. "It was—"

"Like gunfire," Jussi finished.

"I can't...it was so long ago, and still I can't...I am ashamed."

Marilyn kept her face devoid of emotion. She looked, instead at Viktoria, who met her gaze but that was all.

"Jimmy is coming back," Jussi said after a while. He looked at Ivor.

"Ice cream!" Ivor said. *Well done,* Rabbit told Ivor. *Now thank him.* "Thank you, young man. That is just what I needed."

#

At nine-thirty, having seen everything twice (except, Ivor pointed out, the show in the "Harlem in Havana" tent at the end of the midway), the family sat again at the table behind the Bottle and waited for the car draw. At nine-forty-five, they heard the grandstand speaker blare out the winning number. Jussi tore up his ticket.

"Well," he said, "it's maybe time to go home."

"I have a dollar," Ivor said. "I'm going to see the jig show. That Claxton—boy oh boy—he knows how to run a show! I will walk home," he said.

Jussi shrugged.

"Go straight home after the show," Viktoria said. "Remember last year."

Jimmy waited until the family was in the car and driving away from the circus before he asked, "What's a jig show and what happened last year?"

"Never mind what is a jig show," Viktoria scolded, her Swedish grammar interfering with the English.

"It has girls and dancing," Jussi said, enjoying the situation. "Girls in outfits that look like underwear. And there is even a one-legged tap dancer. Havana is in Cuba, and Harlem is in New York, so the music is very fast."

"Like rock 'n' roll?" Jimmy asked.

"Faster," Jussi said.

"What happened last year?"

"Never mind what happened last year," Viktoria said. "Ivor made a fool of himself."

Marilyn, who was in the back seat with Jimmy, gave him a light poke in the ribs and put her finger to her lips.

Jussi saw her in his rear view mirror and tried to smile ruefully for Viktoria's benefit. "I'm sure he will behave himself this year," he said in what could not quite pass for a serious tone.

In a few minutes they were home. Viktoria briskly led the way into the house.

#

Later, after both Marilyn and Jimmy were asleep in the upstairs bedrooms, Viktoria lay awake beside Jussi. "I have to say something," she said, waking him.

Jussi turned to her, instantly alert. "What's the matter?" he asked. "Did you hear something?"

"No," Viktoria said. "What you told Jimmy in the car—when he asked you about the jig show—you should not have said what you said. He is too young, and he looks up to you. You made it sound as if you approved of having dancing girls perform in their underwear."

"They don't dance in their underwear," Jussi said, defensively. "I was being funny."

"You do not have to be funny in that way," Viktoria said. "And how do you know what the show is like?"

"Ivor told me. He saw it last year. He says it is a good show, nothing like what you might imagine."

"You called it a jig show. *Jig* is not a nice word."

"He didn't ask me what it meant. It's just a word."

"No, it is not just a word. It is like...*wop* and *DP* and *hanky*. When you find out what they mean, you feel ashamed of using them."

"*Honky*," Jussi said.

Viktoria ignored him. "You should not have said it. You know better. You remember when...I cannot remember his name, the one you said called you *butcher* and *overcoat* at the bush camp. You did not like it one bit."

"He called me *turncoat*."

"See? Words matter. This is almost thirty years later, and still you remember."

For a long time they both lay awake.

Finally, Jussi said, "I have to tell you something. Rabbit thinks he saw the man who writes the letters."

"Where?" Viktoria asked.

"At the circus. That's why he and I went up the midway. We were trying to follow him. It wasn't just the shooting gallery that sent Rabbit back into the war."

"Did you find him?"

"No. No, we didn't. What is odd, though, is that Rabbit didn't see anyone with him. The man must have come to the circus all by himself."

"So?"

"Nobody does that."

19 • FACE TO FACE

THE LETTER, addressed to *Herr J. Mantere* and mailed this time, arrived on Monday. There was no return address. Viktoria recognized the handwriting, and quickly put the envelope in the bedroom. Neither Marilyn nor Jimmy, she knew, would go into the room without asking permission. Jussi saw it on the night table when he changed out of his work clothes. He opened it immediately.

> *Herr Mantere*, the letter began, *I would like to meet with you soon. There is too much that I want to say to you for a letter. The time is not enough. Thursday I was very afraid when I saw you and your family at the CLE but I have to talk.*

Jussi read the letter quickly, his eyes skimming over the words to find the important parts, but the letter dissolved into a rambling narrative about how its writer had decided to go to the fair with his son but had felt uneasy about going.

Jussi skipped to the bottom. The last words were *Please be so kind to* but there was no second page, no signature. And the letter had not been checked for mistakes. *Odd*, Jussi thought.

Supper was already on the table when Jussi went into the kitchen. Marilyn and Jimmy were at their places; Ivor was not there.

Viktoria looked up and caught Jussi's eye.

He shrugged. *Later*, his body said.

"*Farfar*," Jimmy began, his mouth already full of food. A quick look from Viktoria stopped him. He raised his finger to signal that he was going to chew and swallow before speaking. "*Farfar*," he said at last, "in last night's paper there was an ad from Gibson Motors. It said that if you buy a 1955 Ford now, then give it back to them in November, December, or January, they'll give you a 1956 Ford free. How can they do that?"

"I'll tell you after supper," Jussi said. "Just let me eat in peace for a

219

while. But in the meantime, you think about it. See if you can come up with some possible answers."

"I'd be interested in knowing that, too," Marilyn said. She cut a piece of potato, picked it up with her fork, and let it hover over the plate. "And I'd like to know what's going on with the Baptists."

"Oh?" Viktoria said.

"In the same paper, there was an ad for yesterday's church service at Calvary, and it said that the sermon was going to be on what a Christian's attitude toward communism should be." She put the potato in her mouth, chewed, and swallowed. "And," she said, "the evening talk was entitled 'Wake up or Blow up.'"

"Is Calvary one of the churches near the cenotaph?" Jimmy asked.

"No," Jussi said, "but it should be."

"Jussi," Viktoria said, an edge to her voice. "That is only what the topics were. You do not know what the man said in the sermons."

Marilyn steered the conversation into safer waters. "Calvary's the one that's a block from here, at the top of the hill where Franklin Avenue meets John Street."

"You knew that already, didn't you?" Jussi asked Jimmy.

"Yes," Jimmy said, and he smiled mischievously.

"*Gud i himmel!*" Viktoria said, and she gave Jussi a light poke in the ribs. "He is going to be just like you when he grows up!"

"And like his father," Jussi said.

Amusement ran around and across the table, followed by a wisp of sadness that even Jimmy could feel.

#

Marilyn and Jimmy had been asleep for well over an hour when Viktoria compared letters.

"They are not the same," Viktoria said as they sat propped up by their pillows. She looked from one letter to the other. "The first is written more neatly, as if he was trying to make a good impression. But this second one, the one addressed to you, was written quickly. He did not bother to check it when he had finished writing. And where is the last page? How could he forget to include it?"

"I don't know," Jussi said. "But I'll bet you it comes tomorrow. He's found it by now, and it's probably in the mail already."

"Found it?"

"He was writing in a hurry. I think he was interrupted."

Viktoria did not offer an opinion. Instead, she asked, "Do you think the second page will be signed?"

"Yes," Jussi said. "I think this man is clearing his conscience. He will confess his name."

#

After work on Tuesday, Jussi drove past the shoemaker's shop and glanced at the window. No letter there. When he came into the kitchen at home, however, Viktoria looked at him, then looked toward the bedroom. The letter had arrived as expected.

Jimmy came running down the stairs from his room. "Guess what?" he said to Jussi. "Something about George."

"George has decided to keep speaking English like someone from Britain?" Jussi said.

"Yes, but that's not it. He's going to be a Scout!"

"Isn't he a little young?"

"He's going to join next year so that he can go to the next Jamboree."

"Ah."

"Three hundred Scouts are going from the Lakehead to the Jamboree in Niagara-on-the-Lake. They left today."

"Well," Jussi said. He thought of Anders, the boy tailor-made to follow orders, years ago.

"Did you ever want to be a Scout?"

"No," Jussi said. "I didn't."

"Did they have Boy Scouts when you were my age?"

"Yes, but now I have to change my clothes so that we can eat."

"I asked Ivor to have supper with us tonight," Viktoria said. "He stopped by at noon—"

"With fish," Jussi finished. "I know. He came by work today."

Viktoria raised an eyebrow, and Jussi nodded. Viktoria said only, "Marilyn is late."

"Probably missed the bus," Jussi said. He went into the bedroom and closed the door. He let his fingers touch the letter, but he did not open it.

Marilyn entered the house a moment later. "God, I need a holiday." Viktoria gave her a disapproving glance, which Marilyn chose to ignore. "Betty's talking about opening a second store. That's all she's going to be talking about for the next six weeks, until she realizes she'd lose money on it. Me, I'd like to go to the States—even Duluth—and stay in a motel with a coin-operated TV that gets *The $64,000 Question*. Now *that* would be a holiday."

She started for the stairs. "But I'll settle for a change of shoes before supper. These ones are killing me. And tomorrow Owen is taking me to the Finn Hall for dancing again. And I can hardly walk."

There was a knock on the side door, and Ivor came in. "Am I late?" he asked.

#

In bed, when Jussi and Viktoria were sure that Marilyn and Jimmy were asleep upstairs, Jussi opened the letter. There was a note with it, a piece of newspaper on which in block letters the writer had scrawled in pencil *SORRY THIS IS REST OF LETTER*. He showed it to Viktoria, then reached over to the night stand, opened the drawer, and took out the previous day's letter. He gave it to Viktoria, then looked at the new one.

"What were the last words?" he asked in a near-whisper.

"They are *Please be so kind to*."

Jussi continued, "*meet me. You can pick where and when. I will come. Put reply in shoemaker's window.* That's all."

"He signed it," Viktoria said, looking at the letter, "but I cannot read his name."

Jussi reached into the drawer once more and retrieved a magnifying glass. "The first letter is *A*, and the last name is *My*, double *l*, I think, *y* once more, then *silta*. *Myllysilta*. Jesus Christ!"

"What?" Viktoria sat up straight. "Is it someone you know?"

"Yes, in a way." Jussi said.

20 • MYLLYSILTA

THE NEXT DAY AT NOON, Jussi left his workers to have their lunch and drove past his home and into George Burke Park. At the end of the road he parked his car, got out, took off his work boots, waded across the creek, then put his boots back on.

In fifteen minutes he was at the clearing where the shacks stood, their tarpaper walls and roofs catching the sun's fierce rays. He knocked twice on Rabbit's door. After a moment Rabbit opened it.

"Well." Rabbit let puzzlement creep into his voice. "What brings you here?" He opened the door wide to let Jussi in. A book lay overturned on the small table with its single chair. "Come in, come in."

"Who else is around?" Jussi asked as he entered, ducking a bit to clear the top of the doorway.

"They've all gone to town," Rabbit said. "It's cooler by the lake than it is here in the bush."

Jussi sat down on the bench that Rabbit had fastened to the wall beside the door. A pair of rubber boots rested under the bench. Rabbit remained standing.

Jussi said, "He agrees to meet me. I get to say where and when."

"The letter-writer?"

Jussi nodded. "We got a letter from him yesterday—the second page of one he had sent two days ago." Before Rabbit could say anything, Jussi added, "He signed it this time. Myllysilta."

Rabbit frowned. "I know that name," he said. "I know it from somewhere. Did he give his first name?"

"Just the initial – *A*. No return address."

"*Aate?*" Rabbit ventured. "*Aksi, Alar, Akseli*—no, two syllables—*Alpa?* I know this name, there was a boy—*Antti!* His name is *Antti Myllysilta*. I met him." He took a breath. "*We* met him, Karl and I. On the train. He was going to Vasa on the train when Karl and I joined up to fight."

223

"That could be him," Jussi said. "What else do you remember?"

"He was nice," Rabbit said. "He could speak a little Swedish, enough to get by. He was with someone called Erik, a Finland-Swede. Karl and I went on to Vilppula. I don't know where Antti was sent. I remember that he didn't have a gun, and neither did I."

Rabbit suddenly stopped speaking. "*Mylly* is *mill*," he said, and sat down on the chair. "What is *silta?*"

"*Bridge*," Jussi said.

"Millbridge. He is Owen Millbridge's father?"

"I think so."

Be careful, Rabbit said to Ivor. "But Antti was friendly," Ivor said to Jussi. "He was funny."

"He was flying detachment," Jussi said. "Fifth column. It was his brothers who killed Fredric Svensson. And my mother."

"Did Antti...?" Rabbit couldn't finish the sentence.

"In his letter to Viktoria, he said he had nothing to do with my mother's murder."

"Do you believe him?" Ivor asked.

"I don't know. Words are only as true as the man who speaks them. He agrees that we should meet. That's all I know. The rest...." Jussi shrugged. "*Tulee mitä tulee.*"

Ivor gave a small laugh. "Vilho says that's what God said after he created Eve. Even He didn't know how things would turn out after that bit of work. Whatever would be would be."

Jussi didn't laugh. "What do you think I should do?" he asked.

Ivor didn't hesitate. "Meet him," he said. "But in a place where everyone knows where you two are, but they can't hear what you're saying."

"Such as?"

"You'll think of something."

Jussi considered, but for only a moment. "The meeting room upstairs at the Hemmet? I'd close the door."

"Perfect," Ivor said. "You'll have the advantage." *Well done*, Rabbit said. *Thank you.*

That evening, Jussi and the family got in the car and drove to Shuniah School for an outdoor summer concert by the MacGillivray Pipe Band. As the band marched into the school yard, Jussi could think of nothing but Mannerheim's parade in Helsinki. He hated the sound of the pipes, the beating of the drums, but he smiled and applauded with the rest of the family as the band marched by.

#

No Myllysilta was listed in the phone directory and, Jussi discovered, no Millbridge either. He wrote a note, put it in an envelope, and took it to the shoemaker on his way to work the next morning.

"Are you going to tell me what this is all about sometime?" the shoemaker asked.

"No." Jussi said, his voice neither friendly nor unfriendly.

"Suit yourself." He went back to his stitching.

Around three o'clock in the afternoon, Jussi told his men they could go home. The temperature had climbed above eighty-five degrees, the work was hard, and he was afraid someone might get heatstroke. And, he told himself, he needed the extra time to think out what he was going to say to Antti Myllysilta.

#

Friday brought a thunderstorm. The temperature rose into the mid-nineties, then dark clouds rolled over the city, and at noon, as Jussi entered the Hemmet, heavy rain began to fall.

He tipped his hat to the two women behind the long counter, said hello to one of the regulars who sat on a stool at the counter, and went up the stairs to the Meeting Room. If Myllysilta failed to show up, he decided, he would have lunch at the counter and then go home.

In the Meeting Room, he sat at the long table, where he could immediately see who entered the room. He left the door open. A couple of minutes later, he heard the creaking of the stairs.

The man who came in was younger than Jussi expected, but his face was drawn, his hands sinewy and lined with blue veins. He was dressed in a loose-fitting but expensive black raincoat, and had a black umbrella hung like a cane over his left arm. He was breathing hard from the climb.

The man said, "Jussi Mantere?"

Jussi nodded, then pointed to the chair opposite his. "Sit."

"Thank you." However, before he sat down, the man leaned his

225

umbrella against the wall by the door, angling it so that its wet fabric would not touch the wall. He hung his coat on the coat-rack beside it. His shirt, Jussi noticed, was light blue, freshly pressed—a dress shirt, not the shirt of a working man. His trousers, black and expensive-looking, had a perfect crease running down each pant leg. In his face Jussi could see something of Owen Millbridge, even a little of the son's softness, but the father's eyes were rheumy—the eyes of someone who knows he is dying.

Myllysilta went to the chair that Jussi had indicated. He put his hand on the table for support, then drew the chair out carefully and sat down heavily.

He asked, "Do you mind if we speak in Finnish?"

"Let us speak in English," Jussi said. "We are not in Finland."

"Very well." There was a long pause as Myllysilta searched for a way to begin. "I don't have long to live," he said at last.

"I can see that," Jussi replied tonelessly. "But death becomes you. Why did you ask to meet me?"

"I wanted to ask your forgiveness," Myllysilta said, "but I can see that would be too much."

Jussi waited a few seconds before answering. "That is true. I can't give that to you. I couldn't even if I wanted to. It isn't mine to give."

"I didn't kill your mother," Myllysilta said. "I wanted to tell you that." He folded his hands on the table, then sat quietly for a moment.

Jussi said nothing.

"My brothers sent me to the village, instead," Myllysilta said at last. "Gamlaby."

"To set up an alibi, I think."

"Maybe. But you killed them all."

"But not you. You're still alive, if not much alive." Jussi leaned back in his chair. "I could forgive you for the harm you did *me*." He considered. "I *could* do that, but I won't. And, unfortunately for you, no one can forgive the harm done to someone else. Even if I wanted to, and I don't, I can*not* forgive you the death of my mother. She has to do that, and since she's dead, she can't. God perhaps could forgive you, but I doubt it. For my mother's death you'll go to your grave with all your sins intact."

Myllysilta stared down at the table for a moment. "I have a son," he said at last.

Again, Jussi said nothing.

"I have a son and a daughter. My son is a good man. He has no mother—she died many years ago—but he is like her, not like me."

"Owen," Jussi said. "Yes, I know."

Myllysilta did not react. "To him, I am both his father and...someone he believes is—was—an upstanding, honest businessman."

"The sins of the fathers—" Jussi began.

Myllysilta cut him off. "Do not have to fall on their sons. God doesn't work like that."

"You believe in God?"

"Sometimes." Myllysilta added ruefully, "When it suits me." He leaned back in the chair. "But only if someone asks."

Jussi kept his face expressionless. "Tell me about your names," he said. "Myllysilta and Millbridge. Which are you?"

"I am Myllysilta in my head, Millbridge everywhere else. I'm Finn most places, of course, but when I was processed at Pier 7 I told them I was a Swede and that I wanted to be Andrew Millbridge. I had stolen a blank baptismal certificate from a church we burned down, and I had filled in the usual stuff, so when I told the officials I wanted my name changed there was no problem. I wasn't Antti Myllysilta on the baptismal certificate I showed them. When I started work in Canada, people called me Andy. Antti is my real first name. I used it even on the train going to Vasa."

"I know."

"Ivor remembered me?"

"Yes."

"Antti is dead. I left the name behind when I emigrated. Every time I hear *Andy*, though, especially when a Finn tries to say it, I think of *Antti*. It's my ghost name." A slight smile played over his lips. His eyes never left Jussi's face.

"What does your son call you?"

"Dad. He never says *Andy* or *Andrew*."

There was no warmth when Jussi spoke, no mercy, no retreat. "I'm curious. When did you come to Canada?"

"About the same as you, I think. I had enough of Finland. The Whites didn't make life easy. Didn't even let us honour our dead, didn't allow us to hold religious services, didn't even let us put up gravestones for a while. And everyone I knew was dead, or in prison, or crippled, and too many people knew that I was *lentävä osasto*. Such knowledge could be traded for bread, you know, and everyone was hungry. It wasn't safe for me to stay. And I had...*acquired*, let us say...quite a lot of money during our little war. Do you know, when you came to Canada you worked for me for a short time?"

Jussi looked intently at Myllysilta. It took a moment before he could see, beneath the pallid skin and haggard face, the features of the younger man. "You were the Finnish kid who was part owner of the lumber company. I never knew your name."

"Yes," Myllysilta said. "I was the kid."

Owen, Jussi thought, had some of the same facial features as the father, but softened, without the malice, without the eyes that spoke of skill in quick deception. He remembered the time in the shoemaker's shop when he had first seen Owen Millbridge and thought he looked familiar. It was not a memory he wanted to share with Myllysilta.

He drummed his fingers on the table then asked, "Why did you write the first letter, the one you sent to my wife?"

"I was drunk."

"I don't think so. I don't think you drink at all."

Myllysilta shrugged. *Believe what you want*, the gesture said.

Jussi stared at him. He waited.

"My son," Myllysilta said at last, "one day he told me that he had met a girl. At a dance. Marilyn Mantere, he said."

"You knew she was my daughter-in-law."

"No. Not then. But later." He was silent for a long time. "I had someone find out who she was, then who you were, of course, and I knew that you didn't know me. But I never...*investigated* you, not until Owen said her name." He didn't continue, but stared at the surface of the table. His left hand rested on top of his right one to keep it from trembling.

"You haven't come after me," Jussi said finally. "Why? Someone like you could easily find someone to kill someone like me."

Myllysilta was slow to reply. "Did you know," he said at last, "when the war started we were told to kill the smart ones first? Begin with the peacemakers, the reasonable ones—like that storekeeper, Fredric Svensson, for instance—the leaders, the intelligent, the influential. You can't have a revolution if no one wants to fight."

Jussi did not answer in the pause Myllysilta provided.

"Shopkeepers, clergymen, school teachers, anyone who might be able to gather followers, organize men, learn tactics. My brothers were not at your farm to kill your mother. They were there to kill you. But you know that, don't you? You've always known that. Felt guilty about it. But you were not home when we came to your house. And here in Canada...well, there was no hope of revolution. There was no need for war between us."

"You were part of the Red Terror," Jussi said. "People like you killed hundreds of Whites in the early months of the war. What makes you think that in Canada, even now, you're safe? Do you think the war happened so long ago that no one remembers it?"

"No," Myllysilta said. "But it's different here. This isn't Finland. And, besides, when the war turned in your favour, you took your revenge. We had killed a couple of thousand of you. You killed five times as many of us. You executed us. You put us in prisons and starved us. You broke our families into pieces and gave away our children."

"Yes, we did. You had frightened us. We did what frightened people do."

"I think you left Finland because of what you saw happening," Myllysilta said. "You didn't want to be part of the White Terror."

Jussi said nothing for a moment. "In your letter you said that you know about Ivor. You made it sound like a threat. Ivor is family, and I will keep him from harm. So do I need to kill you?" He paused. "I could make it look as if you killed yourself, you know. It would be easy to do."

"I don't mind," Myllysilta said off-handedly. "Do what you feel you must. My affairs are in order." He paused. "I know Ivor was in the war, of course. Nothing more. That is all I meant."

"Oh, you know more, I think. So perhaps I will talk to your son about you," Jussi said. "To find out what he knows about you. To let him know the truth about you." He leaned over the table toward Myllysilta. "A son has a right to know his father, wouldn't you say? A good father would have told him. A good father would have told his daughter, too. You have not told me her name."

Myllysilta replied after a heartbeat. "May. Her name is May. Please. I ask you—beg you—leave them out of this. You have no quarrel with them." He leaned forward. "Your quarrel is with me."

Jussi waited a moment and then leaned forward, too. "What year was your son born?"

"1922."

"And his mother—you met her here?"

"Yes."

"A Finnish girl?"

"English."

"What does she know about you?"

"She died in 1925. Tetanus. May was not yet a year old, Owen not quite three. Before my Annie died I told her nothing but lies. Useful ones—the same ones I tell my son."

Jussi did not want to ask who had raised the children. "Your daughter does not live here?"

"Toronto. I am a grandfather."

"And *lentävä osasto*," Jussi said.

"Not anymore. Here I am Andrew Millbridge to everyone."

"Except those who speak Finnish."

"To them, too. None of them come from Esse or anywhere close to it. No one knows my real past."

"Not even the man who spies on my grandson?"

"He knows what I want him to know. Nothing more."

"So what do you want from me?"

"If I cannot have forgiveness, then silence," Myllysilta said. "Just silence."

"What do you give in return?"

"Nothing but silence. I offer silence—the same silence I have kept for over thirty years. The silence that keeps the war at bay."

"And if your son and my daughter-in-law get married?"

"I will not be there to see the wedding. The doctor says I will not need to buy Christmas presents this year. Your silence will be my only gift, my last gift, to my children."

"They won't know they have received it."

"Does that matter? It doesn't matter to me," Myllysilta said.

"I will give you my answer in the usual way." Jussi got up abruptly and left the room, leaving Myllysilta alone.

A few minutes later, Myllysilta rose with difficulty from his chair and maneuvered down the stairs, his grip tight on the handrail. As he passed through the restaurant, he noted that none of the customers were speaking Swedish. It was all English now—not like at the Finn Hall.

#

That evening, after supper, Jussi and Jimmy sat on the lawn chairs outside. The sun was still high in the sky. It would not set for a few hours yet.

"*Farmor* was a cleaning lady when she came to Canada," Jimmy said. "Did she like that?"

"She thought she was lucky to be working," Jussi said. "And she liked being able to learn English. People she worked for always talked to her. One lady even gave her books to read—books in English. *Farmor* saved some money, bought a Swedish/English dictionary and word by word, expression by expression, she would translate a book into Swedish."

"That would have been hard."

"It was. And paper was expensive."

"Did she still work after you and she got married?"

"For a while." Jussi wet his thumb and index finger, pinched off the end of his cigarette and put the stub in his shirt pocket. "The only thing she didn't like about being a cleaning lady was having to speak to her employers in...what is it called? The third person."

Jimmy looked at him questioningly.

"Instead of saying *you*, she'd say *Mrs. Brown* or *Mrs. Smith*. It was more polite. It meant that Mrs. Brown and Mrs. Smith were higher up than their cleaning lady."

"It's not like that now."

"No," Jussi said, "it's not. Times have changed." *And all the old organizations—the Finnish CSJ with its threats and its red passports for workers, the Industrial Workers of the World and its union drives, have turned into sports and social clubs. Beatings and marches and protests have become gymnastics and plays and Finnish language lessons.*

After a while he and Jimmy went inside. The house was still very hot, very humid. *Today,* Jussi thought, *is the last hot day of summer. We have passed the middle of August, and now the earth begins to cool. In a month or so, the leaves will turn, and it will be fall.* Myllysilta had said he didn't think that he would live to see Christmas. Jussi wondered if he would see the last of autumn's colours.

21 • WATER

VIKTORIA SAID QUIETLY, "I am worried about Ivor." It was not what Jussi had expected her to say. He put his pillow behind him and leaned on it. Viktoria did the same. Upstairs, they knew, Marilyn and Jimmy slept.

"Oh?" Jussi said.

"He is talking to himself more and more. He was in the back yard when you were with Myllysilta. He was sitting on the lawn chair by the shed, talking to himself again. Sometimes he addressed Rabbit; sometimes it was like Rabbit was talking to Ivor. Is he going crazy?"

"He's...*divided,*" Jussi said, finding at last the word he wanted. "He's much better than he was right after the war, but still, he has better days and worse days. Did you know that one of the first things he told his mother when he got back from the war was that he died, that he was killed by the ghost of a girl he had shot?"

"No."

"I heard this from his mother, not from him. There are things he cannot speak to us about—cannot tell anyone, anymore."

"And when he talks to himself?"

"Rabbit and Ivor." Jussi was quiet for a moment. "I think Rabbit is the part of him that is always fearful, the child in him, the one that stays in hiding. Ivor is the part that tries to cope—the adult, the part that lives the outward life. Fear makes a man think—and Rabbit's always afraid, always thinking—but fear also lets him look ahead, shows him how to avoid trouble or to get out of it when it comes out of nowhere. A man who knows how to cope is more free to see the funny side of things, so Ivor tells the jokes, and Rabbit never laughs."

Jussi paused for some time before he continued. "I am being far too serious. But, you know, in a war I think that Rabbit would be the general and Ivor would be his aide de camp."

"We call him both Rabbit and Ivor. Is this something we should stop doing?"

"I don't think so. He doesn't seem bothered by it."

"Should we call a doctor?"

"No, there's nothing a doctor could do. Rabbit's bothered by the business with Myllysilta. When we've got that fixed, he'll be back to normal. What's normal for him, anyway."

"At the circus. Rabbit told Ivor to run after Myllysilta—which he did, taking Rabbit with him—and Rabbit was scared by the noise of the train and the shooting gallery. Is that it?"

"I think so."

"I think you could have become one of those psychologists—like Fred."

"Freud," Jussi said automatically. Then, "Woman, are you pulling my leg?"

"Maybe a little. Sometimes you think too much and talk too little."

"It's funny," Jussi said, "Myllysilta said I was the smartest of the smart. He has no idea how clever Rabbit is."

Viktoria adjusted her pillow. "What did Myllysilta want?"

"He wanted me to promise to keep quiet about everything."

"Why?"

"He knows his son is interested in Marilyn, and he loves his son. He says he is not the same person that he was in Finland. He must have been...I don't know...eighteen or nineteen then. Closer to your age." He paused to keep himself from mentioning Karl. "He told me his doctor tells him he'll be dead by Christmas."

"Do you believe him?"

Jussi did not speak immediately. Then slowly he said, "I don't know."

Viktoria put her hand on his arm.

"He seemed sincere," Jussi continued, "but he also said that he knows Ivor was in the war, as if he was hinting that he knows Ivor was a child soldier and an executioner. I pressed him on what he knows about Ivor, and he said that all he knows is that he was in the war."

"Do you think he was telling you the truth?"

"About his illness? Yes, he smells of death to me. And his skin has that cold and shiny look...he can hardly get out of a chair. But about Ivor? I don't trust what he said."

"What did you tell him?"

"I was angry. I told him that if I wanted to, I could kill him and do it so that no one would ever know it was me."

"Jussi! Could you do that?"

"I could have at one time. The day his brothers killed my mother, it would have been easy to kill him. If he had been at our home, I would have killed him with the rest."

"And now?"

"I'm not sure. Maybe. Some days it seems as if my mother was killed yesterday, or maybe even this morning. And Fredric Svensson, he was a good man and his death was never paid for."

Jussi had to talk about Karl now. "And Karl...Karl was not killed by Myllysilta—at least that's his story—but Myllysilta admits to defiling his body."

"By shooting him in the back."

"And taking his boot," Jussi said. "But you know, there's something about Myllysilta's story that doesn't hold water."

"What is that?"

"He says that he took Karl's boot because then he would get paid for a killing. One he didn't do."

"Yes?"

"So how could he still have the boot? Shouldn't it be in somebody else's hands, the hands of the man who paid him, maybe? And something else—the idea that Myllysilta had to collect a shoe or a boot from the victim in order to be paid is absurd. No one would just pay a man on receipt of a boot. Battlefields are littered with bodies and with boots. Myllysilta could have picked up hundreds, no killing required."

Jussi and Viktoria talked, and thought, and talked some more, far into the morning.

#

On Sunday, Rabbit rode to church with the family and returned home with Jussi. They drove past the shoemaker's shop, but there was no note in the window. Jussi didn't expect one—Myllysilta was waiting on a note from him—but he wanted to see anyway.

As soon as Jussi shut off the car's engine in his driveway, and before he could open the driver's door, Rabbit asked, "Well?"

Jussi told him about his meeting with Myllysilta. He held nothing back.

"I think," Rabbit said, but there was a long pause before he next spoke. "The boot. There are too many possibilities. For instance, if Myllysilta's story is all true, he is still holding things back from you, such as the name of the man who paid him. That is significant. If his story is false—"

"There may be no such man. Myllysilta may have been no one's agent but his own."

"True. But another thing. If you were Myllysilta, would you do what he has done? I mean, would you use the display in a shoemaker's shop to attract attention? Send a letter to Viktoria? These are not things a sane man would do."

"You think he's crazy?"

"I think...I don't know what to think. It is possible."

They talked for almost half an hour. Then Jussi remembered. "Dammit! Church." He looked at his pocket watch. "I have to go. We will talk tomorrow. I'll buy you lunch at the Hemmet."

"Excellent." Rabbit got out of the car.

Jussi drove quickly to church, arriving just before the doors opened to let the congregation go home to their Sunday dinners.

"What did Ivor want?" Marilyn asked Jussi as they headed down Pearl Street.

"Just to talk," Jussi said.

"*Farfar*," Jimmy said, "do you think the city pool on Cumberland is going to be open today? The paper said the water in Boulevard Lake is so low that they're pumping water from behind the dam to fill the pool."

"It's been a dry summer. Is the pool usually open on Sundays?"

"I'm not sure," Jimmy said.

"What about that dam you made?"

"There's hardly any water in the creek anymore. And it doesn't rise behind the dam now. It just runs through the cracks between the rocks."

"How shallow is it?"

"Maybe six inches. We can still catch crayfish but we can't swim."

"So go catch them," Jussi said. "All you need for that are your three buddies and four glass jars. Keep your eye on the weather, though. I think we'll get a touch of rain." *He will be safer with his friends*, he thought.

#

After lunch, Jimmy found his friends. By three o'clock in the afternoon they were at Spider Dam, comparing notes about the circus. Jimmy didn't talk very much, so he wouldn't have to explain Uncle Ivor. None of his friends seemed to notice. George was too busy complaining about the heat.

Half an hour later a man, dressed in dark clothing so that they would not see him, crouched down among the trees across the creek. The man watched as they carefully lifted flat rocks from the creek bottom and made the crayfish swim backwards into the water-filled jar held just behind its tail. A short distance away, Rabbit watched the man.

I would not have guessed this, Rabbit said.

Nor I, Ivor replied.

Ivor and Rabbit waited until the boys had finished playing. The man had been waiting too. They followed the man until he crossed the creek at the shallows near the running track and stage of the Finnish sports club. Their quarry continued along Montgomery Street. He would, they knew, walk right past Jussi's home. Where he would go after that was obvious, too.

22 • AIR

"I RECOGNIZED HIM from the Finn Hall," Ivor said. He and Jussi sat at a booth in the Hemmet, keeping their voices low, using Swedish for even more privacy. They had almost finished their meal. "He's one of the 'old boys' there. One of those that went to Karelia in the 1930s to live in the workers' paradise, but came back a few years later. He works some of the dances."

"He may have seen Marilyn there."

"With Owen."

"Ahh," Jussi said. "You think he is Myllysilta's man?"

"I'm sure of it."

"Why was he watching the boys?"

Ivor considered. "He did not seem to be much *interested* in watching them," he said finally. "He is not a man who is...attracted, shall we say...to young children." Rabbit retreated to a place of safety. "He kept taking out his watch, chasing away the blackflies," Ivor said. "He did not want to be there."

"So Myllysilta paid him just to see where Jimmy spends his time?"

"That's what it seems like to me."

"It doesn't make sense." Jussi reached into his shirt pocket, took out first his pack of cigarettes, then the small box of matches. He shook an unfiltered cigarette from the pack, got a match from the box, then lit the match with a flick of his thumbnail.

Ivor let Jussi complete the ritual before speaking. "I think that Myllysilta wants to know what *you* are like."

"By finding out what Jimmy is like?"

"Perhaps. I think he believes that 'the child is the father of the man.' So he looks to Jimmy to see what you were like as a child and, consequently, what you are like now."

"Why does he want to know what I am like?" Jussi asked.

"A man wants to know who is going to kill him," Ivor said. He took a bite of his salt fish sandwich. "This is good," he said, his mouth full.

"You think I'm going to kill him?" Jussi asked.

Ivor laid the sandwich down on his plate. "I think that's what *he* wants," he said, though it was Rabbit's thought.

"He's going to die soon, anyway," Jussi said.

"Sometimes *soon* isn't soon *enough* for a man."

Jussi reached into his pants pocket and put a dollar in coins on the table. "Here," he said, "This should be enough. I have to get back to work." He slid out of the booth.

"You're not having lunch?"

"No time," Jussi said.

"Are you going to meet with him again?" Ivor asked.

"I need to think about this," Jussi said. "But, yes, I'll meet him." As he headed for the door he nodded to the waitress. It was code. Ivor, she understood, had enough money to pay for the meal and she did not need to ask.

Outside, rain had begun to fall, and the wind blowing toward the east carried the smell of the city's incinerator all the way to Bay Street. Jussi pinched off the end of his cigarette and put the butt back into the pack before walking to the car.

#

"Summer is almost over," Viktoria said after lunch.

Jimmy brought his plate over to her so that she could wash it. He got a dish towel from the rack and began to dry the dishes. "It's too soon. It won't be September for another two weeks, though."

"Ten days," Viktoria said. "I will bet the water in the creek is getting colder, is it not?"

"A little bit."

When Jimmy had finished drying he said, "Someone should invent an electric dishwasher."

"And a dryer for clothes that can iron and fold the clothes, too, I suppose," Viktoria said. She gave Jimmy a light poke in the ribs. "And then we could all get fat and sit around watching TV all day until we can't think anymore and have forgotten how to talk."

Jimmy laughed. "It doesn't sound so bad."

Viktoria gave him another poke. "After a while we would probably forget how to cook, too. And then when the police came to the house they would find a lot of dead bodies—skinny ones, their big eyes staring at the oven."

At the end of the day, Marilyn showed up for supper a half-hour late. "Owen stopped by the store at closing," she said. "I missed the bus. I invited him for supper on Wednesday. Is that okay?"

Jussi left the decision up to Viktoria.

"Of course," Viktoria said. "We will enjoy meeting him."

#

On Wednesday, Marilyn was home early, even before noon. "Just one customer all morning," she explained. "What are we having for supper? I'll help."

Viktoria smiled. "Good," she said.

"What should we do first?" Marilyn asked.

"How about you eat lunch?" Viktoria said. "I bought a ham at the Co-Op, but it will not take long to cook once it is in the oven. Relax a while. But not too long. You can take the Electrolux and vacuum."

"Where's Jimmy?"

"Upstairs." She whispered, "He is reading that comic book we are not supposed to know about, so make a little noise before you go upstairs. Give him a few seconds to hide it."

Owen Millbridge arrived at exactly five-thirty. Marilyn was standing at the door as he parked his car in front of the house, got out, and came up the front stairs. She opened the door almost before he knocked. He had dressed in casual slacks, a freshly-pressed light blue shirt, and newly shined shoes. Forewarned, he took off his shoes at the door and put them on the mat inside the front porch.

"I hope I'm not late," he said.

In the living room, out of sight, Jussi rolled his eyes heavenward and got out of his chair. He went to greet Millbridge. Viktoria, who had been inspecting the ham, closed the oven door and came to the front porch with him.

"Owen," Jussi said, extending his hand. Millbridge shook it firmly. "I am Marilyn's father-in-law, Jussi, and this is my wife, Viktoria. My grandson, Jimmy, is upstairs but," he raised his voice enough to carry, "he will be down soon."

The floor upstairs creaked a few times, and Jimmy came down the stairs.

"Mr. Millbridge, my grandson, Jimmy," Jussi said.

"Pleased to meet you, sir," Jimmy said. He and Millbridge shook hands.

"Come to the living room," Jussi said, and led the way. Millbridge and Marilyn followed; Jimmy went back upstairs to his room. Viktoria returned to the kitchen and began to take out the good dishes and cutlery.

"Marilyn," Jussi said as she followed Millbridge into the living room, "perhaps you could give your mother a hand in the kitchen."

"Yes, of course," Marilyn said, a little flustered. She went into the kitchen.

"We have met once before," Jussi said, motioning for Millbridge to sit down on the sofa.

"Oh? I don't—"

"It was in July, I think. You were in the shoemaker's shop on Oliver Road. The shoemaker, as I recall, mentioned that your parents were from Finland."

"Just my father. My mother was born here. She died many years ago."

"I am sorry to hear that," Jussi said. "Millbridge is an odd name for a Finn. Your father changed it?"

"He was a Niemi," Millbridge said. "Niemi, I understand, means peninsula in Finnish, and my father thought that if he called himself Andrew Peninsula—his name is actually Antti—it would sound silly, especially if some well-meaning people tried to pronounce it as a Finnish name, so he chose Millbridge instead."

"Ah. That was wise. Where in Finland did his family live?"

"Well," Millbridge said, "it's not even in Finland now. The family was from Karelia."

"Yes, which is mostly in Russia these days. You have relatives still there?"

Before he could answer, Viktoria called "Supper!" from the kitchen.

Jussi had sense enough to shift the supper conversation to articles that had appeared in the newspaper.

Supper was followed by dessert—rice pudding with a little cinnamon on top. When the meal was over, Jussi and Millbridge went to the living room to continue talking. Marilyn washed the dishes; Jimmy dried them; Viktoria put them away.

"So," Jussi began when he and Owen Millbridge were seated, "Your father's family is from Karelia. Your mother's?"

"That's a bit of a mystery. Her father was a trapper, a Scot. She may have told me once or twice what part of Scotland he was from, but I was very young—she died before I turned three—and I really don't have any memories from that time."

"You have a sister, a brother?"

"A sister," Owen said. "May. She lives in Toronto. She's two years younger."

"And your father, he must have come to Canada around the same time I did."

"When was that?"

"1920," Jussi said. "I told them I was a Swede so I could get in."

"My father did the same thing," Owen said, "though I'm not sure what year. Early, though."

"He speaks Swedish?"

"No, just Finnish, and English, of course. He knows a little—what does he call it—kitchen Swedish. Mostly swear words. Enough to have fooled the customs agents." Owen laughed. It was an unforced laugh, a friendly laugh. "He was a bit of a wild man, I understand, before he married my mother. Drank a lot, swore a lot. She tamed him, though."

"Do you live with your father?"

"No, I have my own place. He values his privacy."

"In Finland," Jussi said, "was your father Red or White?"

"Sorry?"

"When he came to Canada...did he support the Communists or the Socialists?"

"I don't think he was interested in politics at all," Owen said uneasily. "In fact, I don't think he ever voted."

"Hey, Dad," Marilyn called from the kitchen, "no more grilling. Play nice."

"Okay," Jussi called back. "I'll behave." He laughed. "When I came to Canada I went to work in the lumber camps."

"My father had invested in a lumber company early on, I think," Owen said. "He was a silent partner. I can't remember the name of the company, though. Later on he went into wholesaling—selling building supplies, furniture. Then real estate."

"Lots of immigrants—Finns, Swedes, Norwegians—worked in

the lumber camps. In some of them, if you weren't a Red, the guys who supported the Red side in the war in Finland gave you a hard time."

"There was a war in Finland?"

"1918," Jussi said.

"I didn't know that," Owen said. "World War One, though, right?"

"It became part of it," I guess, "Jussi said. But it didn't start out that way. Or maybe it did. The Russians—"

"Jussi!" Viktoria's voice this time. She spoke his name as if she were concerned that Jussi would bore Owen with a long and rambling history of the war.

Jussi realized that her concern was quite different, and he changed the subject.

At last, the dishes done, Marilyn and Owen left to see a movie.

A short while later, Jussi went out to the back yard to smoke.

Jimmy was just starting up the stairs, going to his room to read, when Viktoria said, "Jimmy, come talk to me for a minute." *He is the same age Karl and I were, back at the farm when we were learning* Musta Maija *and* Rabbit *crawled near our feet. I felt so grown-up then, but Jimmy seems so much younger than I was.*

Viktoria had him sit at the table. She had set out a small plate of gingerbread cookies and passed the plate to him.

"What do you think of Mr. Millbridge?" Viktoria asked.

"Cookie, first," Jimmy said, and helped himself. He took a bite then pretended to consider the question he had known she would ask.

"He's very ordinary," Jimmy said after he had eaten a bite. "Calm, and..." he considered, "not flashy." He took a second bite. "He's okay." A third bite. Jimmy let the chewing go on for a few seconds past its due date. "I'm sure we'll get along," he said, and winked at Viktoria.

"Good answer," Viktoria said. "Have another cookie."

A few minutes later, Jussi came back in, and Jimmy went up to his room. He could hear parts of the conversation in the kitchen but made little sense of it, so he put on his 3-D glasses and began reading *Crypt* once more.

Downstairs, Jussi and Viktoria spoke quietly and in Swedish. "Myllysilta's son does not know his history," Jussi said.

Viktoria poured each of them a cup of coffee and they sat at the kitchen table. "His father has given him a story to take its place. One that cannot lead anywhere."

"A lie," Jussi said.

"A wall, I think, set between then and now, between Finland and Canada."

"A lie nonetheless."

"A useful one though," Viktoria said. "A...deliberate forgetting."

"Something to make his son think highly of him."

"Something that does not punish the son for the crimes of the father."

With effort, Jussi kept his voice low. "Do you take his side?"

"Is there a side? Here, in Port Arthur, almost forty years after the war? Are there still sides?"

"Some would think so."

"Well, I am not taking a side, and Rabbit is not, and Marilyn and Jimmy are not, and I do not think you should take one either. There are better things to do."

Jussi stared down into his cup for a moment, and when he lifted it to his lips, his hand shook. "I saw things. I did things. They don't go away."

"I know," Viktoria said. "And for us, for you, but for me, too, it is important that they not be made to disappear. All these things are part of us, part of our...." She paused to search for the exact word she wanted.

"Culture?" Jussi said.

"No, not culture...structure," Viktoria said. She had found the word—*byggnad*. "What we have built, what makes us solid, like those beams you place under a house when you raise it up."

Upstairs, Jimmy put the comic down and sat listening. He did not understand much of what his grandparents were saying, especially when they started using words they rarely used, but he knew from the tone that they had disagreed, and that the disagreement had come to a stop and all was well once more.

Sleep, when it came later, came gently, and he slept untroubled by dreams.

23 • FIRE

ON THURSDAY, Ivor arrived just after supper.

Jussi answered the knock. "Well, you might be late for supper, but you're in time for dessert."

"We need to talk," Ivor said. He made no move to come in. "Can we go for a ride?"

"I suppose so," Jussi said. He called to Viktoria, "I'm going to show Ivor the Lagrue house. Save some pie for me. We'll be back in a while."

"Not too late," Viktoria said. "You have work tomorrow."

He put on his shoes and went to the car with Ivor. "What's this about?" he asked as he got in.

"Did Owen Millbridge tell you anything about his father?" Ivor asked.

"Yes," Jussi said. "For one thing, Owen thinks that Myllysilta's name before he changed it was Niemi, and that he came from Karelia." Jussi started the car.

Ivor laughed. "That's like a Canadian going to Finland and telling everyone his name is Smith, and he lives in Toronto."

"I don't think Owen has any idea of his father's past." When they were on Montgomery Street, Jussi asked, "Where are we going? I told Viktoria I was going to show you the Lagrue house."

"Head there then." Ivor said. "It's as good a place as any."

"For what?"

"I have a story for you. Something Vilho told me."

"What's the story?"

"Wait until we get there. You might have to concentrate on driving."

It took less than five minutes to get to the small house on Secord Street. Jussi turned off the ignition. "Well?"

"I was telling Vilho about Marilyn and Owen Millbridge," Ivor said. "Vilho says, 'Owen's a good kid, but I wouldn't trust that father of his. One day he's reading *Vapaus*, the communist newspaper, and the next he's reading *Kanadan Uutiset*, the social democratic one.'"

"Playing both sides," Jussi said.

"Maybe. Vilho says he plays the violin." Jussi didn't smile, so Rabbit continued. "Or, maybe, he's trying to *get along* with both sides." Ivor added quickly, "Being a businessman."

"What else?" Jussi asked. "That's not all you wanted to tell me."

"No. There are two other things. The first is that Myllysilta got pretty rich pretty fast, and that when Owen was ten or eleven, Myllysilta bought him a horse."

"A Don?"

"Yes! Vilho doesn't know where he managed to get it from, but it was a Don—an honest-to-God Cossack horse."

"That's interesting, but...." Jussi didn't say *this is hardly earth-shattering information.*

"The second thing is that in the early years, just after he first came to Port Arthur, Myllysilta had a friend."

"A friend?"

"Someone who had known him in Finland. Vilho says that every so often, the three of them used to drink together, and Myllysilta always got angry, really angry, when the friend called him Millie or teased him about his violin. And then one day, the friend just disappeared. Vilho thinks—"

Jussi finished his sentence. "That Myllysilta killed him."

"He didn't say that, but that's the idea. The body was found a couple of days later in a burned-out shack that the friend lived in near the John Street gravel pit. Lots of empty glass bottles, some of them melted."

"The fire was hot, then," Jussi said. "What about after the friend disappeared?"

"A year later, Myllysilta met a woman."

"Annie," Jussi said.

"They got married, Owen came along, and Myllysilta became, or pretended to become, a changed man."

"The Don," Jussi said. "Does such a man buy such a horse?"

If he feels safe, Rabbit said. "If he feels safe," Ivor echoed.

"He doesn't feel safe now, I imagine," Jussi said.

"Watch your back," Rabbit said. "Money can still buy someone to do the dirty work."

#

The next day, Friday, after breakfast Jussi wrote a note. *Hemmet*, it said. *Upstairs. Saturday. Noon.* He delivered it to the shoemaker just before lunch. That night, Jussi and Viktoria talked for a long time.

24 • EARTH

MYLLYSILTA WAS ALREADY SEATED at the table upstairs when Jussi arrived. "What have you decided?" Myllysilta asked in Finnish.

Jussi pulled out a chair opposite Myllysilta and sat down. He didn't answer the question immediately. When he did, he spoke English.

"I have heard a number of things about you," he said. "Most of what you have told me is...what do the English call it? A fabrication. A ready-made lie. And I have spoken to your son, and asked him about you. He knows almost nothing of your real past. You are a skillful liar. You know how to weave one lie into another and leave no holes. I think he believes everything you have told him."

"I think you have spoken to your friend, Ivor," Myllysilta said in English, leaving the bait untouched. The stumbling English of his letter to Viktoria had cast off its heavy Finnish cadence. Only a trace of the accent remained.

"I think you killed a man and burned his body so that your secrets would not piss out of him when he was drunk," Jussi said.

"Perhaps," Myllysilta said. "That is something I certainly might have done, before I fully became Millbridge."

"I think you bought your young son a Don because you still like to remember the feeling of being an outlaw on a warrior's horse."

"A Don is a fine horse. The Cossacks knew how to breed strength and athleticism into both their horses and themselves."

"Is that what you pretend to be—a Cossack? You are no more a Cossack now than you were the day you rode away from Svensson's murder."

"Was that the storekeeper's name?" Myllysilta's eyes bored into Jussi.

"You know it was. You said it the last time we met. And it is the name you used in your letter, when you claimed to have killed him," Jussi said evenly. "You didn't take part in the killing, though. Except

247

to act as a spy for your brothers, I think. You were the boy who rode away. Weren't you? One of your brothers stole some candies for you, didn't he?"

"If that is what you want to believe."

"At the time I thought you had been one of the killers. But you weren't. You were just a boy told to keep your eyes open and not get into trouble."

"I was young."

"Were you also the boy acting as lookout the day my mother was killed?"

Myllysilta shrugged. "Yes. But I had no part in the killing. My brothers would not let me. They thought I would not have killed a woman, but I would. I did. Several. Just not your mother." He paused and then, as if the question had something to do with Jussi's mother, he asked, "Are you a member here? A member of the Scandinavian Home Society?"

"I'm not a joiner," Jussi said.

"A legacy of the war I think," Myllysilta said. "No church, no political party, no fraternal organization—not even Kansallisseura, the Loyal Finns. No boss telling you what to do. Just you, just your decisions. No Red, no White, no visits to 'the old country.' All because of the war."

Jussi stared expressionlessly at Myllysilta for a few seconds, then said, "Tell me about your friend, the one who died, the one whose body you burned."

"He died," Myllysilta said. "He drank himself to death. I didn't need to kill him. I just needed the story of his death to be useful. I had gone to his shack to ask him to do a job for me and found him dead, so I burned down his shack, and every time I was asked about his death, I smiled and said I knew nothing." Myllysilta laughed ironically. "People became afraid of me, for a while. But they didn't pass on what they thought they knew to their children. And no one ever spoke to Annie about it either."

"Vilho thinks you killed the fellow. Are you saying that he knows only that part of the story?"

"And coughs it up whenever he feels the need. Vilho knows what I want him to know, what *everybody knows*," Myllysilta said, "and he does what I ask him to do." He paused as if considering, then mockingly he said, "It is in the *stories*, you know—not in the truth—

that the power lies to change men's lives." He smiled impishly then became serious once more. "Vilho believes what I tell him. Such men are useful."

"Not to a dead man, Antti Myllysilta, and you, for all your bluster, are surely dying."

"That I am." Myllysilta folded his hands on the table and leaned forward. "In dying, a man has to give up much. I will not die forgiven, I know that, but will you, for all my supposed wickedness, agree to keep my past a secret from my son? My death is of no concern to me, but his life is. And I think it is of concern to you, too."

"You never speak of your daughter. Why is that?"

"We are...I do not know the word...*vieraantuneet*."

"Estranged."

"Is that the word? She will have nothing to do with me."

"Why is that?"

Again, the shrug.

The steps outside the upper room creaked. Both men kept silent as one of the waitresses came up the stairs.

"Do you men want anything?" she said, poking her head in at the open door. "Coffee? Pie?"

"Coffee," Myllysilta said. "With cream. My throat is dry. And...do you have lemon pie?" The thick Finnish accent was back; both *th* and *d* had once again become *t*.

"We do."

"Double it up," Jussi said.

"It won't take a minute," the waitress said, and she headed back down.

Jussi waited until he was sure that she was downstairs again. "Did you know that rage makes a man see only what is in front of him? When I killed the last of your brothers I felt like I was peering down a tunnel, and the bullets went exactly where I was looking."

"Interesting," Myllysilta said. "That isn't how it is for me."

"You learned to kill in the war," Jussi said, "but not in rage." It was almost a question.

"No, not in rage. There was no tunnel. I knew exactly what I was doing. And felt almost nothing. A little excitement, perhaps. Sometimes pleasure. But I didn't kill your mother."

Jussi raised his right hand, his fingers making the sign for *one minute.* The waitress was coming back up the stairs. She came into the room with two cups of coffee in one hand, two pie plates and a small pitcher of cream in the other, and set them down on the table without spilling anything.

"If I tried to do that," Jussi said to her, "there would be broken china on the stairs and lemon pie from my elbow to my chin."

The waitress laughed. "Practice, practice, practice," she said. "Sugar's on the table. Enjoy the pie." She went back down the stairs to the hubbub of the restaurant.

"It is easy for a young man to kill," Myllysilta said.

"Not for most," Jussi said. "Most need to practice."

"When I met Annie, my life changed."

"You came to Jesus, did you?" Jussi's voice was wry but not bitter.

"No, nothing like that. I walked out of a cold room and into one where a fire was going, there was coffee on the table, and the smell of cinnamon in the air."

"Not lemon?"

Myllysilta sighed. "No, not lemon. Apple pie is still the best, with lots of cinnamon. But this is not a day for apple pie, nor for Annie."

"Is it a day for truth? Or are you going to tell me once again that you were paid by a man who gave you money for a soldier's boot?"

Myllysilta drummed his fingers. Then he stopped and said, "It doesn't really matter, does it? I was paid or I was not. I lie or I tell the truth. All that matters to me, and to you, is that my child will be happy." He splayed his fingers on the table like cards laid down. "So. Will you keep my secret?" he asked.

For a moment, Jussi didn't respond. *My secret* triggered a memory of the Grafton gun. He smiled. Long ago, the guns had turned him and Anders into hunters, yes, but also the hunted. They could hunt moose only if they could fool the Russians, who were looking for the guns. Once, they had been stopped, and the cart with its secret compartment had been searched. The compartment had worked as promised.

Jussi made himself look serious. He and Viktoria had made their decision the previous night. It was hard to remember that Viktoria had been about Jimmy's age when Jussi had gone to see Anders about the guns. She had grown into wisdom.

"Yes," he said. Owen should not be punished for his father's sins.

He leaned back in his chair and stared at Myllysilta. "But I have one condition—*you* must keep it as well. I want you to promise me, on Annie's soul, that you will never confess your secret to your son, never tell it to your daughter, bear it to your grave. I am not granting you mercy, Antti Myllysilta. If there is a God, I want you to die unshriven, unforgiven, unable to escape into a merciful death."

Jussi took his fork and lifted a small piece of pie to his mouth, savoured it, and swallowed. "When the gates of Hell gape open, I want the fires to eat you whole. I want to stand over your grave and smell the sulfur and gunpowder rise, reeking, from the soil beneath my feet."

Myllysilta waited a full minute before he spoke. "So be it," he said. He nodded. "You have poetry in you, Jussi Mantere. And, for what it is worth—I know it's not much—you also have my word. Thank you. The pie is very good, don't you think?"

25 • LABOUR DAY

ON LABOUR DAY, early in the afternoon, Ivor showed up breathless at Jussi's home. Jussi and Viktoria were sitting in the back yard; Jimmy and his friends were at the creek; Marilyn had gone with Owen to Boulevard Lake to sit in the sun and enjoy the day.

"Myllysilta's killed himself," Ivor said. "At the Hanging Tree. I saw the body."

"Oh, my God," Viktoria said. "Has anyone gone to find Owen and let him know?"

"No one else knows," Ivor said, carefully slowing his speech so that all the words would come out as normally as possible. "I go there sometimes. It's a quiet place. He wasn't wearing his left shoe."

"No one else knows yet?" Jussi asked.

"No one."

"One shoe missing?"

"Yes."

Jussi turned to Viktoria. "If Marilyn and Owen come back before we do, say nothing to them about this. Tell them I've gone to have a look at the job so that I can get the boys organized when we start work again tomorrow."

Viktoria nodded.

Jussi turned to Ivor. "There's something not right about this," he said. "We need to go look."

Riverside Cemetery off Oliver Road was on the main route west out of Port Arthur. Because the city limit was just past the cemetery, the "last stop" with its "hanging tree" was, literally and figuratively, the last stop before leaving.

As the car approached the cemetery, Ivor said, "Park in the cemetery parking lot like visitors do. There is a shortcut we can take."

Jussi pulled over and stopped just outside the cemetery gates. He and Ivor got out of the car. Ivor leading, they entered the cemetery grounds and walked toward the river that ran close by the cemetery's

252

western edge. They scrambled down the drop to the river's edge, then followed the river when it turned west.

"A few hundred feet and we're there," Ivor said. A minute or two later they were at the tree.

Myllysilta hung lifeless from the rope, his feet inches above the ground. He had soiled himself in death, and his body stank of the fluids and feces it had released.

Ivor pointed. "See, his shoe is gone. I looked around a bit, but it's not here."

Jussi did not bother searching. If Ivor said the shoe was nowhere to be found, a search would be fruitless. "How did he get here, do you think?"

Rabbit considered the problem. "Either someone dropped him off at Oliver Road, or else he walked here from his home," Ivor said. "To walk all this way, though...it's a long way for a sick old man to walk."

"I think that's just what he did," Jussi said. "He walked here. He lives—lived—on High Street, but if he used the streets along the top of the city, instead of going down the High Street hill and then up the hill on Oliver Road, the walk would be relatively easy, no hills at all, and it wouldn't take longer than the time it takes Jimmy to go downtown with his friends to see a movie. Forty minutes, maybe. Myllysilta was sick, but if he was determined enough, he could do it."

"You really think he walked?"

"Yes," Jussi said. "Last night, maybe. And if he told no one that he was going to do this, nobody would know about it, nobody would take one of his shoes."

"I don't understand," Ivor said. *I think I do*, Rabbit whispered.

"Let's follow the path he used—back to Oliver Road. I think I know where the shoe is."

Two minutes later they emerged from the bush.

Jussi said, "The shoe is going to be right across the road." He looked left and right for signs of cars, saw none, and went across the road. Almost immediately he found the shoe in the grass and brought it back. "Let's get back to the tree before someone comes along," he said. Just where the path began, however, he stopped and looked down. "See the print?" He pointed.

There in the soft soil were the footprints—the print of a man's bare left foot, and a step farther ahead, the print of a right shoe.

Ivor shook his head. "He stole his own shoe. He took his sock off, then put it back on before he hanged himself."

They followed the path back to the hanging tree, retraced their route along the river, climbed the hill to the cemetery, and went back to the car. Jussi took care to keep Myllysilta's shoe out of sight.

"Now where?" Ivor asked.

"To the shoemaker's," Jussi said. He started the car, pulled out of the parking lot, and headed for the shoemaker's shop at the bottom of the Oliver Road hill.

"It's Labour Day," Ivor said. "He won't be open."

"I think he will," Jussi said. "I think he's expecting us."

At the shoemaker's shop, the bell over the door announced their arrival, and the shoemaker looked up from his work.

He saw Myllysilta's shoe in Jussi's hand, and chuckled ruefully. "I told him you'd catch on, but he insisted. And, yes, I was supposed to come for the shoe and put it on display. And, yes, I've been amply compensated. The boot, by the way, has something you might be interested in."

The letters, Rabbit said. Ivor got Karl's boot from the window and looked into it. "Letters and notes," Ivor said. He pulled one out, glanced at the handwriting. "Yours," he said. He passed the boot to Jussi.

"I liked the old guy," the shoemaker said. "Did he really...?"

"Yes," Jussi said. "At the Hanging Tree. Do you have a phone?"

"Not at the shop," the shoemaker said. "I have one at home though. Do you want me to call the police?"

"Yes. Just let them know where to find him. You don't need to identify yourself. They have to do this from time to time. They'll take care of things."

"I liked him," the shoemaker said again. "He was a little—you know." He tapped himself on the side of the forehead. "Funny. I never knew his name. I don't think he had any family in town."

"Probably just as well," Jussi said. "I'll keep the shoes, if you don't mind—the one from the display, the one you were sent to find, and the boot as well."

The shoemaker shrugged and wrapped them in brown paper. Jussi tucked the bundle under his arm as he and Ivor left the shop.

In the car, on the way back home, Ivor said, "I don't understand why Myllysilta wanted the shoemaker to fetch the shoe and put it in the window."

"Maybe Myllysilta wanted me to think that, despite his confession, he wasn't really the man who shot Karl in the back and took his boot. He wanted me to think that maybe the man who actually stole the boot is still alive and well and living in Port Arthur. Perhaps he wanted me to spend the rest of my life watching my back and worrying that the family was in danger."

"But why would he do that?"

"Maybe because I killed his brothers. Maybe because I didn't kill him. Who knows? He could also have been trying to set me up somehow as his murderer. The shoemaker, after all, knew about my letters to Myllysilta."

"Myllysilta was crazy."

"Yes," Jussi said. "Yes, he was. Crazy but smart. Trying not to be stuck with the last card. We're all a little scared of that."

"*Musta Maija,*" Rabbit said.

Jussi nodded. They drove for a minute or so before he spoke again. "But he loved his son," he said, "and so must I."

Rabbit waited for Jussi to speak the rest. He knew what was coming.

"The daughter, too," Jussi said, "if she can let me. Who knows what came between them, what he may have told her."

"What he may have *done* to her," Rabbit said. "In any case, it may be difficult for her."

#

When they got home, Ivor said goodbye to Jussi and headed along Montgomery Street toward the creek. Jussi watched him walk. As Ivor neared the end of the street, he raised his hand without turning around, knowing Jussi would be watching. Jussi smiled.

He opened the front door quietly but could hear nothing out of the ordinary. Viktoria must still be in the back yard. That meant Marilyn and Owen had not yet returned. They would soon.

He went into the bedroom. Kneeling on the floor, he pulled out a box from the very back corner of the closet and took off the lid. He unwrapped the brown paper bundle and took out Karl's boot. He carefully laid it in the box with its mate.

Then, from the wrapper, he took out the old shoe, worn by one of the men who'd killed Frederic Svensson, and the new one. He sat on his heels, looking at the final shoes for some time.

Yes, they too belong in this box, Jussi thought. *But not touching the boots.* He tore away some of the brown paper and wrapped the pair of shoes that had belonged to Svensson's killer, and placed them in the box. Then he wrapped Myllysilta's shoe and laid it along one side.

He sat for a moment, looking at the pair of boots, and the single shoe and pair of shoes in brown paper. He nodded. Then he replaced the lid on the box, and returned the box to the far back corner of the closet.

He took a deep breath and went outside to sit with Viktoria and smoke, and wait for Marilyn and Owen to return.

#

That evening, Jussi and Viktoria went for a walk to the creek. Jussi said little except to point out the Saskatoon bushes that grew along the north side of the road. The berries would be ready for picking in a week or two.

At the creek, dragonflies darted and soared, catching mosquitoes. Occasionally a fish nosed the surface of the water and took down a fly.

They stood and watched for several minutes before Jussi took a deep breath and told Viktoria about Myllysilta's death, about finding the shoe, about what Myllysilta seemed to have been planning.

They stood in the quiet evening, not saying anything, for some time.

"He was crazy," Viktoria said at last.

"That's what Ivor said." Jussi took Viktoria's hand in his, and they turned around and began to walk home.

#

The funeral a week later was poorly attended, just Owen, Marilyn, and a few of the old Finns from the Finn Hall. Myllysilta's man was there, but he never introduced himself. Ivor came, and so did Vilho. Both had been drinking, but just a little.

Jussi and Viktoria also came. Jimmy was in school. The shoemaker was not there. Neither was Myllysilta's daughter. She had told Owen that she would not attend. No clergyman was present. Owen gave the eulogy. He mentioned going back to his father's house on the day he died, and finding his violin, broken, on the kitchen floor.

In the spring, Owen and Marilyn were married. A year later they had a daughter whom they named Abigail. They liked the name because it meant "my father's delight."

#

Jussi died in 1963, Ivor a year later, Viktoria in 1980.

When Marilyn and Owen were cleaning out Viktoria's house, they found a cardboard box in the bottom of the downstairs bedroom closet. It contained, wrapped in brown paper, an old pair of men's shoes and a single shoe from the 1950s, and an old pair of leather boots.

Marilyn threw out the shoes and the boots but kept the cardboard box to pack up the things she wanted to keep. There were no letters. There was, however, a picture—the first one that Jimmy had taken—of Ivor, holding a plastic glue bottle with a paper rocket on its nozzle. Ivor was smiling.

The day Viktoria died, Jimmy was flying the CF–104 Starfighter in the Canadian Forces. He was given leave to attend her funeral. A few years later, he flew the CF–18 Hornet.

In the years after Jussi and Ivor died, Viktoria had asked Jimmy once about flying. "What is it like, to be like a bird?"

Jimmy smiled down at her. "It's exciting to fly, but it feels safe. Like years ago, going in the car somewhere with *Farfar*."

Viktoria nodded, not listening so much as watching him speak, watching his smile, so like Raimo's, lost in Belgium. She wished for better for Jimmy.

Her wish was granted.

Jimmy never had to fly in combat.

Never had to go to war.

ACKNOWLEDGMENTS

This novel could not have been written without the help of many people. I am indebted to Kaarina Brooks for her editing suggestions and her help with Finnish expressions. Ahti Tolvanen tracked down some wily Finnish military commands for me. Elinor Barr shared valuable information and gave me a glimpse into her own archives. To Freda Karioja (one of my elementary school teachers), Donna and Melvin Johnson, Lillian Erickson, Carol Vukovich, Signe Ranta, Beth Boegh, Gordon Aegard, and other members of Thunder Bay's Scandinavian Home Society, I owe much of the cultural and social information about Port Arthur's Scandinavian enclave in 1955. Thank you so much for your time and interest in this project.

Reconstructing the Finnish Civil War proved a monumental task. I read J. O. Hannula's *Finland's War of Independence*, an early "White" work on the war written in 1939 (with excellent battle maps, by the way), and Anthony F. Upton's *The Finnish Revolution 1917-1918*, a remarkably well-balanced history of the war written in 1980. These two works gave me the "feel" of the war. D. G. Kirby's *Finland and Russia 1808-1920: From Autonomy to Independence* let me have a look at some of the important documents from the time. The second volume of Väinö Linna's brilliant trilogy, *Under the North Star*, gave me the "smell" and the "taste" of the war. The internet, of course, coughed up countless articles and images that helped me paint the settings and scenes in the book, and also allowed me to research the many questions that arose as I worked on the novel. The "answers," culled from various sources, were frequently contradictory and always in need of weighing and weeding. I created the village of Gamlaby and its environs, but other cities are real. In recounting incidents from the war, I have tried to be fair, and any inaccuracies that remain are unintentional.

The boy on the cover of the book is named Onni Kokko. Fighting in the White army, he was 14 when he was wounded in the battle of Tampere. Before this young soldier died, Mannerheim granted him the 4th Class Cross of Liberty. He was the youngest to receive this award. Another photo of Onni shows him on his deathbed, his head wrapped in bandages, with the award on the pillow beside his head.

Creating a believable Port Arthur, Ontario, in the year 1955, was almost as daunting as rendering the Finnish Civil War. In the summer of 1955 I turned ten, and consequently I had only a ten-year-old's memories and impressions of the year in which the novel's main characters are adults—and "old" adults at that. At the Thunder Bay Public Library branch on Brodie Street, I went through all the microfilm copies of the *Port Arthur News Chronicle* for that summer. The newspapers provided the news, ads, prices of goods, names of current movies, photographs of locations, entertainment options, and more. I learned what people were talking about, what mattered to them, what they worried about in 1955. The library also provided me with a useful map of the Lakehead—one with the old street names from the days before Port Arthur and Fort William amalgamated into Thunder Bay and had to rename half the streets in each former city. There are, by the way, still two Lincoln streets in Thunder Bay.

While I was working on the 1955 section of the novel, I read *A Century of Sport in the Finnish Community of Thunder Bay*, published by the Northwestern Ontario Sports Hall of Fame and the Thunder Bay Finnish Canadian Historical Society. It was invaluable. As was Kaarina Brooks's and Raili Garth's *Trailblazers: The Story of Port Arthur Kansallisseura Loyal Finns in Canada 1926-2002*. Beth Boegh's monograph, *Immanuel Evangelical Lutheran Church 1906-2006,* was a key that unlocked a lot of memories.

Dave Cano's website, *www.hotrodsandjalopies.blogspot.com*, was a marvelous find. Though mainly a celebration of stock car racing at the Lakehead, it's also loaded with anecdotes and photographs of life in the Lakehead's "good old days."

A book that was exceedingly valuable in helping me create the feel of Finland before and during the Civil War was *Through Finland in Carts* by Mrs. Alec-Tweedie (Ethel Brilliana Tweedie). It is a tourist's record of the sights and sounds of Finland in 1897. Her descriptions of ordinary life in the country and, in the 1913 edition of the work, the political situation were fascinating and incredibly useful.

I am grateful to the leaders of the Northwestern Ontario Writers Workshop for their hard work—their contests, readings, and publications during the past twenty years have provided many opportunities for me to create, revise, and share my work. Similarly, Thunder Bay's 10x10 Theatre Project has let me challenge myself to write in new directions.

Author and designer H. Leighton Dickson not only created an amazing cover but also generously provided guidance throughout the production process. Thank you, Heather!

This novel received very welcome support from the Literature Office of the Ontario Arts Council through what is now called its Creators grant.

Most of all, I am indebted to my wife, Marion Agnew, who is not only an exceptional writer, but a talented editor as well. Her insights and suggestions were invaluable. Thank you, Marion, for your incredible patience with me when I would recite yet another "fascinating" story about the Finnish Civil War.

Roy Blomstrom
Shuniah, Ontario, 2017

ABOUT THE AUTHOR

Roy Blomstrom, born in Port Arthur (now Thunder Bay), Ontario, is the son of Finland-Swede parents who lived through the Finnish Civil War and later emigrated to Canada. He has published poetry, stories, and essays, and his ten-minute plays have been produced locally, in Finland, and at the Brighton Fringe Festival. He is grateful for support from the Ontario Arts Council for several of his works, including *Silences*. He lives and writes in Shuniah, Ontario, just outside Thunder Bay. More information about him is available at www.shuniahhousebooks.com and at www.royblomstrom.ca.

www.ingramcontent.com/pod-product-compliance
Lightning Source LLC
Chambersburg PA
CBHW030400020726
47493CB00003B/892